# Burn

## HOMECOMING HEARTS
### BOOK THREE

## HJ WELCH

Burn © 2018 by HJ Welch

All rights reserved.

ISBN-13: 978-1-9997067-5-3

This book is a work of fiction. Names, places, and incidents are either products of the author's imagination or are used fictitiously. Any resemblance to actual events, locales, or persons, living or dead, is entirely coincidental.

All rights reserved. No part of this book may be used or reproduced in any manner whatsoever without written permission, except in the case of brief quotations embodied in critical articles and reviews.

Cover design by Joe Satoria

Also Available

BY HJ WELCH

**Paddle Creek College** (Daddies and kink)

#1 Heaven Sent

#2 Yes, Sir

#3 Little Pleasures

#4 Four Play


**Pine Cove** (Small town)

Complete Box Set


**Homecoming Hearts** (Former Boy Band)

Complete Box Set


**Bears-4-U** (Daddies and bears multi-author shared universe)

Keep Me


BY HELEN JULIET

**Contemporary Fairy Tale Adaptations**

The Fairy Tale Collection (Beauty and the Beast, Cinderella, Rapunzel)

Daddy's Fairy Tales (Daddies and kink – Goldilocks, Little Red Riding Hood, The Three Little Pigs, Puss in Boots)

# CHAPTER

## One

### RAIDEN

RAIDEN SLOWED TO CATCH HIS BREATH AS HE NEARED THE house. He rested his palms on the small of his back and took in several steadying gulps of air. A run around the ranch's grounds was one of his preferred ways to start the day, but he'd pushed himself extra hard that morning.

The sun hadn't even properly risen yet. The sky was a beautiful blend of soft pinks, baby blues and a hint of lilac and orange. He let his gaze drift over the horizon as he filled his lungs and slowed his heart rate.

It was difficult to stay grumpy when he got to experience beauty like this every day. Sometimes, he just needed to remind himself of that.

He wiped his brow and began walking up to his parents' grand farmhouse, the focal point of the property aside from the stables themselves. Even after two years living back here, it still didn't quite feel like his home.

It was more than comfortable, though. Raiden would never want to sound ungrateful for the opportunities he'd been given. But he was in one of those moods, the ones that had been hanging over his days more and more often.

It was just the repetition that was getting to him, he told himself like he usually did. His life had changed so much over the past several years, but this was the longest he'd stayed in one place for a while. The isolation was bound to get to him from time to time.

He rolled his shoulders and shook his head. There were so many people out there who would kill to be able to do what they loved for a living. So what if it wasn't *exactly* what Raiden wanted to be spending his time on. For now, he was earning good money and that, combined with living with his folks, meant he had stability.

He knew a lot of people who craved that even more than doing a job they liked.

Raiden stopped to stretch his legs on one of the many white picket fences that ran all along the grounds, dividing the paddocks up for the horses. He'd tied his hair back, but strands still dripped perspiration onto his face and down his neck.

Stability was good. It just wasn't what he was used to. After five years almost constantly on the road, it had been hard to adjust to life back at home.

Maybe he needed a vacation? He'd been so busy working he hadn't taken much time off. The last couple of years seemed to have vanished before his eyes in a blur of one project after another. A few weeks away on a beach somewhere might be exactly what he needed to snap him out of this funk.

Maybe he'd meet a girl?

He smirked and headed back up the path. If he ever bothered to head into Lexington or even one of the smaller towns between the ranch and the city, he'd probably have no trouble meeting someone nice. But after his last relationship fizzled out, he hadn't had the energy to pursue anything new.

He was just lazy, obviously. He pushed his way into the

large, gleaming kitchen and grabbed a bottle of water from the fridge, thinking as he chugged it back. If he had more drive, he'd go out and find himself a nice girlfriend. He might also address his immediate concern of hating almost all the music he was writing and co-producing.

He was such a brat. Songwriting had been his dream since he was a small child. And just because he wasn't particularly keen on the type of stuff he'd found himself doing day in, day out, didn't mean he couldn't still find joy in it.

He sighed and tossed the empty bottle into the recycling.

Days like these and their moods like storm clouds were happening too often. Something obviously needed to change, but he probably wasn't going to have time to think about that today. He had several projects in progress, a few of which had upcoming deadlines that he needed to be aware of.

To start with, he'd take a cold shower and blast away some of this melancholy by force. Then, once he had coffee, he'd take himself down to the studio and lose himself in the music for a while. Even if he was being forced to write knock-off Christmas jingles in June.

He shuddered. At least the pop songs were kind of fun in a monotonous way. He had a knack for album tracks – filler songs that almost never got released but were great for fleshing out records. He wasn't exactly proud of the reputation he'd gotten, but being busy was better than being bored.

"Raiden?" his mother's voice called from further in the house. Possibly his dad's office? Being a working horse ranch, it wasn't unusual for everyone to be up and about at this time of the morning. But her tone caught Raiden's attention.

He was aware he was a sweaty mess, but his mom would know he'd been out running. So hopefully she wouldn't mind. He wandered out of the kitchen, and sure enough, she was dressed for the day and standing in the study.

So was Raiden's dad and the family lawyer, Eric Solomon.

Raiden stopped in the doorway as the three of them looked up at him.

"Um, hi?" he said awkwardly.

"Sweetheart, there you are," said his mom, like they'd been waiting on him despite it only being seven o'clock. "Why don't you take a seat?"

Raiden frowned. She was smiling at him, but it didn't quite reach her eyes. His dad and Eric looked pained, and Raiden couldn't help the nerves that fluttered in his belly.

"What's going on?" he asked. Warily, he did as he was told and sat. His mom took the chair beside him while his dad circled the big wooden desk and took his usual seat with Eric standing by his side.

The room had always felt welcoming to Raiden, never intimidating. It was large and airy with a window taking up most of the wall behind Raiden's dad, looking out over their land. There were framed pictures of some of his dad's baseball idols, several of Raiden's records, as well as family photos. He even had one of those globes that opened up to reveal a decent stash of whiskey that Raiden had been old enough to join his dad in enjoying since he'd come home.

Now though, the room suddenly felt like an interrogation cell.

"Son, I don't want you to worry, but something's happened overnight that you need to be aware of." His dad looked grave. Immediately, Raiden jumped to the worse conclusions.

"Has...someone died?" he asked, not sure if he wanted to know the answer.

His mom let out a little laugh and pulled his hand between her own. She was a small woman, but her grip was strong. "No, darling, nothing like that." She looked relieved, although still sad. "We're sorry, we didn't mean to scare you like that. But it is still sort of serious."

"Do you know what doxing is?" Eric asked.

He'd been the family's lawyer ever since Raiden's dad had retired from the armed forces and taken over the ranch almost fifteen years ago. He was a steady sort of man, in his early fifties with graying hair and neatly trimmed nails. He wasn't a military man himself, but his orderliness obviously appealed to that side of his dad as they worked well together and socialized regularly.

Raiden trusted him. "Yes," he said, dread pooling in his stomach. "It's when someone releases personal information about you online. Usually with malicious intent."

Eric sighed and glanced at Raiden's dad. "That's exactly it. Look, there's no way to sugarcoat this. But last night someone – or a group of someones – doxed a couple of dozen people. They targeted musicians, actors and sports stars."

Raiden looked at his parents. Oh fuck. "And…I'm one of them?"

His dad grimaced. "I'm so sorry, son. But it looks like you were one of the worst affected."

His blood ran cold despite the sweat he'd worked up during his run. He'd always tried to shield his family from the fame that had dogged him while he had been with the band. He would never have thought it would catch up to him now, after so long out of the spotlight.

"What? How?" he demanded.

Eric bent down to type on Raiden's dad's laptop. "The hackers specifically targeted you and these other celebrities. They didn't randomly release your details. There's a dedicated, easy-to-use website that anyone at all can access and search people by name. Yours has the address of the farm, your phone number, email address and a number of sensitive emails. There are also photos which I'm guessing came from your phone or online cloud service."

Raiden felt sick. He swallowed the shame that rose inside him. "Photos?" he repeated. "...*private* photos?"

Eric was professional enough that he didn't look embarrassed. "I'm afraid so. See for yourself."

Raiden's mom squeezed his hand again, then released him so he could check out the website with his own eyes. This was really bad. "We're not judging you," she said firmly. "You were in a long-distance relationship."

But Raiden felt faint. "Can't...can't we take the website down?"

Eric rolled his eyes. "These assholes are good – sorry, excuse my language, Kima."

Raiden's mom snorted. "They *are* assholes," she said with vehemence. "So what? They're stopping anybody from getting rid of the site?"

"For now," said Eric. "Obviously everybody affected probably has a team working on this, and the police are already involved. But every minute the information stays up and public, the more people can copy it to use however they want."

Raiden had suffered his fair share of online hate as part of Below Zero. Internet trolls certainly hated boy bands and anything they construed as being remotely effeminate. But this was decidedly worse.

"They've got Nara's address, too," Raiden said, talking about his older sister and her husband. He opened the top email chain. "Oh no," he said.

He probably sent thousands of emails every year. And yet, somehow, these dicks had managed to find this thread among all the others.

He'd forgotten he'd even written this. But, evidently, he and his friend Joey had got drunk one evening and gone on a rant about the appalling state of the music industry. They'd ravaged several artists and dragged them for having no talent, obviously thinking no one would ever, *ever* see their words.

Most of the singers were clients of Raiden's.

"Fuck," he said.

In his defense, the artists he'd been infuriated with at the time were *not* nice people. Shallow, petty, demanding divas, the lot of them. But Raiden was supposed to maintain a professional relationship with them regardless of his personal feelings.

"We'll fix this," his dad insisted from across the other side of the desk. "Raiden, you've done nothing wrong."

"I have, though," he said numbly.

He had left his phone upstairs when he'd gone on his run, so he used his dad's computer to check on his social media accounts.

It was already looking very bleak, but there was no sense putting it off.

Fans of the people he and Joey had insulted were already up in arms. Poor Joey. Raiden really wished he hadn't been dragged into this, too. But at least Raiden was taking the brunt of the fury.

The artists themselves were calling him out on Twitter – quite rightly calling him a nobody and a has-been. Saying they would never work with him again. A quick glance at his work emails confirmed as much from the producers, agents and managers already contacting him.

"This is awful," Raiden's mom said, reading over his shoulder.

He should have shielded her from it. "People always say terrible things from the safety of their keyboards," he said, trying to convince her as well as himself. "I'm sure it's nothing really to worry about."

His mom raised an eyebrow at him, then pointed to one of the tweets further down the page.

*I know where U fukcing live now U prick I'm going to kill U and UR whole family itll do the world a favor. What do U think about that, U smug cock?!??*

"Okay," said Raiden. "That might be something to worry about."

# CHAPTER

## *Two*

### LEVI

LEVI LEANED AGAINST THE BAR AND SURVEYED HIS surroundings. His senses were on overload and he knew he probably shouldn't drink much more. But his buddies kept buying the beers, so he kept knocking them back.

After so many months away from civilization, finding himself in a city was a little much. Not that he couldn't take it, but it was hard to switch his brain off.

Stuttgart was a far cry from Baghdad or Qaim, but that was a good thing. Even though Levi had been counting the days until he started his journey home, it had still come as a shock to arrive at the German military base. He and the guys had wanted to make the most of their brief time in Europe before going their separate ways back in the U.S., so he shook himself and clinked his bottle with the four or five men who offered theirs up.

"*Prost!*" he cried.

"*Prost!*" they shouted back.

They were good guys. He'd been proud to serve with them, and part of him did feel a pang that he was leaving all this behind. But it was time to hang up his dog tags, of that much he was certain.

"Sergeant Patterson!" One of the lance corporals, a young guy named Brad, elbowed his way to the bar to squeeze next to Levi. "You too good to buy me a beer now?" he asked with a grin.

Levi rolled his eyes and handed him a bottle. "Like I'd ever hear the end of it," he groused. But it was all in jest. Brad was a good kid.

"Ain't you gonna miss all this?" he asked Levi, sincerely.

Levi snorted into his beer. "They have bars back in Kentucky, man," he said with a chuckle.

"Yeah, Serge," said Brad, "but don't you live in Buttfuck, Nowhere?"

Levi nudged him with his shoulder, which, considering how big his arms were, almost sent Brad's beer flying. "I'm not your sergeant anymore," Levi said good-naturedly. "And if you think for one minute I'm staying put in Buttfuck, you're sorely mistaken."

He'd promised himself a little while to get settled in Williams Pike once he got back. His mom would appreciate having him around. But he was sure he'd soon relocate to Lexington or somewhere else more metropolitan.

Home had too many memories. He didn't want to come face to face with one every corner he turned.

Levi stood with Brad for a few moments, just watching the busy bar. It was a traditional sort of place, all wooden finishes and wine-red leather on the seats. The wall behind the counter was entirely covered with an impressive amount of spirits. Levi had to admit, the Germans did know how to drink.

He'd gotten used to the lack of niceties while on tour. When canned ravioli was seen as a rare delicacy, you didn't miss pizza and beer. But Levi had to admit it was good to indulge now they were out of the desert.

People here had no idea how lucky they were. Levi didn't blame them. In his experience, once you showed an average Joe the kind of extravagance he was living in compared to the likes of the Iraqi people, they got humble pretty damn fast. But, on the day to day, they had their own struggles to occupy their minds. Never once considering they might lose it all in an instant.

Levi shook his head. He was one of those average Joes now. At almost thirty, he could finally start living his life, maybe even enjoy it a little.

He just wasn't sure how to do that exactly.

When you were a Marine, you went where you were told and followed orders, night and day. Ever since high school, Levi had thrived on routine. Whether it was on the football field or from his drill sergeant, he always knew his place in the world.

Now…

He took several gulps of his beer. Now was not the time for thinking. He'd made up his mind, and once he made a decision, he damn well went through with it.

"Seriously, though, Serge," said Brad. He wiped his mouth with the back of his hand. "You sure you won't change your mind, come back for another tour?"

Brad was so young – he wouldn't even technically be allowed to drink at a bar back home, but Europe's laws on alcohol were less stringent. Yet here he was, already a veteran of war. He still had that fire, that spark in his eyes. He was out to save the world.

Levi had done his share in saving the world. It turned out, the world was a more complicated place than he'd thought when he was Brad's age.

He clapped the younger guy on his back. "Gotta leave some bad guys for you to get, buddy."

"Hell yeah," Brad agreed enthusiastically. He sipped from his bottle again. "So, private security, huh?"

Levi shrugged. "For now," was all he said.

The truth was, he hadn't had a clue what he was going to do once he decided to get out of the Marines. What his uncle had done when he'd left the corps was set up his own private security firm back home. He had quite the business now, and a spot was open to Levi if he wanted it.

He wasn't entirely sure he did, but it was something to do in the meantime. Better than resting on his laurels. He was young and healthy. He still had plenty of options open to him. Working for his uncle would just mean he kept a steady paycheck for now. He could change his mind any time.

Some of the other guys weaved their way back to the bar, calling for a round of shots. Levi reckoned, what the hell? He might not ever see any of them again, other than on Facebook.

"It's on me, boys," he said to a chorus of cheers. He flashed his credit card at the pretty bartender. She licked her lips and came to Levi next despite there being other people waiting. It would be so easy to skip the line, but Levi's mom had raised him better than that.

"I believe these guys were next," he said, pointing to the group that had indeed been waiting.

They thanked him graciously in good English. Levi was always amazed by people that could speak another language.

His guys might have been pissed if they'd noticed him sending the bartender on before serving them, but they were so distracted by all the tail in front of them they could hardly concentrate on anything. Levi chuckled, sympathizing. He was fully intending on finding a hot chick to hook up with later that night.

The men in his unit had commented several times that European girls, especially Germans, were often up for anything. Levi wasn't sure that was much more than wishful thinking after months on end with only their hands for company. But all Levi really craved was a bit of human contact.

He licked his lips and turned away as Brad began chatting up a girl slightly older than him with great tits and short, choppy hair. She had a look in her eyes that made Levi think she'd eat Brad alive. Levi got the feeling he'd love every minute of it.

Just human contact, that was all it was. Lips on skin, hands between legs. It didn't necessarily matter who.

Which was why he purposefully didn't seek out Gunnery Sergeant Collins. He was there, somewhere in the bar. Or maybe he'd left already to find somewhere more suited to his tastes.

Collins was a good guy. Great at his job. Reliable.

He also had a mouth made for sin.

Levi readjusted himself and focused on catching the bartender's attention again once she'd finished with the group of locals.

A man could be forgiven for a lot of things out in the desert. Collins wasn't exactly out, but most people knew which way he swung when it came to sexual preferences. He was a big enough guy and lethal enough shot that most men knew not to fuck with him, though. Except if you actually wanted to *fuck* with him.

There was nothing wrong with accepting a blow job from someone eager to give it. Obviously, Levi had made sure it stayed strictly between the two of them. No one needed to know their sergeant liked to get head off other guys. That kind of thing could mess with the order of things if you let it.

That didn't mean Levi was ashamed or thought any less

of Collins. He just liked to keep certain things private. That was his right, after all.

What he needed was a nice girl to take his mind off things. It had always been the same with Collins. A quick blow job while Collins jerked himself off. They both left happy, and there wasn't much talking involved. Certainly no kissing. Levi knew what he needed now was a warm body he could touch all over.

Levi got him and the guys Jägermeister, seeing as they were in Germany. He got one for the bartender too. "What time do you get off?" he asked her, shouting over the noise of the crowd and the music.

She looked him up and down. "About fifteen minutes after my shift ends, I hope." She quirked an eyebrow suggestively.

It took him a second to realize what she'd said, then he laughed. "I'm Levi."

"I don't care, soldier boy," she said with a wink. "See you later?"

He grinned and picked up the beer he'd got with his shot. "I'm sure as hell not going anywhere," he told her.

Perfect. Now he could enjoy the rest of his night. This was just what he needed to get him back on track.

In a few days, he'd be back on American soil, preparing to face the rest of his life. But for right now, he could just kick back and enjoy the minivacation he'd earned himself. The rest of his life could wait.

# CHAPTER
## *Three*

### RAIDEN

RAIDEN SAT IN HIS STUDIO, ALONE.

It was a beautiful room with a large window behind the mixing desk that looked into the currently empty recording space. It had been empty for a couple of weeks now.

Raiden had the mood lighting on to try and get himself in the zone. The pinewood finish on the floor and walls was bathed in blues and purples that normally inspired creativity. But today was just leaving him feeling like the only one left at a nightclub when the house lights came back up. It was depressing, so he gave up and flicked the regular recessed lights back on.

He rubbed his chin and sighed. If he couldn't find his happy place down here, he was pretty screwed.

It had come as a surprise to almost everyone just over two years ago when Below Zero had been dropped by their record label. Raiden had loved being a part of the band, but as sad as he was to see that end, he had known it was the perfect gateway for him into the music industry. His true passion had always laid with making melodies, not just singing them.

His dad had helped him invest his savings into transforming the basement area of the farmhouse into the studio he now worked in. Despite his increasing frustrations with the kind of tracks he had been working on, it was still his sanctuary.

Even now he had nothing to work on.

That wasn't quite true. Not *all* of his clients had pulled their business away from him. Just the most high-profile ones.

Amid the avalanche of hate mail he'd received in the week since the hack, he had also got many messages of support from people who agreed with his opinions. There were people who had hailed him as a trailblazer, agreeing that the cycle of covers and samples that flooded the radio stations these days needed to be pushed aside in favor of new material.

The trouble was, there were ten times as many people who only needed the barest of excuses to terrorize him, and thanks to that goddamned website, there was no longer anywhere he could hide.

Of course he wasn't the only person to get affected by the hack. Far from it. But since he'd been out of the limelight for so long, he'd gotten used to a certain amount of anonymity.

It was insane the levels some people could take their hatred of a person they had never met. Whose only 'crime' was to sing songs you didn't like, or to look in a way you thought was unmanly, or heaven forbid to have an opinion about anything slightly political or social.

At the height of Below Zero's popularity, Raiden and the other guys had sadly got accustomed to daily death threats. But now they were being mailed to his house.

And Raiden didn't even have work to distract him from this gigantic fuck-up. Any projects he'd managed to cling on to he had whizzed through already in his need to keep his mind off the hack. Now, all he had was time to think about his lack of prospects.

For the first few days, he had been worried sick over his and his family's safety. His sister had already handed in her notice on her lease. She and her husband were both lawyers, so they were more than prepared to break their contract and move immediately to protect their location for their clients' sake as much as their own.

But Raiden's parents couldn't do that. Apple Blossom Farm was their business as well as their home. They owned fifty acres and weren't about to up and sell, even with all these threats.

As soon as the website finally got taken down, though, Raiden was immensely relieved that the intimidations began to taper off. He didn't care who said what on Twitter or Instagram, he could always block obnoxious people there. His dad had contracted the IT company that Eric's law firm used. Apparently, they had some expert programmer who was already scrubbing the internet for any of the files that had been leaked from Raiden's computer and phone as well as any trace of his address. In fact, he was in a meeting with Raiden's dad and Eric now.

Raiden had offered to help, but he had no technical expertise when it came to computer programing whatsoever. He knew every in and out of the software he used for mixing music, but anything beyond basic HTML code was out of his grasp. He'd just felt in the way, causing even more problems than he already had.

So he'd disappeared to his sanctuary. He told himself he now had the freedom to work on whatever he wanted. Without the pressure of churning out a mediocre pop song every couple of days, maybe he could finally start working on one of those epic rock ballads he'd always promised himself he'd write. His finances were okay enough that he could take the loss of income for a while.

Except, of course, now was the time his inspiration had totally deserted him. He sat at his mixing desk, idly pushing sliders, not doing anything much.

This was his own fault. He'd been mad at his lot in life, and karma had swooped in and kicked his ungrateful ass.

The only silver lining that he could see right now was that he'd been able to keep the focus on him. He'd done everything he could to shift the attention from Joey, his former bandmate and close friend, as well as any of his ex-girlfriends caught up in the leak. This mess was of his making, and as long as he could take the majority of the fall-out, he felt slightly less shitty about the whole thing.

The door at the top of the stairs clicked open. He looked up in surprise.

"Son? You down there?"

Raiden muted the few tracks that had been rumbling quietly along, then looked back again. "Yeah, sure, come on down."

He was expecting his dad and maybe Eric. His mom was at work, teaching, and wouldn't be back for a few hours.

His dad and Eric were indeed the first ones down. But then they were accompanied by two other guys, both big fellows wearing black suits and white shirts. Raiden spun his chair around and stood, regarding them with interest as they gathered in the small studio space. There wasn't really enough room for five men to stand together, but it appeared they were going to do it anyway.

His dad was the odd one out of the newcomers in his jeans and button down. He'd always been a cowboy at heart, happy to swap his camouflage gear for a Stetson once he'd served his time in the Marines. But the other three men were all suited and booted. Raiden tried not to feel intimidated in his old sneakers and Superman t-shirt.

He vaguely recognized the older guy standing by Eric, but not the younger one that drew his interest the most. He was maybe late twenties, so a bit older than Raiden himself. The man was stacked, obviously concealing an impressive body under the suit that Raiden instinctively guessed wasn't his or was very new from the way he adjusted it awkwardly once they were all standing together. He had icy blue eyes and dirty blond hair. Raiden considered him a fraction longer than he should have, then looked cheerily back at his dad.

"Well, this is quite the gathering," he said with a laugh. "I'd offer y'all seats, but I only have two."

"Sorry, maybe we should relocate upstairs?" his dad said, looking around. In fairness, nobody but Raiden came down here much. His dad had probably forgotten how small it was.

"No, no, that's fine," said the older guy. "This shouldn't take long."

Raiden found himself next to Mr. Blue Eyes. The guy was determinedly looking at the older guy. Presumably, they had come together.

"Raiden," said his dad. "I don't know if you'd remember Kurt Patterson? I served with him and his late brother James during the First Gulf War."

"Sure," said Raiden. Even if it was only a vague recollection, he did remember his dad talking about the Patterson brothers in the past. "I'm so sorry to hear about James."

"Thank you," said both Kurt and Mr. Blue Eyes together.

Raiden risked looking at him again. Something about the guy was mesmerizing. Raiden wasn't sure if it was the no-nonsense attitude radiating off him, his size, his eyes, or a combination of all three.

Kurt clapped the guy on his shoulder. "This here's James's boy, Levi. He's come to work for me."

"That's why we're here," said Eric pragmatically, addressing Raiden.

"Kurt runs a private security firm out in Lexington," said Raiden's dad.

"Best in the city," said Kurt proudly, rocking on his heels. Now Raiden knew they were related, he could see the family resemblance. Still, the guy, Levi, didn't look at him.

His dad's words sank in. "Hang on. Private security?" Raiden repeated.

The three older men nodded. "It was your mother's idea," said Raiden's dad, somewhat apologetically. "She has a point. It can't hurt to take a look at the state of this place, what with all the comings and goings around here."

Raiden looked between them all. "And the death threats," he said. "I mean, that's what you really mean. This is because of me."

Eric raised an eyebrow. "This is because someone violated your privacy and now you and your family have been subjected to dozens of threats that the police consider serious enough to require elevated attention."

Raiden glanced at Levi again. He might as well have been a statue, standing with his hands clasped behind his back, staring straight ahead. It irritated Raiden for some reason he couldn't quite put his finger on.

"Okay," he said, clapping his hands and looking around at the men before him. "Let's define elevated attention. What does that mean exactly?"

"Tighter security around the domestic property," said Kurt firmly. "Not permanently, necessarily. But for now, you can't just be letting anybody walk in here. And increased protection. It's not a great idea for you to be wandering around by yourself right now, Mr. Jones."

Raiden could feel his eyes widening. "You're not serious?" he said. Horror grew in his guts and he purposefully didn't look at the ice man standing to his side. "You're not suggesting a *bodyguard,* are you?"

"Son," said his dad patiently. "This is a serious matter."

"It's a couple of losers writing letters in between their busy schedule of trolling feminists online and jerking off in their mom's basements!" he cried. "Dad, no, this will all blow over. I understand beefing up security. But I don't need a babysitter."

"Um, excuse me?"

The group turned to see a meek-looking guy in his mid-twenties halfway down the stairs. "Yes, Glenn?" Eric said pleasantly. "Everything okay?"

He was the IT contractor that Raiden's dad had brought in from Eric's company to try and clean up the rest of the digital mess left by the hack. A borderline genius, by all accounts. His scraggly goatee and un-ironed shirt didn't give the most striking impression, not to mention that he stank of cigarette smoke. But if he got the job done, Raiden was more than happy.

Glenn smiled and twirled a pen between his fingers. "Uh, yeah. I think so? It was quite the tangle. But we definitely made progress. I'll email you my report?"

"Make sure you CC in Mr. Jones Sr. as well," said Eric, nodding towards Raiden's dad. "Thank you."

"See," said Raiden as Glenn jogged back up the stairs. "Mr. Robot has reset the Matrix. This will all go away soon enough."

The idea of having someone hovering over him was cringeworthy, to say the least. Especially if it was going to be this Levi guy, as he suspected. The brief spark of intrigue Raiden had felt upon first meeting him had now been firmly replaced with the knowledge that they had absolutely nothing in common. The guy was clearly military and wouldn't even look at a lowly creative like him.

His dad raised an eyebrow. "I know it seems extreme," he said. "But need I remind you of what happened to your friend Blake?"

Damn. He had a point.

"That was a very specific case of a nut job with a crush," Raiden tried to argue, referring to his former bandmate's stalker from a couple of years ago. "I'm pretty sure none of these whack-a-dos are in love with me."

"He almost killed Blake," said his dad somberly. "They didn't realize how serious it was until it was almost too late. Your mother and I aren't prepared to take that risk."

Raiden sighed and chewed his lip. They did have a point there. Especially when it wasn't just him at risk. They had the address to his family home and business. There were kids' riding lessons and birthday parties on the grounds all the time, not to mention the regular members of the public that stabled their horses here.

This wasn't just about him.

"So, am I going to get stuck with G.I. Joe here?" he asked. Levi might not want to look at him, but Raiden was going to make him.

Sure enough, Levi Patterson bristled, finally acknowledging his presence.

His dad and Kurt regarded Raiden coolly. Normally, Raiden was extremely respectful of their military service. But he was frustrated with the situation he had found himself in, and when he got irritable, he was liable to speak without thinking.

"No disrespect intended," he added, dropping his gaze.

His dad sighed. "Yes. We're proposing that Levi offer you additional protection. I get that you're unhappy," he conceded. "No one here blames you. You're the victim in this attack. But now we have to make sure we act appropriately. Set up a proper defense."

Raiden nodded. "Sorry. You're right." He turned to smile at Kurt and Levi. "I'll play ball, do whatever you say."

Because they were right. No one had taken the letters Blake had been sent seriously and it almost ended in disaster. Raiden could maybe gamble if it was just his safety on the line, but not when it was his family's and so many other innocent people's as well.

Kurt nodded. "That's the spirit, son. We'll get through this. Before you know it, life will all go back to normal."

Levi simply regarded him with those stunning blue eyes.

Eric rested his hand on Raiden's dad's back. "That's settled then. What do you say we go hash out the details?"

Raiden's dad nodded. "You're more than welcome to stay for dinner," he offered the Pattersons. "I could get the grill on, and we could crack open some beers."

Kurt smiled as they headed for the stairs. "Sounds great, Sam," he said sincerely.

Levi hung back, allowing the older generation to head up first.

Raiden stuck his hand out, feeling awkward. "I guess we'll be getting to know each other pretty well," he said.

It wasn't an apology and he knew it. But it was the politest thing he could muster just then.

Levi raised an eyebrow, then slowly took the proffered hand, shaking it only once. "I guess," he drawled. He turned and followed his uncle up the stairs without so much as a backwards glance.

Raiden watched them disappear, the door swinging shut behind them.

"Well," he said out loud to himself. "Isn't this going to be fun?"

# Four

## LEVI

LEVI SIPPED HIS BEER AND DID HIS BEST TO BEHAVE. THIS wasn't exactly what he'd had in mind when his Uncle Kurt had offered him a job.

He'd been keen to start as soon as he landed from Germany. Keeping busy was what he needed. If he stopped, he thought too much, and that wasn't good for anybody. So when he'd stepped off the plane to a voicemail from Kurt announcing he had the perfect first assignment lined up, Levi had done what he always did and just accepted it.

He should have guessed by his uncle's unwillingness to divulge any further details that it was going to be utter horseshit.

Levi knew that Kurt's usual clientele were businessmen, diplomats, that sort of thing. He operated out of Lexington and Louisville, sometimes as far as Nashville or St. Louis. The last thing Levi expected was to be stuck here in Williams Pike.

The Apple Blossom Farm was technically just outside the town, he supposed, but this guy was hardly a politician.

He was hardly even a guy.

Levi watched Raiden as he hovered by the barbecue, standing in his socks with an old comic book t-shirt on. Levi vaguely remembered Sam Jones's boy from when he was growing up, but if he was honest, he'd always thought his name was pronounced ray-den: like the character in the Mortal Kombat video game.

Turns out it was the traditional Japanese way: rai-den. Like try or fly. Levi had to keep rolling it around in his head so he wouldn't make a mistake.

Because even if everything else about this assignment was going to be a joke, he was at least going to be a professional.

This kid wasn't in any real danger. He even said as much himself. This was all just a stunt to make his parents feel better. The only consolation was that it would probably blow over in a few weeks, a month or two at most, then Levi could move on to a real job.

There wasn't anything really wrong with Raiden Jones per se. Other than he was evidently very privileged. He'd grown up with money and opportunity and had continued to amass it into adulthood. Levi guessed he was a few years younger than him, in his mid-twenties.

Levi was accustomed to military grooming standards. Raiden's black hair was thick and shiny, falling around his ears almost to his shoulders. It seemed frivolous and unnecessary, and every time Raiden ran his hand through it Levi felt a spike of irritation.

Not least of all because every time Raiden touched it, a traitorous part of Levi wondered what it would be like if *he* were to touch it. Hair like that was made to be grabbed during a blow job.

He scowled and took another swig of beer. Thoughts like that one hundred percent fell into the 'unprofessional' category. What the hell? He wasn't in the desert any longer. He had plenty of opportunities to meet women now he was back in America. There was absolutely no reason to look at a dude in that way. Especially not one he was going to be stuck guarding whenever he left this damn house.

At least that wasn't all that often, from what he understood so far. They had discussed Raiden's typical daily routine, and aside from the run he usually took around the grounds each morning, he often confined himself to his studio to write.

How did you even write music? A book maybe Levi could get, but how did you picture sounds in your head and make them into a song? He shook his head. No doubt he'd get more than enough insight into that over the next few weeks, whether he wanted to or not.

He realized he was staring when Raiden glanced over. Levi quickly shifted his eyes as casually as he could, giving the impression that Raiden had just seen him sweeping his gaze over the patio space.

It wasn't so much a backyard as the back of the house opening out into the grounds of the ranch. By the patio was a kidney-shaped pool with a jacuzzi attached. A clump of trees to the right gave the area some definition, but then it just rolled out into grass as far as the eye could see, with more trees and picket fences in the distance.

It was beautiful, and ordinarily, Levi suspected it was a very calming vista. But at that moment it set his teeth on edge.

His mom's house was fine. It was the same two-bedroom place he'd grown up in on a quiet street in Williams Pike. Levi couldn't imagine what growing up in a place like this would feel like, thinking that was normal.

Raiden had been some sort of pop star, though, so he was probably used to caviar and Champagne and having things whenever he clicked his fingers. Levi hadn't heard of Below Zero, but even if he hadn't been overseas on and off for the past decade, he had to admit that boy bands really weren't his sort of thing.

And now he was a songwriter with a big mouth. Levi had seen all the damaging personal information that had been leaked, so he'd read all the shitty things he'd said about a bunch of singers he'd worked with. Maybe if he hadn't been so rude, he wouldn't be getting so many death threats now.

Levi's gaze lingered on him again as he talked with his dad. On closer inspection, he wasn't skinny so much as slim. There was still a fair amount of muscle definition under that faded t-shirt. At least he knew how to work out. Levi could understand that. People who sat on their asses all day were incomprehensible to him.

In theory, Levi didn't need to understand Raiden, he just needed to protect him. But in Levi's experience, the more you knew a guy, the easier it was to predict their actions. He needed to anticipate how Raiden might react under fire.

Not that it was ever going to come that.

Levi raised his eyebrows as his uncle came to sit beside him. "So," he murmured low enough that he wouldn't be overheard by the Joneses. "Would you say this assignment was a hundred percent bullshit, or maybe just fifty?"

His uncle tutted at him and swirled the beer around in his bottle. "No assignment is bullshit," he said, his tone low but firm. "If a client feels in danger, we assess that danger until we feel it is clear. Some situations may just be more serious than others."

Levi shook his head. Smells from the grill wafted over and he realized how hungry he was. "This is a training wheels operation for me, isn't it?"

Kurt shrugged. "Just something to get your feet wet. I know you can handle it."

"So that's a yes."

Levi snorted. Whatever. Maybe a simple mission would

be a good idea to get him in the swing of things. His unit had specialized in reconnaissance, but it was going to require a different skill set to protect assets in the U.S. than it had dealing with insurgents in Iraq and Afghanistan.

"Hello everyone," a cheery voice called as the patio door slid open.

Hekima Jones was a petite woman of Japanese heritage, although she'd been born right here in Kentucky. She and Levi's mom had gotten along quite well when he'd been little, but after his father's passing a couple of years ago, the two women had less in common. He hadn't seen her for years.

She was dressed in a smart shirt and dress pants, but at the threshold of the door she kicked off her pumps and slipped on a worn pair of flip-flops to step outside. "Kurt," she said with a sigh and made to hug Levi's uncle first.

"Kima," he said just as warmly. "You're looking wonderful."

She scoffed. "After a day of lectures, I doubt it." She winked playfully at him, though. "My goodness, Levi?"

She raised her eyebrows and Levi stood to greet her as Raiden came over to join them.

"Yes, ma'am," he said, holding out his hand. "It's been a while."

She batted his hand away and pulled him in for a hug. "I'm so glad you're home for good. You did your country proud, and your dad. But now…"

She trailed off as she let him go and patted his chest with her small hands. It was clear to see where Raiden got his willowy figure from. She gave him a watery smile.

"Welcome home."

"Thank you, ma'am."

She shook her head and fished a beer out of the ice bucket, popping the top off with ease of the side of the table.

"It's us who should be thanking you. We appreciate what you're doing for us – for Raiden."

Levi caught Raiden rolling his eyes, but he ignored him. If he wanted to be a brat, let him.

"It's no trouble at all," he told Kima.

"Absolutely," said Kurt. "It's our job and we'll do it to the best of our ability. I promise you, you're in safe hands." Levi nodded in agreement.

No matter how dumb he thought this assignment was, he wasn't going to risk his uncle's reputation or that of the company he'd been building for years.

"How many people can boast buddies like that," Sam said from over by the barbecue. He saluted his bottle at Kurt, who returned the gesture.

It was obvious how close a friend he considered Levi's uncle, despite his dad being his best friend.

Levi wondered if Sam missed him as much as Levi did. In those last years, Sam would have seen far more of his dad than Levi, thanks to his deployment. The thought stung, even though it was unreasonable.

"We are lucky to know a private security firm as friends," Kima agreed. She took a long pull on her beer and closed her eyes with a sigh. "It's good to know we can keep this ugly business in the family."

"I'm sure this will all be over soon," agreed Kurt. "We're still working with Eric's IT guys, so we're going to tackle it from both sides."

"That sounds like something to toast to," said Raiden convivially enough. He raised his bottle. "Here's to getting this thing wrapped up as fast as possible."

Levi caught his eye as the others chinked glass. *Here's to parting ways as soon as possible,* he added mentally. Just because their dads had been best buds didn't mean they had to spend any more time together than was absolutely necessary.

He should have learned now not to tempt karma. Even when you didn't say things out loud, she was evidently still listening.

Kima and Raiden busied themselves for the next few minutes bringing out salads, rolls and condiments from the kitchen to go with the meat on the grill. Levi hovered while his uncle helped Sam sort out the various cuts and patties, then Levi ferried plates over to the table when they were cooked.

"This smells amazing, Mr. Jones," he said sincerely.

"Call me that again and you'll get none of it," Sam told him playfully. "Just because you're helping us out doesn't stop me from being Sam, okay?"

That caused an odd pang in Levi's chest. Like it somehow brought him a bit closer to his dad again, like when he was a teenager. "Sure," he said with a nod and twitch of a smile. He wasn't used to feeling like the youngest in the room, not for a long while.

Of course he wasn't, as he was reminded when Raiden came back out with Kima. Although the more Levi looked at Raiden, the less like a kid he seemed.

"I've had a brilliant idea," Kima announced as she set down a bowl of potato salad. She had a twinkle in her eye, but the way that Raiden frowned at her made Levi think he didn't know what she was going to say any more than the rest of them.

"All your ideas are brilliant," said Sam, kissing her cheek.

She rolled her eyes. "Yes, but this one's especially brilliant." She winked at him, then turned to Levi. "While you're working for us, instead of commuting back and forth, you should just take one of the guest bedrooms. That will make your job easier as well as more effective."

Levi's blood ran cold.

Logically, of course, it was a perfect idea. It would be much easier to protect Raiden if Levi was here around the clock. Also, he could prove the threats weren't that serious faster the more he was here.

And as much as he'd missed his mom, Levi's dad was present in every inch of her house. Staying here would be a lot less stressful for Levi.

But that meant seeing way more of Raiden than he'd bargained for. Raiden, who hadn't ever done a proper day's work in his life. Who had been sheltered from the real world and had absolutely nothing at all in common with Levi.

Raiden, with his gorgeous hair that he shook back from his eyes *again*.

This was a very bad idea.

"That's a great idea," he said, forcing himself to smile.

Because that was the last time he was going to let personal feelings get in the way of his job. It didn't matter that he found Raiden irritating as well as mildly attractive. All that mattered was showing his uncle that he'd made the right decision when he'd invested in him.

The general chatter among the group was that this was an excellent plan. They moved to take their seats and dive into the feast that Sam and Kima had prepared for them, and Kurt handed out another round of beers.

That was when Levi finally looked at Raiden and met his eye. They held each other's gaze for a second before Raiden arched an eyebrow and turned away.

Levi guessed he was as unimpressed with the situation as he was. But for the meantime, there wasn't much they could do about it.

They'd just have to get on with it.

RAIDEN CHEWED ON HIS THUMBNAIL AND TRIED NOT TO fidget. He was perfectly capable of driving himself places, but it seemed he'd lost that luxury along with almost every other aspect of his privacy.

That was being dramatic and he knew it. The house was big enough that he and Levi were no more on each other's toes than he was with his parents. But still, having him there irked Raiden.

Levi was just doing his job. Raiden could acknowledge that on a sensible, logical level. It just might be easier to put up with if Raiden wasn't so keenly aware how much the ex-Marine disliked him.

The dude would barely look him in the eye. He obviously thought Raiden was a pathetic waste of space, a delicate creative who was incapable of looking after himself. He'd never said anything to that effect out loud, but it was clear from the silences and lack of eye contact.

Levi Patterson considered him to be beneath contempt.

Raiden didn't really care what other people thought of

him. It was just tiring to be around that kind of energy all the time.

At least for the first few days, Levi had been busy with his uncle updating the ranch's security. That Raiden absolutely appreciated. It was a sensible precaution regardless of any stupid death threats. They had kids and families on the premises all the time, so it was in everyone's best interest to beef up security.

But now that was all sorted, Raiden had to put up with his own personal, six-foot-four, two-hundred-and-twenty-pound shadow. Everywhere he went, Levi was there, insisting he go through the door first to assess the room for any potential risk.

Every time he spoke to Raiden it was in short grunts or clipped sentences to inform him that the space was clear (of course it was) and that was that. It was driving Raiden crazy.

As was the silence in the big, black Jeep they were currently driving down the highway in. This was the first time in the weeks since the doxing that Raiden had needed to leave the ranch for any reason, so he and Levi were stuck in the car together making the forty-five minute drive.

"Do you mind if we put the radio on?" he finally asked after twenty minutes. There weren't much that stressed him out, but driving without music was one of them. The lack of conversation would be manageable, so long as they had some beats to fill the void.

Levi looked at him from the corner of his eye and raised a brow. "Sure," he drawled, as if he found the concept both ridiculous and boring at the same time.

He made no move to switch on the stereo, so Raiden leaned forward and pushed the button to bring it to life, then began flicking through stations. "What kind of music do you like?"

Levi shrugged, eyes on the road. He had a striking profile,

Raiden had noticed. A long face with strong cheekbones and straight nose. Now he'd been out of service for a few weeks, his hair was a little longer on the top, but he kept the back and sides short. It suited him.

"Anything," he said in response to Raiden's question about the music.

He wouldn't have known it, but that was one of Raiden's pet peeves.

"Oh, so you like Austrian folk music?" he goaded. "Scream metal? Opera?"

That earned him another raised eyebrow, along with a scowl. It was better than being ignored.

"No, wait," said Raiden, clicking his fingers. "I bet you're a disco diva. Bit of that old Saturday Night Fever. Am I right?"

Levi licked his lips. They were kind of pouty, but the fact they were almost always turned down in a sneer diminished any attractiveness they might have held.

Attractiveness? That was an odd thing to think about a guy. Levi really *was* driving Raiden crazy.

"Just…put on some rock," Levi said through a clenched jaw. Raiden would have bet anything there was an unspoken 'asshole' he wanted to tag on the end there.

Raiden flicked through the radio stations until he found one playing some Bon Jovi. He glanced at Levi, but there was no reaction to his choice.

"I bet you're a Chili Peppers kind of guy," he mused. He leaned back against the car door, studying Levi for any response. "Foo Fighters, that sort of thing."

Levi sighed. "Not really into music, kid," he said. He focused on the road as he switched lanes.

*Kid?* But the thing was, Raiden *was* feeling childish. He wanted Levi to pay attention to him. It was depressing, but since the majority of his work had dried up, Levi was the only other person he interacted with most days aside from his parents.

"You don't like music?" he asked. "Nah, I don't buy it. Everyone likes *something*."

"What can I tell you?" Levi said in that bored rumbling tone of his. "Not much opportunity to listen to the radio when you're driving around in hostile territory."

Raiden rubbed his chin. He'd let his stubble grow out a little bit, more due to laziness than anything else, and it was prickly under his fingers.

"Don't you soldier types usually have a guitar or something? Or is that just something they do in the movies?"

Levi didn't answer for a minute, and Raiden figured he was probably going to be ignored. But then Levi shifted in his seat and huffed.

"Yeah," he conceded. "Someone always has a guitar. And guys often like singing together while we drive."

"Really?" said Raiden, intrigued.

He stared at Levi intently, even though he didn't look back at him. It was still interesting watching the muscles in his jaw work.

"You have a unit of five guys," Levi eventually said. "You work together and always travel in the same vehicle. So, yeah, it gets boring seeing the same old desert and hamlets over and over. You find ways to pass the time."

Raiden jabbed the power button on the radio off again. "What songs do you know?" He could see this was pissing Levi off, and for some reason that tickled him.

Levi reached forward and turned Bruce Springsteen back on. "Not in Iraq now," he growled.

"Yeah, but singing is the best," Raiden argued, willing Levi to agree. "Such a release."

Nothing. Levi just kept his eyes on the road.

Fine. Raiden turned the music up instead and sang along

at the top of his lungs. That at least earned him a tut of irritation. "Come on, man, everyone knows The Boss."

Levi turned the radio back down. "Just because I know it, doesn't mean I have to sing it."

Raiden sighed. "You're no fun," he grumbled.

"I'm not here to have fun with you, *sir*," he said. He might as well have spat the 'sir' out, it was said with such scorn. "I'm here to keep you safe. That's all."

Raiden scoffed. "Safe. We both know this is a glorified babysitting gig. I hope my parents are paying you well enough, at least. You must be bored out of your mind."

Levi said nothing.

"Look," said Raiden, filling the gap after a minute or so. "I mean no disrespect. But you've got to agree that this twenty-four-seven business is excessive. No one is going to jump out and shoot me. The online harassment has already tapered off substantially."

"Until my uncle deems the threat neutralized, I will continue to act as your personal security," Levi said. "So until then, I suggest we not antagonize one another any more than necessary."

So Raiden was getting under his skin. Excellent. Maybe if he pissed Levi off enough, he'd convince his uncle to stop this bullshit sooner rather than later.

"Sure, whatever you say, Betty."

Levi fingers curled a little tighter around the steering wheel, the rest of his body very still. "Excuse me?"

"You know? Betty? Don't tell me you don't get it."

Raiden knew he was being a dick with the slightly obscure reference, but was having too much fun to explain himself.

Levi licked his lips. "If you're having trouble remembering my name, you can either call me Patterson, or feel free to keep your mouth shut altogether."

Raiden snorted. He'd bet anything that that was *not* how Levi was supposed to speak to clients. Of course, Raiden wouldn't rat him out to his uncle or anything. But it was very rewarding to know he was rattling the big ogre's cage.

"Sure, Betty, whatever you say." Levi went to open his mouth, but Raiden pointed ahead. "Oh, look! We're here."

# CHAPTER

## *Six*

RAIDEN

Logically, Raiden knew it was probably a supremely idiotic idea to antagonize an ex-Marine. But it was also fun.

He watched as Levi ground his teeth and made the turn down a dirt track where the GPS indicated. It appeared he was going to let the new nickname slide for now.

Raiden had been to this rehearsal space numerous times over the years. It was basically a glorified garage attached to a cluster of buildings that stored farming equipment. It had power, a feeble attempt at AC and minimal soundproofing. The fact it was surrounded by fields meant that anyone playing here could generally make as much of a racket as they liked.

It wasn't much. But then the hourly rates were cheap, so a lot of bands who were just starting out booked it for days at a time.

It had been a while since Raiden had hung around here. He'd maybe been once or twice since his Below Zero days. But he still had a deep fondness for the place.

In his teenage years he had been a part of several cover bands. They had come here when they could afford it rather than piss off any of their neighbors by practicing in any of their parents' garages. Raiden had also started a rock band that had played several local gigs before he'd gone for the boy band audition. Singing was singing as far as he'd been concerned. Never in a million years had he thought he'd make the cut. He still wondered what might have happened to that band if he hadn't left them behind.

As far as he knew, those guys had all gone off to college. It felt funny that Raiden should find himself back here after all these years. Like his life had gone full circle.

At twenty-six, that was slightly depressing. He shook it off. Being back here didn't mean the end of anything. In fact, he hoped it would be a beginning.

He and Levi stepped out of the Jeep into the strong Kentucky sunshine. At Raiden's indication they headed towards the door to the studio, Levi going first, of course.

A few days ago, Raiden had got an email from someone he'd never met before. She'd introduced herself as Pearl and her band as the delightfully named Glittergasm. It was a succinct message, saying that she thought Raiden and she could work well together, and that he should check out their demos then come meet them.

Raiden had liked the directness of it. There was no chit-chat about those awful emails that had been leaked, no agreeing that the music industry sucked. He'd got so many messages that roasted other mainstream artists in one sentence, then announced that whoever the person was was the real deal, a *genuine artist,* in the next.

Raiden hadn't responded to any of those. Sure, he should never have said what he did about Elsie Hadden or Funkolove, but those artists had treated him like dirt. When people tried to sound clever by laying into singers and musicians Raiden knew for a fact were hard working and talented, he had no time for that. So what if they made by-the-numbers pop? They sold records, so good for them.

Pearl hadn't mentioned any of that. She just said that she felt like her band might be of interest if Raiden was looking to work on something a little different. She also, correctly, guessed that he'd probably have extra time on his hands now, so didn't have anything to lose.

He liked her spunk. Not many people just told it as it was. So he'd listened to what the band had done so far and was surprised when he really liked it. It was rough around the edges, for sure. But he saw a lot of potential in their pop-punk, glam-rock style.

And seeing as he really *didn't* have anything to lose right now, he figured he might as well take a chance and work on a project that genuinely interested him for once.

He followed Levi through the door into the practice space that seemed very dark after the summer sun. But as soon as Raiden took his shades off and blinked a few times, his eyes gradually adjusted to the dim light.

Five people were scattered around, all of whom looked to be in their late teens at the most. A guy and a Hispanic girl were jamming with guitars on the same beat-up couch Raiden himself had sat on several years ago. It looked even more stained than he remembered and a few more pockets of stuffing were trying to escape, but other than that it looked to still be functioning.

A white girl with multicolored dreads was sitting behind the drum kit, circling a drumstick in her hand. Another guy was lying behind a speaker with a toolkit by his side, his long, shaggy hair pooling on the ground around him.

The girl who stood to greet them, though, was obviously Pearl. Raiden had learned over the years that lead signers often exuded a certain air of authority, and this chick had it in spades. It was the kind of vibe that let everyone know that this was their baby, these were their people, and you fucked with either at your own peril.

She had a slim, boyish figure underneath an outfit that would have looked at home in any Japanese Manga comic. Chunky boots, thigh-high socks, a skirt that barely covered her ass and a strappy top that seemed determined to fall off her shoulders. So many bangles she jangled with every movement and just as many piercings. No tattoos, though, which was interesting.

Raiden didn't find the look sexual. He was sure a lot of guys would, but to him, it just screamed *'fuck you, world.'* He liked it.

Her most striking feature though, and what he immediately saw as a crucial marketing tool, was the lilac hair that fell in large rolls to her shoulders. Coupled with a full face of shiny, glittery makeup, he immediately recognized her value as the face of the band.

"Hi," he said, sticking out his hand as she approached. "You must be Pearl."

"You must be Raiden," she said, pronouncing his name correctly. That made a nice change. "I don't know who you are, though?"

She looked Levi square in the eye. Raiden chuckled.

"Oh, this is my buddy, Kevin. You don't need to worry about him."

Levi ground his teeth, clearly not getting that movie reference either, or getting it and being pissed off even more.

"My name is Levi Patterson, ma'am. I'm here as Mr. Jones's private security. I hope you won't mind if I give the room a quick once-over."

The guy by the speaker sat up. "Like a bodyguard?" he asked. "Cool."

"Do you have a gun?" the girl with the bass guitar asked from the sofa. She had a deep voice for a girl and was dressed simply in jeans and a t-shirt with a cartoon duck on the front.

Levi flashed her a smile. "Of course, ma'am. I wouldn't be much use if I couldn't protect my client."

The girl giggled.

Raiden scowled. Of course G.I. Joe was nice to her. Would it really kill him to treat Raiden with anything less than strained civility?

"Well," Raiden said loudly, clapping his hands. "This is the band, huh? I like the tracks y'all sent over. I guess you're looking to work on some more?"

Pearl looked him up and down, then retrieved a dog-eared notebook from a backpack by the sofa. "Yes," she said, walking back over to him. "We currently have two singles and an EP out. That's been enough to land us some gigs, but we need to get an album out soon if we're going to capitalize on that work. I thought we could maybe collaborate, see if we can get some songs together in time for the tour."

"Y'all have a tour booked already?" Raiden was impressed.

"Five dates over two weeks," said the girl at the drums proudly. "Over three states. "We're opening for Dyrnoir when they play Madison Square Garden."

"Isn't that insane?" said the guy with the guitar, his eyes sparkling.

"Dyrnoir?" Raiden repeated. "Fuck, that's incredible y'all!"

It really was. Dyrnoir had been around for over a decade and had sold millions of records worldwide. Their pop-rock style and equally charismatic front woman matched up nicely with what Raiden had seen of Glittergasm so far. Basically, they couldn't have asked for a better band to open for.

"I'm actually going to die when I meet Janel Rider," said the bassist, referring to Dyrnoir's lead singer. She even got a little teary-eyed.

Raiden felt a warm sensation of pride for the kids. Their enthusiasm was infectious.

"We want to polish some new songs by then," said Pearl. She handed Raiden her notebook, something he guessed she didn't let just anyone look at. "I'm the main lyricist, but you do music and lyrics. We figured, if you liked our sound, you could help us get a few more tracks together in time."

"I do like your sound," Raiden agreed. Christ, he couldn't remember the last time he felt so excited about a project. "When do you want to start?"

"Now?" Pearl suggested, gesturing towards to the couch.

The guitarist and bassist hopped up to perch of the arms of the sofa, allowing Raiden and Pearl to sit side-by-side. Raiden looked around, fixing on Levi as he finished his walk around the room. Having failed to locate any incendiary devices, he took up position by the door, hands behind his back, eyes straight ahead.

Raiden wondered if he was bored already.

He smirked, getting a small, perverse kick from that. If Levi had been nicer to him, maybe he'd have more sympathy. But seeing as he insisted on being a jackass, Raiden could take a tiny bit of joy from forcing him into the world of music that he claimed to hate so much.

Nobody *hated* music, Raiden was convinced of that. If he was going to be saddled with Levi for the time being, perhaps he'd get a chance to prove that to him.

Raiden did like a challenge, after all.

# CHAPTER
## *Seven*

LEVI

THE POUNDING ON THE DOOR HAD LEVI AWAKE BEFORE HE even knew what was happening. His feet swung out of the bed and his hand flew to his gun on the nightstand as he raced over and yanked the door open.

Raiden froze with his fist in the air. His eyes went wide with shock as he took in the gun Levi had raised. Then his gaze swept down Levi's almost entirely naked body.

Levi would have been thankful he was at least wearing briefs, if it wasn't for the glaringly obvious morning wood he was sporting.

He refused to get embarrassed. He couldn't help what his damn dick did when he was unconscious. So he stood there, defiantly, until Raiden's eyes eventually flicked back up to Levi's face.

"May I help you?" Levi asked, his voice rough with sleep.

To his credit, Raiden didn't blush. He cleared his throat and put on a decent smile.

"I came to see if you wanted to go for a run?" he asked. "I've been a very good boy and used the treadmill since this whole thing started. But if I don't get a real run in the fresh air soon I'm going to get murderous. And not the fun kind."

Levi arched an eyebrow and rubbed the sleep from his eyes. Thankfully, his cock was calming down.

"There's a fun kind of murderer?"

"Would you like to find out?" Raiden asked, his eyes sparkling.

He was wearing a simple pair of shorts, a t-shirt and some sneakers that looked like they'd been well loved. His hair was just long enough that he could tie it back, which made sense to keep it out of his eyes. Except there were a few strands hanging free that were infuriatingly inviting Levi to tuck them behind Raiden's ears.

Yet again, Levi reminded himself that Raiden wasn't cute. He was an annoying little brat, as was obvious from the puppy dog eyes he was currently throwing Levi's way.

"The treadmill is infinitely safer."

Raiden pouted. "But it's so *boring*. Come on, if you run with me, I'll be fine, right? My route doesn't go out of the grounds, and y'all made the compound all super secure now, right?"

Levi sighed and rubbed his head. Truth be told, he'd love a proper run. He still hit the closest gym as often as he could, but there was no substitute to pushing through a few miles in the open air.

"You have to do exactly as I say," he said, pointing a finger at Raiden's face as it lit up with excitement. "I'll stay a couple of feet in front. And under *no* circumstances is there to be any chit-chat. The only reason I want you to open your mouth is if you see the glint of a sniper rifle."

Raiden hopped from foot to foot. "Yes, yes," he cried excitedly. "Scout's honor, I promise. Let's go, let's go."

Without a word, Levi stepped back and let the door close on Raiden. He could still hear Raiden chittering and jumping about in the hall as he yanked on a shirt and pair of shorts himself. Levi wasn't joking about making him keep his mouth shut. If he tried to jabber on about anything while they were out, Levi would have to take him to task.

For a horrible second, he wondered what that would entail exactly. Grabbing Raiden by his collar, perhaps, making him look Levi in the eye while he scolded him.

For some ungodly reason, that image made Levi's dick twitch to life again.

"Knock it off," he grumbled, glancing down at it.

He then looked at the gun where he'd laid it down on top of the dresser. It would be a pain to bring it, but in the end, he decided on a holster. Better to deal with the rub from the straps than go out unprepared.

After gulping down half a bottle of water, he opened the door again to find Raiden just as keen as when he left him.

"So, um, cool tats," Raiden said with a grin before Levi even had a chance to close his bedroom door. He looked at Levi's chest where moments ago his body ink had been on display.

"What did I say?" Levi asked with an arched eyebrow.

Raiden mimed zipping his mouth shut, locking it, then tossing away the key.

"Good boy," Levi murmured.

They jogged their way through the house and stretched in silence on the patio. Then Raiden pointed towards the path that took them in front of the property, the direction of the stables, and Levi set off at an easy pace.

Despite his stern words, Levi felt more natural falling into step beside Raiden rather than running in front of him. He told himself it was because he could protect him better with him in his line of sight, but the truth was it just felt rude to ignore him like that.

By the time they got into a good pace, the house diminishing behind them, it was about oh-six-thirty. The sun had risen for them, bathing the grounds of the estate in hazy light. Birds and insects chirped in a dawn chorus, and Levi felt a calm he hadn't experienced in a long while. Things were so much simpler when it was just your feet slamming against the earth in the otherwise quiet of the day.

"So, you've lived here your whole life?" he found himself asking Raiden before he even realized what he was doing.

Sure enough, Raiden raised his brow and gave him the side-eye. Levi knew what he'd said about chit-chat, but it was different if he was the one asking the questions.

"Most of it," Raiden answered after a minute or two. "I was about ten when we moved here. My dad's always been keen on horses. The ranch came with an impressive stock. He loves it here."

"But not the rest of you?" Levi asked.

Raiden shrugged. "We're all more academics. Into learning and technology and such." He chuckled and shook his head. "Luckily Dad's not the sore type, or he might have got upset no one in his family wanted to go camping or hunting with him."

Levi thought of his own dad with a pang. "So he got himself a whole farm instead?"

Raiden jutted his chin over to the stables. "He's probably out there now, working with the crew, looking after the horses. He always did like to get his hands dirty." He wiped sweat from his forehead. "I think you visited our old place before we moved here. Or so my mom says."

"Yeah?"

Levi wasn't sure how to respond. Discussing anything about their dads' friendship was like stepping into another life. Even though it had been a couple of years since his passing, it still hurt to talk about how things used to be.

"He and your mom came to my sister's wedding," Raiden

continued. "It's kind of funny, how our dads were best buds, and we're only just getting to know each other now."

Levi wanted to reply that they weren't getting to know each other, that they weren't friends. But even if that wasn't his intention, thanks to the proximity of the job he *was* finding out more about Raiden.

He knew how he took his coffee, he knew he didn't like potatoes and what his shoe size was. Levi was getting familiar with the way he moved, what his different little sighs meant. All kinds of stupid stuff he normally only ever noticed about the guys in his unit, the ones he spent night and day with.

This was probably how it would be with every client, he figured. He'd step into their world for a time, get to know them inside and out, then move on to the next. For a reason he couldn't quite put his finger on, the idea made him sad.

"I guess you must miss your dad, huh?" Raiden continued. "I'm really sorry, man. I know I said it before, but I can't imagine what that's like. To lose a parent."

"I didn't lose him. I know exactly where he is," Levi snapped. He knew it was a douche reaction, but Raiden was right. He *didn't* know what it felt like. So maybe he should just leave it.

"Sorry," Raiden mumbled.

Levi sighed. He didn't want to be the bad guy. "Yeah, I miss him," he conceded.

He glanced over at Raiden and caught the small smile he offered him. Levi didn't want anyone's pity. Sometimes things just happened in life. You may not like them, but you just had to get on with it.

Raiden left it, though. He didn't probe any further, asking what had happened, like most people did. He just jogged on in companionable silence. Levi appreciated it.

They didn't go far, maybe only covering a couple of miles.

But Levi knew it did his legs and lungs good, and he imagined Raiden felt the benefit too. He was certainly glowing by the time they made it back to the house, his cheeks flushed and his skin covered with a light sheen of perspiration.

"Good work," Levi said to him as they approached the back door to the kitchen.

Raiden quirked a smile at him. "Thanks," he said. "I appreciate you letting me out."

That made him sound like a naughty dog and Levi rolled his eyes. "Well, now I know you can behave yourself, perhaps we can do it again sometime?"

Raiden pulled the sliding patio door open. "I'd just like to inform you that you look all gross and sweaty and the urge to push you in the pool is *real*. I should get credit for resisting temptation."

"You're hardly an oil painting yourself," Levi lied. Some people did indeed look grim after a workout. But others, such as Raiden, simply looked healthy after working up a sweat. It suited him.

Raiden laughed, a full, throaty sound. "You gonna throw my ass in the pool then?" he led them into the cool A/C of the kitchen. "To be fair, that would be way more likely than me besting you."

"You know it," said Levi, heading to the fridge for water. As reluctant as he was to admit it, he was kind of having fun.

He swallowed down several gulps from the bottle he'd opened, then threw another to Raiden. He wasn't here to have fun. This was work, no different to out in the desert. The second he forgot that someone could lose their life at any moment was the instant they were in real danger.

He didn't really believe Raiden was in any danger, certainly not like his battalion had been on any of his tours. But still, he couldn't lose sight of his primary mission. He needed to put some distance between them again.

He opened his mouth to tell Raiden he was going up for a shower. But before any words came out, the sound of the front doorbell rang through the house.

Raiden raised his eyebrows and Levi held his hand up to steady him. Considering the time, both Mr. and Mrs. Jones would have already left the house for work, so it was just the two of them aside from any staff on duty.

"I'll get it," said Levi.

He wiped his hands dry on a towel, conscious of the piece still strapped to his side. He didn't want to scare the mailman shitless, but he knew better than to approach the door unarmed.

Raiden followed him to the front of the house. The bell rang again as they entered the lobby.

"Someone's eager," Levi murmured. He unlocked the deadbolts and pulled the door inwards.

Pearl, the girl from the band Raiden had been working with, was stood on the other side.

Despite the hour, she was fully made up with her purple hair expertly styled. Her outfit looked more suited to shooting a music video than it did running early morning errands. Levi noted the old but well-kept car parked in the driveway that he assumed to be hers.

"Hi," she said, tilting her head. She wore heart-shaped pink sunglasses that she peered over to assess Levi. "You're the bodyguard, right?"

"Yes, I am, ma'am," he confirmed.

She nodded and removed the shades. "Good, I probably need to speak to you as well. Where's Raiden?"

"He's here," Levi said warily. "Can I ask what this is regarding – hey!"

She slipped under his arm and into the house. He had to stop himself from grabbing her arm and hauling her back. She was just a kid, after all. But he was still irritated.

Unfortunately, Raiden's excitement undermined his ability to scold her.

"Hey, girl," he cried, pulling her into a hug. "This is a surprise."

Pearl nodded, her gaze wandering around the front of the house. "Sorry, I know it's early. But time is a factor and I like talking to people in person. May I come in?"

Levi and Raiden both looked at each other. She wasn't a security threat, Levi was certain, so this was a social call. That left the decision up to Raiden. Even if Levi was pissed.

"Oh, sure," Raiden said after a beat. "Come on in. You want something to drink?"

"Tea would be very nice," she said. Her head turned from side to side as if she was cataloging everything she saw as they walked through the house. "Why are there horseshoes everywhere?"

Raiden smiled despite the fact Levi felt the question was slightly rude. "My dad's thing. He collects them. Cool, aren't they?"

Pearl took off her glasses and didn't reply.

Raiden didn't seem all that bothered, though. He gestured for her to take a stool at the island counter and routed around in the cupboards. "English breakfast okay?"

"Perfect. Milk and sugar, please."

Pearl perched on one of the seats and watched Levi take another halfway down the table. He was here merely as an observer. By all rights, Raiden could tell him to get lost now they knew there was no danger. But he didn't, so Levi stayed. Besides, Pearl had said something about wanting to talk to him too, whatever that meant.

"What brings you down here, then?" Raiden asked.

"We got some extra tour dates," said Pearl without any preamble. "We hit the road in a few days."

Raiden looked up from the tea he'd been preparing. "Oh," he said. "Well, that's fantastic."

Levi knew right there and then he was definitely spending too much time in Raiden Jones's company.

He could see, clear as day, the disappointment that flitted across his face. Levi may not understand about making music, but he got how much it meant to Raiden to have been working on the kind of stuff he really liked. If Glittergasm were off on tour, presumably that meant their progress would be greatly slowed.

"I guess I can keep working on the tracks from here and we can email," Raiden said, proving Levi's theory. Raiden brought the tea over to Pearl with a smile. Levi respected him putting on a brave face.

Pearl blinked, confusion lining her features as she took the proffered cup. "That wasn't what I was suggesting."

Raiden glanced at Levi, probably because he was the only other person in the room and Raiden needed some support. "Oh, sorry. Sure, what did you want to know?"

"How many other clients do you have right now?"

That was a bit invasive, Levi felt. But Raiden simply shrugged. "None, really. I've got the odd project here and there, but y'all are the only ones I'm working with seriously. Was, I mean."

Pearl frowned, as if Raiden was making no sense. "I don't get why you're sad. This means you can come on tour with us and finish the record, like I hoped."

Raiden sat back as Levi immediately considered what she was saying. Going on tour would be a security nightmare.

"What?" said Raiden. His eyes had lit up with happiness again, though, like when Levi had first taken him to work with Glittergasm. "Are you serious?"

"Of course." Pearl took a sip of her tea. "The record label is loving what we've come up with so far. You'd have to arrange your own travel and accommodation, but I assume that won't be a problem." She glanced around at the house and the grounds beyond the window, then gave him a knowing smile.

Raiden chuckled. "No, that would be fine. Geez, I haven't been on tour in so long."

Fucking hell. Levi really didn't want to be the bad guy. He knew his client's safety was the only thing that should matter, but it was obvious how much this meant to him.

"Raiden," he said, his tone resigned. "I'm not sure this is such a good idea. Not right now."

Why did the way his face drop hit Levi like a damn sucker punch?

"Oh, come on, man," Raiden said, slipping out of his seat. "You can't be serious. I'm not going to stop my whole life because of these stupid threats. It's not like there's one psycho who's targeting me more than all the others. It's not like it was with Blake."

He came and stood in front of Levi, resting his hip on the island. His hair was still damp from their run and he smelled very male from all the perspiration. It tugged unfairly at the parts of Levi that wanted to let him have his way and damn the consequences.

"What will it take for you to okay this?" Raiden asked.

"How about if he comes too?" Levi and Raiden both looked back at Pearl. She shrugged. "I also assumed that would be the plan. Sorry, it seems I'm jumping to too many conclusions."

"Me?" said Levi. "Go on tour with a rock band?"

The grin returned to Raiden's mouth. "I've heard crazier ideas," he said. "Plenty of them." He slapped Levi's knee and hopped on his toes. "What difference does it make if you're haranguing me here or in some hotel room? I promise I'll be so good, I'll do whatever you say. We can even share a room if it'll make you feel better."

The very notion had Levi's gut twisting. He would *not* be sleeping beside Raiden.

The point was moot, anyway, because he had to say no. This was insane.

'No' wasn't the word he heard coming out his mouth, though.

"I'll have to clear it with my uncle," he said slowly. Raiden threw his arms around Levi's neck before he even finished speaking.

"Oh, thank you! Thank you!" he cried, quickly pulling away. Which was a very good thing, as inhaling so much of his scent in one breath left Levi feeling heady. For fuck's sake, he needed to get his body under control. This lust or crush or whatever the fuck he was suffering from was getting out of hand. Especially if they were looking at spending the next few weeks cooped up together, even more so than they already were in the house.

"I'm not promising anything," he warned. "I still have to convince my uncle."

Raiden nodded enthusiastically, whereas Pearl just raised an eyebrow.

"Oh, I'm sure you'll have no trouble," she said with a smirk.

"ARE YOU KIDDING ME?"

Raiden grinned up at Levi in the bright morning sunshine. "What?" he asked innocently, shoving another bag into the back of the Jeep. "I need all this stuff."

"I can assure you, you don't." Levi folded his arms, showing off his muscles and tats.

Raiden assessed the situation and tucked his laptop bag into a convenient little nook between a few other bags. "You've never been on tour before."

"I've done several tours," said Levi coldly.

Raiden rolled his eyes, unintimidated. "Not with a *band*," he said. "This is different. It's part vacation, part work. I have to bring gear if we want to record anything while we're writing. Clothes, toiletries and grooming products – it's so easy to become a total bum on the road if you're not careful. You have to make a home away from home. It requires a lot of stuff."

Levi slipped the solitary backpack from his shoulder and dumped it in the trunk on top of all the luggage Raiden had already stored there.

"No," said Levi. "It really doesn't."

He stalked off to the driver's seat, leaving Raiden to bundle the last of his things inside the Jeep. He wouldn't put it past Levi to start the engine and pull off without him, so he jammed the last couple of bags wherever they would fit and slammed the lid of the trunk down.

"See, it's no big deal," Raiden said as he slipped into the passenger seat, buckling up. "Everything fit just fine."

Levi didn't reply. He just turned the keys, bringing the car to life with a roar of the engine. "You got the address?"

Raiden tutted and fished his phone out so he could get the address for the hotel they were staying in later. The first gig was in Cincinnati. It wasn't ordinarily a city Raiden would be this excited about visiting. But it happened to be the hometown of his former bandmate Blake and his fiancé Elion, and they were coming to watch the show. The tour would move them on tomorrow morning, but at least Raiden would get to see his buddies for a few hours. It had been far too long since he'd seen them both.

Levi copied the address into the GPS and handed Raiden back his phone. Then they were driving out of the grounds, heading to the highway.

Once they reached Ohio, they would check into their hotel, see the show, then hang out. At least that was Raiden's plan, so he guessed Levi would just have to tag along. It was going to be harder to navigate this bodyguard thing while they were traveling. Between the two of them, they had got into an okay routine around the house. But out on the road, they would no doubt face a lot more challenges.

Raiden really wasn't convinced he needed a bodyguard at all, but his parents weren't taking any chances. In fact, they only agreed to let Raiden go if Levi was with him. It wasn't like Raiden was a kid anymore. In theory, he could do what he liked. But his parents' support meant a lot to him, so if they wanted to pay for this, he would behave himself and put up with it.

After Cincinnati, they had a couple of days before they needed to be in Pittsburgh. Raiden hoped he and Pearl could get some writing done before the next show. Progress on the new songs was going extremely well. It was like playing with electricity. Every time a riff or a harmony came together, Raiden got giddy. He didn't think he could feel that way anymore, that he'd become too jaded. But when a song started forming with these guys it was like being a kid at Christmas again.

"Mind if I put the radio on?" he asked, not waiting for Levi to respond before he punched the power button. By now, Levi knew this was non-negotiable. But by asking each time, Raiden kept up the illusion for Levi that he was still in charge.

It was important for Levi to be in charge, he had noticed. That wasn't all that surprising given his military background, but Raiden didn't like being bossed around. This way, he could fool himself that he still had a bit of control over the situation.

He sang along to Green Day. He wasn't a total asshole: he always put on a rock station for Levi. But he hadn't yet coaxed him into belting out a number with him. "Come on, Betty. Everyone likes Time of Your Life."

"What's with this 'Betty' shit," Levi growled. "It's not even funny."

Sometimes Raiden could swear Levi grew up on another planet. It was like he was allergic to pop culture. It wasn't like there was a huge age difference between them either. Levi was only three years older than him, despite how much he wanted to call him 'kid.'

"You really haven't worked it out yet?" Raiden asked.

Levi's scowl intensified and he kept his eyes firmly on the

road. However, Raiden felt like being generous and threw him a bone.

"What if I said that by being my bodyguard, Betty, that would make me Al?"

Levi frowned. "Isn't that from a song?"

Raiden clicked his fingers at him and wriggled a bit. "Bingo! You Can Call Me Al."

He took the small quirk of Levi's mouth as a huge victory. "Okay, yeah, I get it," Levi said. "Simon and Garfunkel, right?"

"Just Paul Simon, actually," said Raiden, feeling triumphant. "But yes, that's it. It's a great song. Iconic music video as well."

"Never seen it," Levi admitted. But there wasn't any rancor in his voice. Raiden took that as an even greater win.

"Oh," Raiden said, shaking his head. "It's so simple, but it's genius. I'll show you when we get to Ohio."

Levi raised an eyebrow as if to say he had better things to do with his time than watch old music videos from the eighties. But he didn't say no either, so Raiden fully intended to inflict it on him at some point over the next few days.

He enjoyed teasing and tormenting Levi. He really was too easy to wind up half the time. But he'd rather see Levi smiling at him than scowling.

Levi looked good when he smiled.

Levi looked good all the time. His hair was growing fast now he wasn't buzzing it short every day, and he was already sporting an undercut that really suited him. There was no missing his hot body either. Raiden was somewhat fascinated by all his muscles and the way they moved. When they ran together, his legs were like pistons on a steam engine.

And then, of course, there had been his cock.

It wasn't like Raiden had never seen another guy's junk in his underwear. Hell, trying to make TJ keep his pants *on* had been trouble enough on tour. But something about seeing someone you knew with a hard-on, up close and personal, was sticking in Raiden's brain. He couldn't stop coming back to the image over and over again.

There had been times, late at night, where he'd idly speculated what it might *feel* like.

He'd definitely not wondered that before. Not about anyone specific, anyway.

Raiden wasn't fussy with his porn. He watched anything that took his fancy, which could be wildly different on any given day. So he'd seen plenty of guys fucking each other. There was undoubtedly something hot about watching dudes bang, and porn stars always had big cocks. Naturally then, there had been times in the past where Raiden had got off to that, thinking about what it might feel like to have another guy's dick in his ass.

But it had always been abstract. Until he saw Levi's cock, larger than life in front of him, and now he had to be careful he didn't dwell on how heavy it might feel in Raiden's hand. In his mouth.

Considering his best friends were now out as queer and in serious relationships with other guys, it wasn't surprising that Raiden might speculate on his own sexuality. Deep down, he felt everyone probably had the capacity to fancy people from their own sex or gender. He'd just never had the theory put to the test.

Being intrigued by Levi's cock was not the same as being attracted to him as a person. But there was no denying the more Levi loosened up, the more he smiled, the more attractive he became.

Raiden needed to watch himself. A macho guy like Levi would probably beat the shit out of him if he caught a whiff of any vaguely homosexual inclinations.

Except...would he? Having spent the past few weeks together, Raiden couldn't claim to know his bodyguard inside and out. But he felt confident enough to hope that, no, Levi Patterson would not be that kind of jerk.

But he was almost certainly straight, so Raiden needed to keep any wild fantasies he had to himself. Levi was also technically *employed* by him, so daydreaming about his cock was grossly inappropriate.

The thing was, he had good intentions. But as they traveled down the interstate, there was no getting away from the fact they were going to be spending almost every waking moment together for the next few weeks. A lot of that time was going to be like this. Side by side, in the car.

There was no way Levi wasn't going to be present in Raiden's thoughts almost constantly. So this newfound fascination with his body was going to be very difficult to ignore.

Of all the times to start exploring his sexuality, Raiden could have probably picked any time other than now. But there was no escaping it. He was just going to have to jerk off a *lot* and keep things as professional as he could between him and Levi.

He suspected that might be easier said than done.

"So, what made you leave the Marines?" he asked after a while. "If you don't mind me asking?" He needed to stop thinking about sex before his dick got excited. Thinking about war would certainly help with that.

Levi shrugged. "I'm surprised you haven't asked before."

Raiden played on his phone, updating his Instagram. "Didn't want to pry," he admitted.

He couldn't fathom what would make a man join the armed forces in the first place. That was his dad's thing. But Levi was obviously more like his own dad as well as Raiden's than Raiden would ever be. So *leaving* the Marines was logical to him. He was just curious as to what had pushed Levi in the end.

Levi just shrugged. "It was time, I guess," he said. "So, now

I get 'Betty.' I don't like it," he added with a sideways glance at Raiden. "But I get it. What about 'Kevin'?"

Raiden accepted the change of conversation topic. He'd rather not talk about military stuff. It wasn't like he had much he could add on the subject anyway.

"Are you telling me you can't think of a single film involving a celebrity getting private security after receiving death threats?"

Levi groaned. "Kevin Costner. The Bodyguard."

"Yahtzee," said Raiden. "Pretty funny, huh?"

Levi's arched eyebrow suggested he didn't think it was quite as hilarious as Raiden did. "You do realize that makes you Whitney Houston in this scenario?"

Raiden scoffed. "Hell yeah. Damn, that woman could *sing.*"

Levi licked his lips and glanced away from the road long enough to consider Raiden properly. "You know, most guys wouldn't be okay with being the chick."

It was Raiden's turn to arch a brow at him. "I think you need to hang out with better guys if that's the case," he said candidly. "It's a hypothetical. If a dude can't handle being compared with one of the most talented artists of the past century, they must have an extremely fragile ego. Do you really consider being likened to a woman an insult?"

Levi surprised him by chuckling. "No," he said flatly. "I don't. But a lot of guys would, that's all I meant."

"I'll take that as a compliment, then," said Raiden, staring straight out the window at the tarmac racing under the car. "I guess it's all pretty macho in the Marines?" he asked.

Levi dragged his lower lip through his teeth. "Yeah. Lot of talk about fucking women, and the F-word gets thrown around as the go-to insult."

"Homophobia as well as misogyny," said Raiden, nodding. "Good to know." Not all that surprising, really.

Levi shrugged again. "It's all very intense. You have to blow off steam where you can. Sometimes, you just say the most shocking things to get a kick out of it. There's a lot of fights, too."

Raiden nodded. "Makes sense," he conceded. "The music industry has a lot of issues, but at least there's a fair amount of diversity too. Not so much pressure to be a manly man."

Levi glanced at him, eyes narrowing.

"What," Raiden asked.

"I want to ask something, but I don't mean it as an insult."

Raiden laughed. "I'm pretty hard to insult," he said. "The whole world pretty much has tried its best. After so many thousands of messages telling me to go kill myself, the bar to shock me has risen substantially."

Levi seemed to think for a minute. About what, Raiden couldn't really guess. Then he flicked his gaze briefly towards Raiden before watching the road again. "Are you gay?"

Raiden laughed, loudly. "You're right," he said good-naturedly. "That's not an insult, but those 'some guys' you mentioned before might very well see it as one."

He rubbed the back of his neck, glad to see Levi's expression was relaxed. There was even a small smile on his lips. Great, at least they hadn't managed to piss each other off. Again.

"No. I mean, I don't think so," he said. He tried to will his cheeks not to blush at his earlier thoughts about cock. About *Levi's* cock.

"You don't think so?" Levi repeated.

"Yeah," said Raiden. "I mean, I know I'm not gay, because I like women. But, who knows? I could like guys too. If I met the right one, I think I'm definitely open to that. For example. Channing Tatum: not kicking him out of bed."

Levi chuckled. "Okay. So, you're telling me you might be a little bit gay?"

"There's more than just gay and straight, isn't there?" Raiden countered. "There's a spectrum. One of my best buds is bisexual. I think it's more common than a lot of people want to admit." He flashed a devilish grin Levi's way. "Just think. If we all chilled out about this sexuality stuff, we could be fucking twice as many people. Wouldn't that be awesome?"

Levi didn't reply right away. "That's a novel way of looking at it," he said finally.

Raiden hoped he hadn't freaked him out with his honest opinion. But he wasn't getting a bad vibe off of Levi. In fact, he seemed to give serious consideration to what Raiden said.

They listened to the radio for a while in comfortable silence, then chatted a little about favorite sodas, of all things, after Raiden pulled out some snacks for them. The afternoon was stretching out before them, but Raiden figured they had plenty of time to make it to Cincinnati in time for the show.

After a couple of hours cooped up in the car, he found his eyelids drooping. It wasn't like Levi was relying on him to keep him awake, so he decided it would be okay to take a quick nap. The rocking of the vehicle helped him doze off. He always did like sleeping while traveling. It certainly made time pass quicker.

Unfortunately, that wasn't a good thing in this instance.

An hour or so later, he woke to Levi tapping his knee. "Hey, kid," he said gently. "We're coming up on Knoxville."

Raiden blinked as consciousness came slowly back to him. *Hang on, what?*

"Knoxville?" he repeated, suddenly very awake. "Levi, what the hell do you mean, *Knoxville?*"

Levi frowned at him. "We're getting near the hotel," he said, pointing at the display on the dash.

"I highly doubt that," said Raiden, looking wildly around

for any road signs to help him out. "Because the hotel is in Ohio, and we appear to be in *Tennessee!*"

"I put the address you gave me into the GPS," Levi snapped, scowling. "If we're in the wrong state, this is your fault."

"I told you we were going to Cincinnati first!" Raiden shot back. He was absolutely furious. "Why the hell didn't you notice we were going in completely the opposite direction!"

"We're going to several different states," Levi argued back. But there was something defensive in his words too. "It's not my job to double-check every step of the way. You gave me bad intel."

"Fuck," Raiden cried. He pulled up their location on Google Maps on his phone. Sure enough, they had been traveling down the wrong way along the I75, and they would never make it to Cincinnati in time.

Raiden berated himself for not noticing before. But that wasn't his job. Levi was the goddamned reconnaissance Marine. How the hell did he not check they were going the right way?

Well. This tour had got off to a great start.

**CHAPTER**

*Nine*

LEVI

Levi couldn't decide what was worse. How infuriated he was that Raiden had given him the wrong address, or the fact Levi had failed to remember they were supposed to be heading north instead of south.

He didn't have any defense. This was what happened when he blindly followed instructions like a good little soldier boy. This was also precisely the fucking reason he got out of the Marines.

"Well," said Raiden through a clenched jaw. "There's no point trying to make it back up to Ohio now. We might as well stop the night around here and then head to Pittsburgh in the morning."

It might have been manageable if Raiden was just pissed, but he was obviously upset as well.

"Look," said Levi. "You're right. I should have remembered the city you told me we were headed to first. But you gave me that address. This is both our fault."

Raiden angrily dug his phone out of his pocket again. Levi could only glance at him as he was still driving. There wasn't much point continuing to the destination if it was the wrong one, but for now, he didn't have much else to do.

"There." Raiden held up his phone where he'd zoomed in on the Cincinnati hotel address. Then he pointed to the one on the GPS where they were currently heading towards.

They were totally different.

Levi didn't know what to say. How could he have got it so wrong?

"I get this is all a big joke to you," Raiden bit out, locking his screen and putting the phone away again. "But this is my job, so I'd appreciate if you took this tour a little more seriously from now on."

Being scolded by his client pissed Levi off no end. To have Raiden reprimand him, though, just when they were starting to get along, was utterly humiliating.

Levi didn't trust himself to respond, so he addressed a different issue instead. "We should get a motel for the night," he said. "Unless you want to push and drive onto Pennsylvania?"

Raiden scoffed and shook his head. "If you can manage to navigate us to a nearby *hotel*, I think that would be for the best. Don't you?"

Levi thought keeping silent this time would be better for both of them. He jabbed at the GPS until it listed all the nearby hotels, then quickly picked the most suitable looking one. Price wasn't an issue when it came to Raiden, so he went for one with a good rating so as not to irritate him any further.

Fuck him. Why should Levi care that Raiden was furious with him? Levi was sure he'd typed in the address he had shown him back at the ranch, so Raiden just must have pulled up the wrong hotel or something. But while Raiden was convinced it was all Levi's fault, he was probably going to stay fuming.

Levi shouldn't have been as bothered by that as he was. Raiden was privileged and wouldn't last a day out in the desert. However, that didn't seem to stop Levi from feeling bad, which was annoying.

They didn't exchange another word as they pulled up to the front of the Hampton Inn. It wasn't the most glamorous of places to stay, but it wasn't a Motel 6 either. Four stories of mostly cream brickwork in the middle of a parking lot and lawns on all four sides. Basic, but pleasant enough. The American flag fluttered on a pole by the front entrance as Levi swung into one of the many vacant parking slots.

Raiden stormed out of the Jeep and headed inside presumably to book them a couple of rooms. Levi resigned himself to getting the luggage. Luckily, he had noted which of Raiden's half-dozen bags was his overnight one, so he grabbed that as well as his own backpack.

It was fine. Once they both cooled off, they could have a calm conversation about this. Until then, time apart in separate rooms would do them some good. It was already evening, so they could each order room service for dinner and not have to speak again the rest of the night.

Security wise, it wasn't ideal to remain out of contact for that long, but this was a totally spur of the moment detour. They should be safe enough. However, there was going to be one stipulation he insisted on.

He smiled at the clerk as he approached the front desk inside. Raiden was obviously almost done making the booking. "Sorry, miss," he said politely. "Did my friend mention we need rooms side by side?"

The woman smiled up at him. "No, he did not, but that's no trouble at all to fix." While she clicked away with her mouse, Levi ignored the glare Raiden was giving him. "Okay, there we go. You're on the third floor. If you need anything at all, dial zero to speak to the front desk."

Levi and Raiden both thanked her, then took their respective keys from the counter and bags from the floor where Levi had left them. They walked to the elevator in silence and Levi reached out to call the car down.

"Look," Raiden said. "I get why we have to be next to each other, but I'd appreciate a little alone time tonight."

"Fine by me," Levi replied.

This was ridiculous. He shouldn't be letting Raiden's anger affect him this much. Levi told himself on the ride up to the third floor and the walk to their rooms it was because he wasn't looking forward to admitting this fuckup to his uncle. If he couldn't even chauffeur a client to the correct *state*, what good was he?

But he knew he was pissed off that Raiden thought less of him. Levi should be able to impress a civilian like that well enough, but he'd gone and shown himself to be an incompetent lemming, blithely doing as he was told. He should have checked the damn directions.

He slammed the door to his room a little too hard, he knew. But he was pissing himself off now. Why should he need to impress Raiden at all? He was perfectly capable of looking at almost every guy without his cock coming to life. That deal with Collins had just been to benefit them both out in the desert.

Same with Musgrove on the tour before last. And Jimmy Burke the last year of summer camp.

Fuck Raiden for putting these ideas in his head. He wasn't bi. He just liked getting his cock sucked. Maybe other guys were bi or gay, that was fine. It just wasn't him. He was straight. He liked pussy.

He threw his bag on the floor then dropped onto the bed, bouncing slightly against the mattress. He balled his hands into fists and pressed them against his closed eyes. One long, slow breath in and out, and he felt marginally better. He was cranky from the fuckup as well as driving half the day, not to mention hungry.

Room service, that was what he needed. Thankfully, the menu had the burger and fries he was craving, as well as a side of slaw and beans. He asked for a couple of beers for good measure. He just needed to take the edge off this foul temper he was in.

He was better than this. Levi was trained to keep a lid on his emotions, keep cool under pressure. He did his best to switch his brain off when his food arrived, focus on nothing but delicious carbs, cold beer and dumb reality TV But the vision of Raiden clenching his jaw and blinking back tears was tormenting him.

After his second beer, he made a really bad decision.

"Raiden," he called after knocking on his door on and off for a good minute, maybe more. He didn't want to be an asshole to any guests that might be in the rooms around them. But at the same time, now he was up and had made a dick of himself, he wasn't going to back down. "Come on. I know you're in there."

He better be in there. If he had left without telling Levi, Levi was going to tan his hide, argument or no argument.

He raised his fist to pound the wood again, when the click of a lock stopped him. He stepped back.

"What?" Raiden demanded as he yanked the door inwards.

Levi cleared his throat, determined to remain calm. "May I come in?"

Raiden rolled his eyes, turning and walking back into the room. Levi took the fact he left the door open as an invitation to follow.

"I'm sorry," he said, shutting the door behind him. He had no idea why he said that. He'd had no intention of apologizing when he'd come over here. "I do take your career and this tour seriously. I honestly have no idea what happened with the GPS."

"Okay, whatever," said Raiden, rubbing his eyes.

"No," said Levi, his irritation rising despite his best efforts. "Not whatever. I didn't do this to you on purpose. And, quite frankly, it's not like you're part of the band. They were still able to go on stage without you."

Raiden let out a hollow laugh. "I don't know why I expect you to get it. It's not about being on stage, man. It's about the community, the unit. I wanted to be there because I feel responsible for these guys now. Like…like they're my little protégées or something. I was proud, all right? And yeah, it looks like they smashed it just fine without me. But for a second there, I mattered again. I was doing something with meaning."

Levi ground his teeth. "It's just music. I don't appreciate you dragging me over the coals like something serious actually happened."

"Oh, fuck you," Raiden snapped. "I don't have to explain this to you. Get the fuck out of my room."

"Christ, you're such a brat," Levi snarled stepping closer. "You need to calm down and get some perspective."

"My whole life got turned upside down and inside out by some fucking sicko," Raiden spat. He picked up a beer bottle from the nightstand. It appeared Levi hadn't been the only one to order from the hotel bar. "I was going to see my friends in Cincinnati as well. People I trust to look out for me. Guys I really wanted to see and just shoot some shit with. Instead, here I am, with you, in fucking Knoxville."

"You know what," said Levi, throwing up his hands. "Sorry I bothered. I'll just leave you to your pity party and try again in the morning."

Raiden scoffed. "Yeah, tell you what, let me get the door." He pushed past Levi, bashing their shoulders together.

"Watch it," Levi growled, grabbing his arm and spinning him around.

Raiden slammed the bottle back down. "Or what?" He pushed Levi's chest. Levi gritted his teeth and stepped back, absorbing the blow. "What you gonna do, tough guy?"

"Stop that," said Levi.

But Raiden pushed him again. "I never wanted you around. This whole bodyguard thing is just for show. So go on, leave, get out."

"I'm trying," Levi said, exasperated as Raiden shoved him, *again*. "You're in my way."

"So?" said Raiden. "Do something about it. You're a man of action, aren't you?"

He grinned and licked his lips, damp from the beer. Without thinking it through at all, Levi pushed him aside. Not enough to hurt him by any measure, but seriously over the line for what he should do with a client.

Raiden responded on what felt like instinct, grabbing Levi's arm and tugging him back.

Levi spun, seizing Raiden's wrists, and pinning them to the wall above Raiden's head.

They were both breathing heavily. In a flash, the adrenaline pumping through Levi's system changed in nature. The fight in him morphed into lust.

He needed to back the fuck off, right now. The last thing Raiden needed was to feel Levi's cock getting hard in his pants. Raiden was trying to antagonize Levi. That was all he'd been trying to do since he'd started this ridiculous assignment.

Except their chests were rising and falling together, touching with each breath. Raiden's gaze raked down Levi's body, and he figured he might be too late to conceal that erection.

"I'm sorry," he said, dropping Raiden's hands and stepping away.

Raiden grabbed his face and kissed him.

Levi was so shocked he couldn't move for a moment. But Raiden gripped his jaw with both his hands as his lips molded Levi's, his tongue slipping out to probe against Levi's mouth.

There was only so much restraint one man could exercise. Levi clutched Raiden's narrow waist and crowded him back against the wall, kissing him back with fervor. Raiden made a needy sound at the back of his throat and had Levi quivering.

Their cocks rubbed against each other through their jeans. For all his bulk, Levi was only a little taller than Raiden, so their bodies matched up neatly as they rutted against the wall. Nothing about this felt neat, though.

Raiden attacked Levi's mouth with his lips, tongue and teeth, his fingers digging into Levi's back as they frotted. Levi didn't have time to consider what the hell he was doing, his climax building hard and fast.

As much as he didn't want to come in his pants like a damn teenager, it seemed he was going to get little choice in the matter. Raiden's hands dropped and slapped against Levi's ass, digging into the cheeks through the denim. He used the extra purchase to thrust faster, chasing his own release and rubbing against Levi's cock to create the perfect friction.

Levi gnashed his teeth and groaned, plundering Raiden's mouth again between gasps. He screwed his eyes shut as his orgasm peaked.

His grip was so tight he worried he was going to bruise Raiden's arms as he came. But Raiden was crying out too, arching his back and banging his head against the wall they'd been shamelessly making out against.

Reality came crashing down pretty fast.

"What the fuck?" Levi whispered as he tried to catch his breath. He let go of Raiden and staggered backwards, wiping his mouth.

He wasn't going to blame Raiden for initiating that madness. They had both taken part with equal enthusiasm. But a nasty part of him wanted to lash out and accuse him, if only to take the heat off himself.

Raiden was still panting, looking up at him with those big, dark eyes.

"I should go," Levi managed to utter, taking another step back. "I – I'm sorry."

Raiden didn't say anything. He just watched Levi make his escape for the door.

Once back in his own room, Levi barely had the door locked before he was stripping naked, fumbling to the bathroom and twisting the shower faucet on. Hot water slammed against his skin as he stepped under the stream.

He had just fucked up big time, and he knew it.

Raiden was less shocked by the revelation that he was, in fact, *not* a hundred percent straight, and more disturbed that he had practically forced himself on Levi.

With his size, he had no doubt that Levi could have stopped him at any second, so he must have been into it on some level. But the look of horror as he'd left Raiden's room made it pretty clear that he wasn't thrilled with what they'd done.

Raiden slept poorly that night, tossing and turning. No matter what he told himself, he really hadn't been that drunk. Just enough to be reckless. But he'd been completely in control of his actions.

It scared him that he would be attracted to someone who clearly didn't like him, and was apparently straight. He'd met so many nice guys over the years, gorgeous men with fun personalities, interested in the creative arts, like him. So why did Levi drive him so crazy?

That was probably it. Raiden liked a challenge, and he and Levi did nothing but aggravate each other. Hopefully, now he'd scratched this itch, he could forget about it. They'd made each other come in an embarrassingly short amount of time. He now knew what Levi's mouth tasted like, so that was it.

Just because he hadn't gotten to see his cock didn't matter. He and Levi weren't going to date. This was a one-time mistake and it was going to be awkward enough for the rest of the tour without dwelling on it any further.

It was light enough outside to call it morning. He would love to have gone for a run, but that meant asking Levi to come with him, and he couldn't face that. Instead, he rolled out of bed and did some jumping jacks. He could get a good stretch in the room and do some crunches to work up a little sweat. Anything physical would help distract his body from how exquisite it had felt to be pinned down by Levi.

Raiden couldn't say he'd been into that much before – being bossed around in the bedroom. Of course he'd gotten off to dominatrix porn. He got off to most things. But he'd never asked a girl to push him around before.

The way Levi had pinned him to the wall, though, made his whole body shiver now. He scowled and flipped over to crack out some push-ups. If he pushed himself to the point where he started to tremble from lactic acid, rather than desire, he might be able to shake these feelings off before he had to face Levi.

A cold shower later and he was standing outside Levi's door. He ground his teeth. There was no sense him checking out if Levi was still asleep. He needed to know.

With a deep breath, he knocked twice on the door, loud enough he was confident he'd be heard, but not too aggressive. At least he hoped.

Levi opened the door a few seconds later in sweats. It looked like he might have been working out, too.

"Hi," said Raiden, determined to tackle this head on. "I was wondering when you'd be ready to go?"

Levi nodded. "Ten minutes."

"No rush," said Raiden, raising his hands. "Just knock on my door when you're ready."

He took a breath, ready to bring up last night. But Levi nodded again, then closed the door in his face.

"Damn." Raiden sighed and rubbed his still-damp hair before going back to his room.

He didn't have any of his gear. Levi had left that all in the car. Raiden assumed it would be safe enough overnight as the trunk was concealed from the outside. But it meant he couldn't distract himself with work while he waited. He flicked on the TV and fiddled with his phone instead, partially succeeding with occupying his mind with thoughts other than the way it had felt to come pressed up against Levi's solid body.

He and Pearl had swapped several messages since yesterday evening. It looked like the show went great with a welcoming crowd. They had a reasonable following of fans already from the EP and few singles they had released, but it was hard to predict how many of those would show up to a small gig. Raiden still wished he could have been there, but at least everything went well in his absence.

Blake and Elion had been pretty gutted they hadn't been able to get together. With Blake's hectic performance and teaching schedule and Elion's college classes, it was hard for them to negotiate time to see each other. Raiden felt guilty, but they'd been understanding, naturally. They were great guys. Raiden had promised them that once this tour was done, they would work something out.

Raiden's phone pinged. It was a text from Levi.

*Meet me at the car.*

Raiden huffed and snatched up his overnight bag. Typical. Levi was probably just going to ignore him as much as humanly possible now. Well, tough shit. They were going to be stuck in a car together for the next several hours. He'd have no choice but to talk to Raiden at some point.

Raiden checked out at the front desk without really paying attention to what he was doing. He was brewing a storm inside again, even though he wanted to stay calm. But would it really have killed Levi to wait and walk down with him? What about all his security measures?

"Don't worry," he said by way of a greeting as he opened the car door. "I didn't get taken out on the way down to the lobby. I know my safety is your top priority."

"I didn't think you would," Levi murmured. His attention was on the GPS display integrated into the dash of the Jeep. "Come here, check this out."

Raiden bit back a sarcastic response and threw his bag onto the back seat before sliding into the passenger seat. "What?"

Levi pointed at the list of previous destinations he'd pulled up on the menu. The second to last one was the hotel in Cincinnati. Raiden was positive. He had re-checked it about a hundred times since yesterday evening. The top one was somewhere in Knoxville.

"You added another address after we left Apple Blossom?" Raiden asked in confusion.

Levi met his eye and shook his head slowly. "No, I didn't change anything after we left the ranch."

"So," said Raiden. "What? I don't get it. How did we end up here?"

Levi licked his lips and looked at the display again. "Someone *else* added a new address."

Raiden laughed. "That's crazy. Why would anyone do that? *How* could they do that? It's not like you let anyone into the car besides us since we left the farm."

"Raiden," said Levi. His tone was grave. It made Raiden stop laughing and pay attention. "You were hacked a few weeks ago. Someone got into your phone and computer files. We still don't know how. Then they did what they wanted with that information." He pointed at the mysterious top address. "GPS runs on satellite navigation. 4G. Signals that can be hacked."

Coldness washed through Raiden. He sat a moment, absorbing Levi's words. "You think," he said eventually. "That someone – the hacker – tapped into the car and sent us the wrong way on purpose?"

Again, Levi considered his words before he spoke. "I can't see any other explanation."

"Why?" Raiden felt sick.

Levi scrubbed his face. "The way I see it, there are two possibilities. One, they're a prankster who enjoys fucking with people for kicks."

"But," Raiden prompted. He could tell there was a 'but.'

"But," Levi said. "My uncle has all our vehicles' software encrypted. This would be very hard to hack."

"A lot of work for a prank?" Raiden guessed. Levi nodded. "So, what's option number two?"

He waited while Levi considered his words. Raiden's skin prickled with gooseflesh.

"Option number two is that they hoped to lure us – you – to a location of their designation before we realized we'd gone wrong. A long shot, but we did almost make it all the way to Knoxville, after all."

"Why would they want to bring me somewhere?" Raiden asked. Despite all the death threats he'd received, for the first time since the hack he felt truly afraid.

Levi shook his head. "I honestly don't know," he said.

# CHAPTER
## Eleven

LEVI

LEVI WAS LOST IN THOUGHT AS HE DROVE. HE AND RAIDEN HAD pulled into the nearest gas station to the hotel and picked up a map to guide them to Pittsburgh. He wasn't risking the GPS again.

It seemed this threat might be genuine, after all. It was clear to him now how lax both he and Raiden had been. They needed to treat this as serious. Deadly serious.

Why indeed would anyone want to trick Raiden into going somewhere? Levi had seen some of the worst in humanity while he'd been deployed, so he could only think this person's intentions were sinister.

He called his uncle from his hands-free on the road and warned him what they thought had happened. His uncle didn't sound happy, but he didn't chew Levi out at least. He was probably already thinking of the hundred actions he needed to take to protect his cars from anything like this in the future, as well as security for the Jones's back at the farm.

"We'll need to go back through every single message and letter Raiden received since the hack," Kurt said. "Probably the weeks leading up to it as well. I'll get Glenn back on the case and see if we can't spot anyone that stands out as having a particular grudge or motive."

Levi nodded and glanced at Raiden. He was staring out the window, chewing his thumbnail.

Christ, Levi had fucked this situation up in so many ways. He agreed with his uncle and ended the call.

"They'll let us know if they find anything," he assured Raiden once he'd explained what Kurt was going to do. He hoped it made Raiden feel at least a bit comforted.

Raiden just nodded and continued staring out the window.

Levi refocused on the road ahead, but there was no escaping the thoughts whirling around his head.

He'd kissed Raiden. He'd kissed another dude. And he'd liked it.

It was just a physical sensation. Kissing and having his dick rubbed through his pants. But, he wouldn't have done it if he was repulsed. The mere thought of doing that with most of the guys he had served with made his stomach flip. Even Collins had never suggested they make out like lovers.

But Raiden just made his damn blood boil, like he was under his skin. His body had felt so amazing pressed all along Levi's. "About last night…" he began.

That got Raiden's attention. "Yeah?"

"I just feel with this new development, we need to clear the air," said Levi. He could only see Raiden out of the corner of his eye, but it was enough to see he was watching Levi intently. "I'm sorry. It was grossly unprofessional."

Raiden laughed. "I'm not gross," he said, a teasing tone to his words.

And just like that, the air *did* clear between them. If Raiden was willing to laugh about it, there was hope.

Levi cast him a small smile. "It probably shouldn't happen again."

Raiden nodded. "No problem, dude. We can just forget about it, things like that happen when you're on the road." He winked Levi's way. "Chalk it up as your first, wild tour experience."

Levi chuckled, relieved Raiden was letting him off the hook. This way they could simply sweep it under the rug and pretend it never happened.

Levi had no right whatsoever to feel remorseful about that. It wasn't like he'd been hoping it would happen again, after all. It *couldn't* happen again, not while Levi was acting as Raiden's protection. Especially after what they suspected had happened with the GPS. So this was the ideal outcome. Maybe they could find their way back to the almost-friendly banter they had before.

"Do you want to put the radio on?" he offered to Raiden. His face lit up and Levi tried to squash down the pleasure that fluttered in his belly from that. His job was going to be much easier if they weren't at each other's throats, that was all.

"So, um," said Raiden as music filled the car. "I will forget about it, I promise. But I just have one question, to set my mind at ease, if you like."

Levi braced himself. His instinct was to slam the lid on this and never, ever open it again. But Raiden looked so hopeful at him, he didn't want to be a dick. "Just one," he said, quirking a brow and holding up a solitary finger.

Raiden nodded. "I guess, I'm worried I sort of...jumped you last night. But, I mean, you didn't seem to mind so much? I didn't put you in an awkward position, did I?"

It was an easy out. Levi could say he felt obliged. But they'd both know that was a big fat lie.

"No, kid," he said with half a smile. "I didn't mind so much. Maybe there's something to that theory of yours?"

"That more people are less straight than they think?"

Raiden asked, biting his thumbnail again. "Yeah, I was wondering the same thing. Okay, so, we're cool. I'm glad."

Levi turned and faced him for just a second. "I'm glad too."

After that, Levi asked Raiden about the messages he'd received post-hack. It wasn't the most pleasant of subjects, but it needed to be done, and they had time to kill. He requested Raiden jot down anything of note, but it felt like they came up with jack shit.

Even if they narrowed it down to just the most offensive messages, they still had hundreds of Twitter users who had said things so vile they either needed therapy or jail time. All it did was leave them both feeling on edge.

Raiden suggested they stop somewhere nice for lunch, on him. He found a quiet little pizza joint in Charleston called Mimi's with rave reviews. It was in a suburban area and looked more like a house than a restaurant itself. It had fairy lights strung outside even though it wouldn't be dark for hours.

"Cute," said Levi. He slipped his hands into his pockets as they walked from the car, past the line of leafy trees and into the little restaurant.

"I know I am," Raiden said with a wink over his shoulder.

That sounded dangerously like flirting, but Raiden didn't follow up on it, so Levi left it. If he called him out on every stupid thing he said, Raiden was going to think Levi was obsessed. Besides, if Levi didn't mention it, it meant he didn't have to acknowledge that he liked it, just a little.

The place obviously had been a house at some point, but it was decorated in vibrant colors now and the smell of cheese, meats, herbs and sauces accosted Levi as they stepped through the entrance. His mouth watered immediately.

"Table for two-" the waitress began to ask before her eyes went wide. "Oh my god, you're from Below Zero, aren't you?

You sang that *'Oh oh ooh'* song!" She turned around and, despite the restaurant being almost entirely full, yelled across the room. *"Hey Flick, check it out! It's Joey from Below Zero!"*

"Um," said Raiden awkwardly, his cheeks going pink. "It's nice to meet you."

Levi arched an eyebrow as the waitress was joined by her colleague, who sprinted to her side, and they both gawked at Raiden.

"Actually, this is Raiden Jones," Levi said with a polite smile. "Not Joey Sullivan."

"Oh, sure," said the girl, apparently not embarrassed in the slightest she had mixed him up. "Can we have your autograph?"

"I have all your records," said the second girl. She was slightly younger than the first, with braces on her teeth. "I love the work you do with Storm Sailor, any of the European DJs, actually."

She looked like she might cry as the first girl handed Raiden a couple of menus to sign and a black marker.

Raiden perked up visibly at the Storm Sailor comment. "Yeah, those guys are amazing to collaborate with," he said as he scribbled his name. "So talented."

He handed the cards back to the second girl, who clutched them to her chest. The first girl plucked two new menus from the rack. "I've got a really good table just come up free," she said in what Levi assumed she thought was a sexy voice. It was adorable. "In the corner, by the window. Give you some privacy," she added with a wink.

"Thank you very much," said Raiden, chuckling.

He didn't seem to mind that everyone in the restaurant was staring as they followed their hostess and took their seats. Levi cataloged them all, about fifty people in total, but he didn't register any of them as being a particular threat. They just seemed like locals, excited to see a celebrity.

"You get that all the time, I suppose?" he murmured to Raiden as they were left alone. He picked up his menu to scan it.

Raiden chuckled again. "Not so much anymore, actually. It's nice every now and again to meet fans, especially when they really care." He glanced back at the younger of the two waitresses, who was not so subtly peeking around a corner at them, and waved. She went bright red and vanished from sight.

"And you don't mind she got your name wrong?"

Raiden grinned as he eyed up the pizza choices. "Name me every member of Bon Jovi."

"Uh," said Levi. "Jon Bon Jovi…"

When he held out his hands in defeat, Raiden nodded. "Just because you don't know their names, doesn't mean you don't like their stuff, right?"

"*Slippery When Wet* got me through my teenage years," Levi admitted.

Still, he would have thought Raiden would have at least corrected the girl when she mistook him for Joey. The humility was very endearing to see.

Raiden wagged his fork at him. "What I want to know," he said, that glint back in his eye that said he was up to trouble, "is how many other members of Below Zero you can name? I thought you'd never heard of us."

Levi refused to take the bait. "I hadn't," he said, sipping the water their waitress brought them. They paused the conversation while she took their order, but when she was gone, Levi didn't change the subject. "You're my client. I needed to do my research." He leaned a little closer. Raiden wasn't the only one who could be playful. "I have been known on occasion to do my job right."

Raiden batted his arm. "I'm sorry," he said, blushing a little again. "I didn't mean to disrespect your job either. I definitely didn't take this seriously enough and went out of my way to be an ass to you."

Levi rolled his eyes. "Okay, no more apologies, from either of us. The past can stay in the past from now on." He didn't just mean about the way they'd argued. He hoped Raiden got that.

He seemed to as he grinned at Levi. "I promise, chief!" He saluted, poorly. It made Levi smile.

"Actually," he said as he folded his napkin into his lap. "I was a sergeant."

"Really?" Raiden sounded genuinely interested. Levi didn't want to talk about his military days, though. He shouldn't have brought it up. But part of him wanted to impress Raiden a little.

"That's in the past, though," he said pointedly. Raiden nodded.

"So it is."

They managed to make enough small talk to last them until they got their pizzas. Once they arrived, neither of them wanted to chat much because their food was just so good. Although, Raiden did pause between mouthfuls long enough to insist he'd picked the best topping with his steak and cheese until Levi made him take a bite of his spicy shrimp and sausage.

Raiden moaned. It was a positively filthy sound. "Okay, yeah, that's good."

They cleaned their plates and got ready to head back on the road again. But when the waitress came scurrying eagerly back over to them, she had a surprise.

"Your meals are on the house, gentlemen," she informed them excitedly. "It's been an honor to have you here."

"Oh, no," said Raiden hastily. "It was so good, I'm happy to pay."

"Honestly, we insist," said the waitress.

Levi saw Raiden's dilemma. He didn't want to be rude by refusing her generous offer, but he didn't want to take advantage of a free meal either. Raiden frowned and glanced out at the other diners. Levi followed his gaze as it settled on a young couple with two small children who looked so tired it was a wonder they were still sitting upright.

"Oh," said Raiden, offering the waitress his card again. "Okay. I'd like to pay for *that* family's bill, then. But please don't tell them it was me. Is that all right?"

She stared at him for a moment. "Um, yeah, I'm sure that's fine. Let me just, uh, take your details." She wandered off, presumably to swipe his card for when the young family came to pay their bill.

"What?" Raiden asked when he caught Levi staring.

"Nothing," he said, feeling the wry smile creep onto his lips.

The rest of the drive into Pennsylvania was pretty much uneventful. They listened to the radio while Levi drove and Raiden navigated. They were able to stick to the highways for almost the whole way through, so aside from heavy traffic at times, it was hardly challenging conditions.

Raiden napped for some of the last leg, but Levi let him. He knew where he was going by that point, and chances were Raiden had endured as restless a night as Levi. He was hopeful now that things between them weren't half as fucked as he had feared. They had the new worry of the hacker getting into their car's system of course, but if they weren't at each other's throats, it would make working together far simpler.

As they got further into Pittsburgh, Raiden roused naturally with the city lights beaming down around them. Levi was feeling tired from two full days of driving, but the fact they were near their hotel perked him up considerably.

Maybe he'd hit the gym or the pool once they'd checked in, then order some food.

Or he and Raiden could always grab dinner together, if he fancied.

He chewed his lip and tried to tell himself that it was so Levi could keep an eye on him for security reasons, and why should they eat alone if they could keep each other company? Except he had to admit that Raiden was kind of fun to be around, and he wouldn't mind maybe hanging out more.

*Keep it in your pants, Marine,* he thought savagely to himself.

This time, he helped Raiden bring all his bags inside, as they were going to be staying a couple of days. Plus, unlike the night before, Levi wasn't pissed off with him. They walked inside the hotel together, side by side.

The guy behind the desk got starry-eyed at the sight of Raiden, but managed to keep a professional manner. Levi wondered if he would need to run out back and scream once Raiden left the front desk. Raiden had called ahead and asked for rooms next to each other, impressing Levi. He was taking his security more seriously now.

"Man, I'm shattered," Raiden said in the elevator as they traveled to the fifth floor. "I didn't even drive. You must be a zombie."

"That's what coffee is for," Levi told him with a wink. "But yeah, I'll sleep well tonight, I'm sure."

The mention of sleeping made him think of beds and things two people could get up to in them. He clamped his mouth shut until the elevator opened on the right floor for them.

"This is me," Raiden said with a happy sigh as they came upon the correct room number.

Levi held his hand out for the key card. "I'll go first, check it's okay."

Raiden nodded and handed it over, stepping back with a yawn. Levi placed the bags he was carrying onto the carpet so he had his hands free, then swiped the card to let them inside.

The room was a suite, and the door opened into a living room area.

There were people waiting for them on the other side.

Before he had time to think, Levi pulled his gun.

*"Freeze!"*

# CHAPTER

## *Twelve*

### RAIDEN

"NO!" Raiden bellowed, shoving in front of Levi. "No, no, Levi, these are my friends," he babbled. Levi had barely registered him. He just bounced the gun back up to point it at the group behind Raiden. "Levi?" he tried again, stepping in front of the gun. "That's two-fifths of Below Zero and their fiancés you are aiming a fucking gun at."

"Three-fifths," a low voice rumbled from the direction of the minibar. "But no fiancé. Cool piece, bro."

Levi seemed to come back to his senses, blinking as he lowered his weapon. "And what," he asked in a voice like ice, "are they doing sneaking into your hotel room?"

"I don't know," Raiden said, bubbling with excitement as he turned around to the very shocked party. "But it's *awesome.*"

He stepped forward as the five guys relaxed a fraction. Most of them still seemed rattled at having a gun pointed their way. Raiden couldn't say he blamed them.

"It's okay, I promise, Levi just got a little overexcited is all. You can chill." Raiden arched an eyebrow at Levi, willing him to back him up.

Levi finished hauling the rest of the bags into the room and closed the door. "Sure," he said, his voice like stone.

Raiden rolled his eyes. "Don't be a party pooper. Come here and meet my friends. They're totally normal."

"Speak for yourself," said Blake. He was the first of the group to recover and come over to meet them. He clapped Raiden on the back. "Some of us are quite exceptional."

"He's talking about me," said Elion as he bounced over and shoved his hand in front of Levi. "Elion Rodriguez, Blake's fiancé."

To Raiden's utter astonishment, Levi smiled as he shook first Elion's, then Blake's hands. "I know all y'all. You do that dancing show. Flaming Feet?"

Blake laughed, showing his dazzling teeth. With his blond hair and impressive physique, he really was an all-American heartthrob. "Feet of Flames," he corrected with amusement. "Wouldn't have pegged a guy like you to be a fan."

Levi shrugged. "The guys on my last tour loved it. We watched it all the time when we could get signal."

"Shut up," said Raiden. "That's amazing."

"That Nessa chick is super hot," Levi said forcefully.

Typical. He didn't want any hint of the fact he might not be straight to even peek out. He could only watch a show if there was a babe to jerk off over. Raiden resisted the urge to roll his eyes. Instead, he turned back to his friends.

"I can't believe you're all here," he said weakly.

"We couldn't let you down, dude," Blake said affectionately.

"Hell no," agreed Elion, rocking on his heels in excitement. "Do you like your surprise?"

"Love it," Raiden said, beaming at the people around him. Elion and Blake had been together almost two years and had recently gotten engaged. "Can I see the ring?" he asked Elion with a grin.

Elion preened and held out his hand. The stones in the silver band were pink to match the tips of Elion's black hair. "My boy did good," he said proudly, bumping his hip against Blake's.

"Okay, all right," said Joey Sullivan, pretending to be annoyed. "But this isn't your bachelor party, is it? You'll get your turn next."

"Joey," said Raiden warmly.

"Ray!" Joey cried, throwing himself at Raiden for a fierce hug. Joey was smaller than Raiden but made up for it with larger-than-life enthusiasm. His unruly curls accosted Raiden's face, making him laugh. "We missed you so much!"

"It's been too long," Gabe, his fiancé, agreed. He took his turn and hugged Raiden as well, then eyed Levi warily. "So… we're not under arrest or anything?"

Raiden scoffed and slapped Levi's chest, purely to irk him. "Nah, Levi's a teddy bear, just like you."

It was true. Gabe was allegedly a librarian. But thanks to a keen interest in rock climbing and many years volunteering as a firefighter, he was stacked almost as much as Levi was.

Gabe and Joey had got engaged just over a year ago and their wedding was taking place in a couple of months. Raiden hadn't expected that they could all get together like this beforehand, not with all their crazy schedules.

Raiden blinked as a shot glass appeared in front of his face. "Good to see you, dude," a friendly voice growled from behind his ear. "We've got some catching up to do."

Raiden knew there was no fighting it, so he took the drink and downed the burning liquid with a spluttering cough. "Missed you too, TJ," he said.

TJ gave a sort of battle cry and picked him up from behind for a hug. He was easily as big as Levi and Gabe with more tattoos and brushes with the law to actually make him seem scary. But Raiden knew better.

"So, who's your friend?" TJ asked when he'd put Raiden down again. He shoved his hand around Raiden and offered it to Levi. "Trent Charles," TJ said.

"Trent?" Joey scoffed.

TJ licked his lips and winked at him. "I'm trying a new thing, little man."

Levi grabbed the proffered hand and pumped it once. His eyes were narrow. "Levi Patterson. I'm Raiden's security."

"You still have security?" Elion asked. Raiden had mentioned Levi a few weeks ago, if not by name. "Is this because of that hack?"

"Are you all right?" Blake demanded. Their concern was warranted after the attack they had gone through a couple of years ago.

Raiden smiled and held up his hands. "I'm fine," he insisted. The last thing he wanted was to spoil this night. He couldn't remember the last time he, Blake, Joey and TJ had all been in the same room together. Possibly not since the band had split. "Levi keeps everything running smoothly. So you can see why picking the lock to my room gave him a heart attack."

He glanced apologetically at Levi, who still looked unimpressed.

It had been pretty hot the way he'd been ready to fuck shit up in an instant for Raiden, though. Raiden knew he shouldn't be having thoughts like that, but he couldn't help it.

"No lock picking," said TJ with a smirk. "That poor guy on duty almost flooded his basement when three members of Below Zero walked up to him. He agreed to let us have a key card."

"I could get him fired for that," Levi grumbled.

"But we won't, will we," Raiden said pointedly. Levi didn't mean it. After all, he was just rattled. "Because it was the best surprise, ever."

Joey hopped from foot to foot. "We thought we could hang in here," he said. "Avoid any hassle from going to a bar."

"I already bought supplies," said TJ, ambling back to the minibar and holding up a bottle of tequila. Presumably, that was where Raiden's shot had come from. "So let's get this party started."

Raiden took a moment to orientate himself as he and Levi moved their bags into his bedroom. Levi didn't seem to want to leave Raiden's side, despite being told everything was okay, and said he'd relocate his luggage to his own room later.

This was the best surprise Raiden could have ever wished for. After the unpleasant shock of realizing their GPS had been hacked and missing the stop in Cincinnati, Raiden had been feeling pretty low. Not to mention confused about what had happened between him and Levi last night. But having the guys reunited felt like stepping back in time into familiar territory where he was safe and loved. Even better, because Elion and Gabe were here too.

And Levi. Raiden glanced at him as he rummaged in one of his suitcases for a fresh shirt to wear. "Are you okay with this?"

"With your very basic security being breached?" Levi muttered, arching an eyebrow. "Not particularly." He sighed and rolled his shoulders. "But that's a problem for tomorrow. Right now, no. There's no issue with you hanging with your friends. So long as none of you tag the hotel's location in any posts. Are we clear?"

His stern tone sent a little shiver down Raiden's spine. It was probably messed up that he liked it when Levi got bossy with him.

"Yes, sir," he replied seriously. "I'll make sure they behave."

Levi snorted, his incredulity breaking the tension. "I somehow doubt that," he said, looking back out where TJ was threatening to light a fresh line of shots on fire. "Just get them to understand about the location thing."

Raiden came to stand next to him. "You're not going to sit like a sourpuss in the corner though, are you?" he asked.

"I'm on duty," Levi said simply.

Raiden rolled his eyes. "Okay, but these are my best friends in the whole entire world. Would it maybe kill you to have a couple of beers and get to know them?"

Levi regarded him strangely. "Why?"

"Because you're a human being and you're allowed to have fun every once in a while," Raiden said with a laugh.

He was aware, though, of what he was saying. He wanted Levi to get along with his friends because he wanted them to like each other. Which was kind of dumb because Levi was just his bodyguard.

The memory of his body pressed deliciously against Raiden's and his tongue thrusting into his mouth was somewhat at odds with that statement.

Raiden wasn't allowed to think about that, though. "Come on, man," he said. "I won't be able to have fun if I feel like you're sitting around judging us. Nothing bad's going to happen. My friends are getting married. It's a celebration."

He knew he was stooping to emotional blackmail, particularly when he gave Levi his best puppy dog eyes. But he didn't care. He wanted to party with his boys and maybe see Levi thaw out a little for once.

Levi licked his lips. "Okay," he said slowly. "But I won't do any shots, of any kind. Are we clear?"

"Crystal," Raiden replied, trying not to sound too eager.

"Are you guys making out in there or what?" Elion's teasing voice floated across the music TJ had put on in the main room. Raiden did his absolute best not to blush. "Come on, you're missing the fun!"

Raiden poked his head around the door. "We can't all be

as naturally pretty as you, can we?" he said, throwing Elion a kiss. "Give the weary travelers a second to freshen up. You *did* crash my room, after all."

"It's fine," said TJ, slapping Elion on the back. TJ towered over most people as he was built like a linebacker. His many tats made him seem intimidating too, but next to beautiful, slim Elion, the contrast was even more evident. He winked at Blake's fiancé. "They can play catch up when they're good and ready."

Levi pulled Raiden back into the bedroom. "No. Shots."

His fingers dug into Raiden's arm, just a little. This time, his whole body shivered. He wondered if Levi noticed.

"I promise," he said.

He was starting to get the feeling he'd do anything when Levi asked like that.

# *Thirteen*

## LEVI

THIS WAS A BAD IDEA AND LEVI KNEW IT, ESPECIALLY AFTER THE breach in security they'd had the day before with the GPS. There was no doubt in his mind that someone had tried to fuck with them, and the fact they'd made contact again since the initial hack made Levi nervous.

Before, Raiden was just one of a dozen celebrities to be targeted in the hack. The fact Levi was there, providing security, was just to set everyone's mind at ease.

Now Raiden had been singled out. Levi would have to wait to hear back from his uncle to see if anyone else had experienced anything sinister off the list. But the chances of them publicizing any further attacks were slim. They weren't going to say anything about Raiden's issue, after all.

So did that mean this threat was more serious than they thought? If so, Levi should not just shrug off the fact that Raiden's hotel room had been violated. What if it hadn't been his friends, but someone waiting with a gun? Or even worse, someone who had entered and left already, leaving a bomb behind?

Yet here he was, walking back into the main room of the

suite with Raiden like they were just going to a frat party, no big deal.

One of the bigger guys, Gabe, raised an eyebrow from where he was sitting on the couch. "No gun this time?" he asked. He was obviously put out by the weapon. Levi had met plenty of civilians who were. It didn't bother him.

"It's within reach," he said. He didn't want a gun sitting around with a bunch of drunk dudes anyway. It was safer to keep it in Raiden's room. "I hope that's not a problem?"

"I'm sorry again if we gave you a fright," Blake said.

Levi hadn't been lying when he said the guys out on tour liked to watch dumb reality shows. They preferred watching fluffy, mindless stuff after all the shit they had to deal with while on duty. So he genuinely did recognize Blake Jackson and Elion Rodriguez.

They seemed like actually nice guys. Their concern for Raiden appeared sincere too, which elevated them in Levi's books.

Because his well-being was Levi's job. Nothing more.

Joey Sullivan and TJ – Trent – Charles, Levi had researched online like he'd said. Gabe, Joey's fiancé, was an unknown. But he seemed like a steady enough guy.

"It wasn't really a fright," Levi said wryly in response to Blake's apology. "More just acting on instinct."

"We're still sorry," said Blake. He pulled Elion to him and arched an eyebrow. "But *some* people were convinced a surprise would be a good idea."

"You're such a spoilsport," Elion grumbled with a smirk that suggested he didn't mean it at all.

Levi appreciated Blake's concern, however. A couple of years ago the two of them had been involved in a serious incident with an obsessed fan that almost got deadly. Levi wondered if Raiden was facing a similar situation now.

Raiden scoffed and accepted a beer from Gabe. "This was honestly the best thing that's happened to me all year."

Joey, easily the youngest-looking guy in the room even without his baby face and cherub curls, leaned forward on the sofa. "But...you worked with Lady Gaga a couple of months ago."

Raiden flashed a grin at him. "What can I say? Bros before critically acclaimed international megastars."

The group laughed. There was an extremely easy dynamic between them all. It made Levi able to relax a little, although he was glad he had bolted the door once he'd brought all the bags in. If he could help it, he didn't want any more surprises.

Which reminded him...

"I hate to be a killjoy," he said. "But is there anything else I should know about before we settle in for the night? Y'all order pizzas?" He swept his gaze over the room. "Or strippers?" It was a bachelor party, after all.

Joey and Gabe, the two grooms, looked horrified. "God, no, no strippers," said Gabe. Then he snapped his head around and glared at Trent, who was quietly setting up a seriously impressive number of bowls and plates of food, not to mention lining up cocktails and shots along the small bar. "Right, Trent," Gabe said pointedly. "Because I know Blake told you no strippers."

Trent smirked, licking barbecue sauce off one of his fingers before casually slugging back a shot of tequila from the bottle. "Nah, dude," he said in a low voice that rumbled from his chest. "To each their own, but I find paying someone to get naked for you a little skeezy." He waggled his eyebrows. "Much more fun to just find a nice girl who wants to do it of her own accord."

"Or nice dude," said Elion, raising his beer. Blake slapped him playfully.

Trent raised his own beer. "Or dude."

"Yes, well," said Blake. "Some of us don't have to try and find anyone to do that anymore, do we?"

He kissed Elion's cheek as Gabe snuggled closer to Joey.

Raiden made a retching noise as the rest of the guys laughed. "Blurgh, happy people are gross. Levi, get over here with the other singles and let's turn up the music."

The room naturally divided into two, with the two couples on the sofas discussing wedding plans and the three single, straight guys gravitating towards the bar.

Mostly straight.

Levi bit his lip as Trent handed him a beer and the three of them clinked bottles. As much as he tried, he was struggling to get Raiden's words out of his head. Could it be that it was more than just enjoying getting his cock sucked? Could he have a thing for guys? Not as much as women, but could it be there, lurking?

If it was, it couldn't happen with Raiden. So he took a swig of beer and committed himself to finding a balance between keeping his wits about him and participating enough so Raiden didn't feel he was being watched and judged.

"This is awesome, TJ," Raiden said. He picked up a slice of pizza that had obviously arrived before they had. "Thank you, man."

Trent leaned against the counter and smiled. "It was a group effort," he said.

He had a similar build to Levi and wore a simple vest that showed off the body art on his light brown arms. Half of his dark hair fell in thick waves to his shoulders and the rest was tied in a knot behind his head. His dark eyes were framed with thick eyebrows that gave him a slightly scary look. Levi could see why he was popular with the ladies. There was apparently a new one on his arm each week, according to the internet.

He resisted the urge to roll his eyes. This job had turned him into a goddamned fanboy.

"It actually worked out better that you couldn't make last night," Trent continued. "This way, we all made it, and as fun as the gig sounded, it's better to just hang. Catch up."

Raiden looked at the others. "Well, almost all of us. I guess Reyse was too busy?" he said ruefully.

Trent arched an eyebrow. "Yeah, he is busy," he admitted, referring to the fifth and final former member of Below Zero, Reyse Hickson. "But I think he finds it hard, don't you? Like, he's feeling guilty he's such a huge success."

"You're hardly struggling for work," Levi commented. "I liked that last movie you did, with the terrorists in Paris."

Like Joey, Trent had gone into acting after the band had split. Levi had never thought much of him, but as part of his research, he'd bothered to watch a couple of the more action-orientated films he'd done. They weren't half bad.

Raiden scoffed and punched Trent's impressive bicep. "Better than the puppy day care one," he said with a snicker.

"Or the one where you voiced an animated trash can," Joey added with a hoot from across the room.

Trent gave them a playful smirk. "You can all suck my magnificent cock," he said to a collective cheer.

It reminded Levi a little of hanging with his guys on tour. Makeshift bunks set up under a tent big enough to house a dozen or two dozen men, all blowing off steam in various ways. Namely ribbing the shit out of each other. For the first time in a long while, he felt somewhat at ease. Like he'd come home.

"Let's just be grateful the four of us could make it," Trent said, presumably returning to their conversation about Reyse. "Hicks will come back to us when he can."

Raiden gave his friend a thoughtful smile and touched his arm. "I'll drink to that."

"Good, because you owe us a shot," Trent said playfully. He vaulted around the bar with surprising agility, scooping up the tequila bottle as he went.

"Another one?" Raiden groaned. "I've hardly eaten anything."

"Do you really think there's any getting out of this?" Gabe said in exasperation as Trent dropped into the seat beside him. "Come on, get over here."

"You too, Levi!" cried Elion excitably.

Trent shook his head as he lined up shot glasses. "Boss man is working, no shots for him. Unlike the rest of you pussies." With a wicked grin, he thrust a bowl of lemon slices into Blake's lap. The large number he'd prepared did not bode well for the evening.

Levi was impressed at Trent's consideration, and Raiden gave him a small smile and pat on the back before heading over to sit on the sofa. But Levi felt an itch at the back of his mind, as if he wanted Raiden's friends to like him, to approve of him. This wasn't high school, so he was a douche for even legitimizing such a thought. But on the other hand, it took a hell of a lot to put him on his ass.

"I think this US Marine can handle one," he said, perching on the sofa arm next to Raiden.

"Yes!" Elion cheered. "That's the spirit, dude. See, Raiden. He doesn't have that much of a stick up his ass."

Raiden froze. "I, uh…"

Levi chuckled. Of course Raiden had told his buddies that Levi was a stiff. That was his job, after all. "I think Ray here needs to do a double for that," he said slyly, arching his eyebrow down at Raiden. Was it his imagination, or did he tremble slightly?

The suggestion that Raiden do two got a cheer and

several whoops from the other guys. "I like this one," said little Joey, who was already a bit worse for wear. He leaned over and patted Levi's knee. "I think you should keep him, Ray."

Raiden laughed, glancing nervously at Levi. He didn't say anything though, instead groaning and complaining loudly as Trent pushed two full shot glasses into his hands.

There wasn't anything to say, anyway. Levi wasn't going to be sticking around. Once the job was complete, he'd leave Raiden and move on to the next client.

That's just the way it was.

# CHAPTER
## *Fourteen*

### RAIDEN

RAIDEN WASN'T THAT DRUNK. HE COULD STILL STAND UP ON his own two feet. He even managed to walk in a straight line when Gabe asked him to. Even though the table got in his way. Someone must have moved it.

When Joey started crying because he loved everyone so much, Gabe bundled him up and escorted him back to their room, making soothing noises as they left. Then Elion got a little too handsy with Blake, so they disappeared as well before they could get indecent. That left TJ, Levi and Raiden.

Raiden should have been getting sleepy after their long day traveling then imbibing a shit ton of booze. But he was alert and fidgety.

He and Levi were on opposite ends of one couch, and TJ on the other. They'd stopped doing shots, thank fuck, and had been playing twenty questions before Blake and Elion had gotten too horny and ditched them. Now Levi and TJ were engrossed in a rather serious beer mat flipping contest. They were each up to six coasters each.

Raiden was trying to sober up a bit with a glass of water and a bowl of pretzels he was currently devouring. He was watching the guys flip their coasters intently, like it was an Olympic sport. He gasped as Levi snatched a pile of seven from the air, then coughed on pretzel bits.

"Nice catch," he wheezed.

Levi shrugged, like it was nothing. "Wanna play?"

Raiden shook his head. "Think I'll leave it to the pros."

TJ stretched then scratched his chin. "Actually, I might head out. You guys are probably beat."

Raiden checked his watch. "You're going to bed already?" That wasn't like him.

TJ winked. "I don't have a room here, bro. Gonna hit a club, see where I end up."

Raiden was going to ask why he hadn't booked rooms like the others, but that would be far too organized for TJ. "You'll need to crash at some point," he said with a frown. He leaned over to find the remote and turned the music off. "Why don't you crash on my sofa?"

TJ gave him his signature raised eyebrow. "And what if I have a lady friend?"

Levi sat up, fishing his key card out of his cargo pants. "Why don't you take my room?" he suggested, offering out the card. "It's still empty. I could take the couch in here."

Raiden's heart skipped a beat. It was just because Levi was obsessed with keeping an eye on him and probably feeling extra jittery after working out the GPS got hacked. The couch was a long way from the bedroom.

TJ gave Levi a lop-sided smile. "Sure, man," he said, glancing at Raiden. "Sounds like a great plan."

Raiden wanted to demand what that look meant, but TJ was already on his feet. He clapped Levi on the back, then saluted at Raiden. "See you later," he said with a grin, then slipped out the door.

Levi stood as well, carefully not looking at Raiden as he brushed his cargo pants down. Raiden's heart was thumping loudly in his chest. Rather than let himself be overwhelmed by it, Raiden lounged back on the sofa, licking salt granules from his fingers.

"So, that was you absolutely, *definitely* not doing shots?" he asked slyly.

Levi scowled and began picking up dirty glasses to take to the mini-bar. Housekeeping wasn't going to hate them, but they had given them a fair bit of work for the morning.

Raiden sighed and hauled himself upright to lend a hand. Levi was doing his best not to look at Raiden and work around him. So naturally, Raiden was doing everything he could to get in his way.

*"Enough,"* Levi growled. He spun around and looked at Raiden after the third time he deliberately got under his feet. "If you're that drunk, I suggest you just go to bed."

Raiden tossed the last cold pizza slice in the trash, then piled the box up with the other recyclables. "All you're stuff's still in there. Don't you want to get it out first?"

"I know how to be quiet," Levi grumbled, stacking up more glasses. "I *was* a reconnaissance Marine."

Raiden was still drunk enough that it seemed like a good idea to ease his way between Levi and the bar. He grinned up at him impishly, spurred on by Levi's obvious irritation. "You know," he said. He rubbed his thumb across his lower lip, like he was deep in thought. "That's a pretty huge bed. It wouldn't be much of a hassle to share."

Levi went still as the color drained from his face. "I'm not discussing this with you."

He tried to move away, but Raiden just shimmied back in front of him. "Why not?"

He touched his hand to Levi's hip, which Levi immediately batted away. "Because we agreed not to."

"But," Raiden whined. "We're stuck in this room together.

It doesn't have to mean anything. Come on, aren't you curious?"

Raiden was more than curious. Despite his earlier promises that he was going to stay away from Levi and keep their relationship professional, in his intoxicated state all he could think of was Levi's mouth claiming his own. How he rubbed his cock against Raiden until he came.

"Raiden," Levi growled. "You're drunk, cut it out."

"I will," Raiden said. He held his hands up. "If you tell me you don't want it. Don't want me."

He studied Levi's icy blue eyes as they flickered back and forth. "This is a bad idea."

"That's not what I asked," Raiden whispered. He slid his hands up Levi's firm chest. He stood still as a marble statue, but he didn't push Raiden away. "I never said it was a good idea. But it could be *oh so good.*"

"How would you know?" Levi said. He stepped forward, forcing Raiden to back up into the bar. "You ever been fucked?"

Raiden's breaths were coming out ragged. His mind flooded with images of Levi fucking him, making him mute for a moment. "You ever fuck a guy?"

"No," said Levi a little too quickly.

Raiden laughed, dizzy with desire. "Oh, you've done something, though, haven't you? This isn't entirely new territory for you, is it, Marine?"

He rubbed his hands over Levi's pecs, feeling his nipples harden under his t-shirt. He was panting too, little puffs that made Raiden's hair flutter.

"I'm offering you more sex," Raiden continued. "Surely you're not going to let the fact I'm a guy stop you?" He leaned in closer. "A tight hole is good no matter where it comes from, right?"

Levi groaned, then grabbed Raiden's shoulders. Raiden

could feel the bulge in his cargo pants, and his mouth watered at the idea of fulfilling his wish to touch his prick this time.

He fisted the material of Levi's shirt. "I want your cock in my mouth. In my ass. If that's not something you want, I'll walk away now and shut the door. Never mention it again." He smirked and licked his lower lip provocatively. "One-time deal, my friend."

Levi's jaw was so tight it looked like it might snap. All the color that had rushed from his cheeks had come back in a deep blush. He looked so fucking hot when he was aroused.

"We can't always have what we want," he ground out.

Raiden rolled his cock against Levi's through their pants. "No. But who says we can't have this?"

"My job."

"You're off the clock," Raiden said, glancing at all the empty beer bottles and shot glasses. He could still taste the tequila on his lips despite the water and pretzels he'd had. "Your uncle never needs to know." He pressed against Levi, who was still not moving, and whispered in his ear. "Tell me you want to fuck me, Levi. *Please.*"

In a sudden flurry of moment, Levi surged forward, seizing Raiden to sit him on the bar. Glasses crashed to the ground as he grabbed Raiden's face and kissed him furiously. Raiden surrendered immediately, clutching handfuls of Levi's blond hair and wrapping his legs around his waist.

"Tell me," Raiden demanded as Levi kissed down his throat, biting at his collarbone. "Tell me how much you want my ass."

"Shut the fuck up," Levi snarled. Raiden just grinned until Levi came back up to savage his mouth again.

Raiden moaned and thrust his pelvis against Levi's hard stomach. "Been thinking about your cock," he mumbled between kisses. "When I saw you. At the ranch. I bet it's gorgeous."

"Are you sure you've never done this before?" Levi asked. He grabbed the back of Raiden's neck to look into his eyes as he panted.

Raiden licked his lips. "Just have an open mind, I guess," he said truthfully. "Come on, G.I. Joe. I'd let you ravish me right here, but there's a perfectly decent bed through there." He wiggled his eyebrows. "And a bag with condoms and lube in it."

It wasn't that he'd been planning on seducing Levi. Far from it. Sex was just something that tended to happen on tour. It was always kind of crazy. Raiden was extremely glad now that he'd come prepared.

Something shifted in Levi's eyes. Raiden felt him stop fighting.

Raiden slipped off the counter, pushing Levi backwards to the bedroom while they kissed sloppily. Levi's large hands roamed over Raiden's back and pawed at his ass. Oh, he wanted it all right.

Raiden was surprised how not nervous he was. He knew anal was supposed to hurt if you didn't do it right, or even when you *did* do it right. And he'd read a fair number of testimonials from guys who had massively freaked out at the idea of having someone inside them. But none of that seemed to bother him as they stumbled back into the bedroom. They tripped and Levi pressed him against the wall as they regained their footing.

This was all he cared about. Feeling Levi claiming him again. Dominating him.

Levi picked him up once more and Raiden dug his fingers into his back and shoulders. He wanted to bruise that beautiful inked skin with marks of his own. He wanted to get Levi's shirt off and maul him.

Spinning the both of them, Levi walked the few steps to drop Raiden unceremoniously onto the bed. Raiden panted and shuffled backwards, pushing his hair from his face. "Well, come on then," he said, hoping to goad Levi into action. He was looking down at Raiden like he was assessing him, summing him up.

Sure enough, Levi crawled on top of him, like a predator who had caught his prey. "You want me to fuck you?" Levi growled.

That was probably the closest he was going to get to admitting that he wanted this. That Raiden turned him on. Raiden felt like they were at the point of no return. They couldn't deny their attraction any longer after this.

He didn't want to. Life was too short, so why not see where this took them. In that moment he knew he was hard as a rock and felt like his skin was on fire. Only Levi could soothe the burn.

"Yeah," Raiden said. "Why not? I bet you give a magnificent pounding."

Finally, he reached out and palmed Levi's own hardon through his cargo pants. Even through the material he felt amazing. Raiden wanted him inside him.

"And I bet you're a filthy fuck," Levi said back at him. He skin was flushed and damp. Raiden was desperate to taste more of it.

A look flitted across Levi's face, like he was thinking too hard about what they were going to do. Thinking wasn't necessary, only action.

Raiden dropped his hands above his head and squirmed his hips against where Levi was straddling him. "Time to put your money where your mouth is, Kevin." He deliberately used the nickname to grab Levi's attention back. It worked.

"You talk too fucking much," Levi said. But it lacked rancor. Raiden could hear the excitement in his words and watched eagerly as he stripped his shirt off in one smooth motion.

Raiden reached up to run his hands over the expanse of muscles. Tattoos were spread over his biceps, spilling across his back and onto his chest. Eagle wings and red roses and names on scrolls. Raiden wanted to know what every single one of them meant.

"Yeah?" said Raiden, raising his eyebrows. "You could shut me up, you know? Plenty of other things I could be doing with my mouth."

"Don't you worry," Levi said. By the look on his face, he could apparently think of several things as well. He pushed Raiden's hands away and hovered over him. "I've got more than enough to keep your mouth busy."

Raiden took him up on that offer, grabbed his neck to pull him in for another searing kiss. Levi's big hands slipped under Raiden's shirt, skimming over his ticklish flesh, feeling the muscles as Raiden squirmed beneath him.

In a flash, Levi yanked his shirt off too, leaving them both naked from the waist up. He dropped back down to continue the kiss, their bare chests rubbing together. "I want you on your knees," he rasped into Raiden's ear as he attacked his jeans. As soon as the fly was unzipped, he shoved both Raiden's pants and briefs down, stripping him naked.

Raiden gasped and lay still with his hands above his head, allowing Levi to inspect his unclothed form. His cock was erect and curving towards his stomach, already dripping precum in anticipation. Levi ran his large hands down the underside of Raiden's arms, along his chest and down the side of his hips, carefully not touching anywhere near his groin.

Raiden might have thought that was on purpose to tease him, but knowing what he did, he suspected otherwise. Levi might have a history with men, but how much cock had he actually touched? That would mean he'd have to definitively acknowledge he was fucking a guy, and if Raiden had to guess, he'd say that Levi had avoided that in the past.

"Suck it," he dared him.

Levi looked like he might defy him. But then he swooped down and swallowed Raiden almost to the root, forcing him to cry out. He really hoped TJ had gone out like he'd said. If not, that the hotel had good, thick walls.

Levi only gifted him with a few bobs of his head before he released Raiden's cock and moved off the bed, standing to drop his own trousers. He looked Raiden dead in the eye as he swiftly unbuttoned himself and shoved the cargo pants to the floor.

He stood gloriously naked as he kicked the clothes away. "Where's the stuff?" he asked.

Raiden gulped and tore his eyes away from Levi's muscular thighs and impressive cock. There was that trickle of fear he'd been anticipating. How was he expected to fit *that* inside him?

He pointed to his overnight case. "In the blue washbag," he said.

Levi moved with purpose, quickly removing one of the packets of condoms and the pump action lube. Raiden had bought a fresh one, and Levi tore the plastic safety wrapping off the top with his teeth.

Raiden flinched. Levi saw. Something dark flashed in his eyes, and he approached the bed again. Dropping the supplies on the mattress to the side of them, he ran his fingertips up Raiden's flank, then cupped his jaw with one hand and hip with the other. His grip was strong, possessive.

"You still sure about this?" he asked.

He looked unflinchingly into Raiden's eyes. Any assumptions Raiden had made that Levi was detached from this experience flew out the window. He was right there, with

Raiden, naked on his bed as they prepared to fuck each other's brains out.

But there was also something caring in his tone. Raiden suddenly felt like one of Levi's guys out in Iraq, relying on him to keep everyone together no matter what. In that moment, he was sure he'd been a great sergeant.

For all his teasing and tormenting, he trusted Levi. So he nodded. "Yes," he whispered. "Tell me what you want."

Levi's blue eyes looked like dark coals in the dim light of the bedroom. He dipped down and kissed Raiden with something that could be mistaken for tenderness if Raiden didn't know any better.

"I want you on your hands and knees," Levi said. He sucked on Raiden's earlobe, then bit it gently. "Can you do that?"

Raiden nodded.

"Good boy."

Raiden took pride in his grooming and kept his intimate areas pristine, more for himself than a need to appeal to anyone else. But as he presented his ass up to Levi, on all fours like an animal, he took some comfort that he looked as best as he could.

Levi stood at the end of the bed, then gripped the front of Raiden's thighs and dragged him suddenly backwards to him. Raiden gasped but stayed in position, sensing that was what Levi wanted.

Was this the way he always had sex, or was he winging it as much as Raiden was? Raiden's heart was hammering in his chest and his pulse thrummed loudly in his ears. He could hear Levi breathing heavily through his nose.

"Good," he murmured, running his hands over Raiden's back, his thighs, his ass and his stomach. He found the ticklish part of Raiden's belly, the softer part beneath his navel that he loved to be touched, and stroked it as he pressed the front of his thighs and jutting cock against Raiden's ass.

"Oh, fuck, yes," Raiden said, the words breathy. He was trembling with anticipation as Levi snatched up the lube, slicked his fingers, and began rubbing his hole. There wasn't much more that turned Raiden on than a confident lover.

Levi had obviously done this before with a woman. There was no hesitation as he eased the first finger in and kissed his way up Raiden's spine. But then he surprised him by using his other hand to fondle his balls, giving him sensations from multiple directions.

Raiden moaned and pushed against him, wanting more. A sudden slap to his ass stunned him.

"Behave," Levi growled. But Raiden could hear the playfulness there.

"Or what?" he asked and wiggled his ass a little.

Levi spanked him again. It wasn't hard, but enough to make the skin tingle. "You'll find out."

Raiden chuckled quietly, then stopped with a gasp as Levi used the opportunity to force another finger inside.

"Are you sure you've never fucked a guy before?"

Levi kissed down his back again. "Are you sure you're never given this tight ass up for cock before?" he countered. "Because it seems to me that you're begging for it."

Raiden bit his lip and whimpered. "Stop pissing around and give it to me then," he said.

Levi withdrew his fingers and slapped the other ass cheek. "Your job here is just to wait and take what I give you."

"Yes, sir," Raiden told him.

His arms and legs were already trembling, but then Levi pulled his cheeks apart and the next thing Raiden felt was Levi's mouth and tongue invading his hole.

"Oh – *fuck*," Raiden cried, scrabbling to get purchase on the bedsheets. He'd had girls play with his ass before while going down on him, but he'd never actually had anyone eat him out before. He thought he might come there and then, especially when Levi reached around and tugged on his cock. His fingers were slippery with the lube he'd been using and Raiden's precum, and Raiden wailed.

He hung on though, gnashing his teeth as Levi kissed and licked his entrance, stretching him further in preparation for his cock.

"Yes," he begged. "Please, just like that, oh my god." He wasn't really aware of what he was saying, just that he wanted Levi to know that he liked this a *lot*.

Levi continued to pleasure him a little longer, then stepped away. Raiden felt bereft as his cock, balls and ass were all suddenly abandoned. He looked over his shoulder to see Levi wipe his face, then pluck the condom from the bed.

Raiden refused to gulp or shiver or any of the other reactions his body wanted to have in the face of Levi rolling the rubber down his big cock. It would fit, it would be fine. Raiden wanted this. He just needed to relax.

Levi lined up the tip and pushed. Raiden dropped his head between his shoulders and moaned.

"That's it," Levi murmured, rubbing his back before using both his hands to pull Raiden's cheeks apart, making it easier for him to gain access. "Easy does it."

Raiden's whole body quivered as he focused as hard as he could on loosening the muscles of his asshole. This was so completely different to having a couple of fingers in there.

Levi kept massaging his ass and even leaned down to kiss between his shoulder blades. This was not quite the fucking Raiden had expected from the grumpy ex-Marine. Gradually, he pushed his way further in, groaning with pleasure as he did.

"Your ass is so tight," he rasped. He gave Raiden's cheek

another slap that made his whole body sing. "Little virgin ass."

Raiden wanted to give him some shit, but he was too focused on getting through the burn as Levi entered further into him. Even with the prep and what felt like half the tube of lubricant, it still hurt like hell. He was sure it would pass. Otherwise, why would people do this? He gritted his teeth.

"Let's shove a fucking eggplant up your ass and see how you like it," he managed to grind out.

Levi laughed. He actually laughed, heartily, and ran his hands up and down Raiden's sides. His breaths were ragged as he eased in a little more, caressing Raiden's skin with featherlight touches.

"You're doing well," he murmured. A compliment. Raiden blinked in surprise.

It made him want to please Levi again, to tease a little more praise from him. So he concentrated solely on his breathing, relaxing his abdomen and the rest of his lower body, allowing Levi to penetrate him.

Levi inhaled sharply and sank all the way in. His balls slapping against Raiden's was a strange but also exhilarating sensation. "Oh, fuck, yes," Raiden growled triumphantly. He felt so full he wanted to cough to try and alleviate it. But the burn was already subsiding and he shifted on his hands and knees where they had gone tingly from being rigid for so long.

Levi groaned and clung to his hips, obviously desperate to move. When he felt ready, Raiden nodded.

"It's okay."

Levi grunted and withdrew his cock enough to slide it back in. Once, twice, three times. With each thrust, it got slightly easier for Raiden to relax around him. Then he touched something that made Raiden scream.

"What the fuck was that?" he said, although he guessed it had to be his prostate. "Holy shit, do that again."

Levi chuckled, happy to comply.

He picked up the pace, keeping his dick angled so it hit Raiden's sweet spot each time, making Raiden yelp and gasp and curse. "Yes, yes, yes," he babbled.

Levi stroked his belly again before capturing his cock, milking it in time to the pounding he was giving Raiden's ass. Before he knew what was happening, he peaked, coming with a wild shout all over the bedspread.

Mercifully, Levi slowed, then pulled his hard cock out of Raiden's overly tender hole. He was still on all fours, his vision blurry and his limbs trembling. The bed dipped as Levi knelt in front of Raiden, his throbbing cock in front of his face.

Raiden didn't ask. He just removed the condom and let Levi feed his big cock down Raiden's throat. Raiden sucked up and down his length, jerking him off with his hand too, just like he'd fantasized about. Raiden loved licking girls out. The way their lips felt on his, the way they screamed and writhed under his tongue. He quickly found he enjoyed sucking cock just as much. The musky taste in his mouth, the heavy weight of it and the velvety texture of the skin.

Levi was panting wildly. "Raiden," he managed to warn, like a gentleman.

Raiden wanted to swallow his cum, though. It was basic and filthy and he loved it. So he sucked harder, laving the member with his tongue and tightening his lips until Levi shouted and grabbed two fistfuls of Raiden's hair. Raiden stilled as he shot his load, swallowing as best he could. But there was a lot, and when he finally leaned back, gasping for air, he had to wipe it from his chin.

Levi watched him as they both slowly came down from

their orgasms, like a man watching a wild beast, wondering if it was going to get skittish.

Raiden felt awash with exhaustion, but he knelt up to face Levi. Their chests rose and fell almost in unison as their cocks softened. "Okay?" he asked.

Levi didn't look away from him. He nodded. "I think I'm going to take a shower."

He got off the bed, picked up his own bag, and walked naked to the bathroom.

Raiden was too tired to analyze anything too closely. He could probably do with a shower as well, but instead he settled for mopping himself up with a few tissues then crawling under the sheets.

He was asleep almost immediately. When he awoke in the morning, Levi was nowhere to be found.

# *Fifteen*

## LEVI

Even after two hours in the gym, Levi was still feeling like absolute shit.

There didn't seem to be a way to turn his brain off. It was like a hive of bees had set up home in his skull. Dripping with sweat and his muscles aching, he stepped into one of the shower cubicles and turned it on colder than it needed to be. He didn't want to take *any* risk of his cock perking up. He was sure he wouldn't be able to jerk off for a long time without thinking of the night before.

He never should have given in to Raiden's advances. But when he had, he should have just fucked him, plain and simple. What the *hell* had been that display he'd put on? He hadn't done anything like that with anyone, not any of the girls he'd seen long enough to call girlfriends or even any of the ones he'd hooked up with that had been into the freakier stuff.

Never in all his twenty-nine years had he been so overcome with the need to dominate a partner in bed. But Raiden pushed him and begged for it. He'd wanted to be bossed around and it had felt so fucking right that Levi's body still vibrated to think about it twelve hours later. He could probably get hard again in a second.

He turned the shower down another degree.

So what? Good sex, that was what they'd agreed on. Nothing more. Raiden wasn't even gay like Collins had been. He wasn't looking for a boyfriend. They had just both come to the realization that they were both somewhere on the queer spectrum and decided to have some fun. They'd done just that. No harm, no foul.

So why couldn't Levi get it out of his mind? Why did he keep picturing Raiden on his knees for him, taking his cock from the front and behind? Levi wanted to grip Raiden's hair and look into his eyes while he swallowed Levi's dick and touched himself. He wanted to pin him against a wall and spank him while they fucked. He wanted to see if he could keep Raiden's smart mouth from talking shit, then maybe a little light punishment when he inevitably failed.

Dear god, he wanted to kiss him again.

Levi rested his palms on the cold tiles and shivered. This was so bad. He couldn't unpick his feelings from the fact that Raiden was, first of all, his client, and second of all, a man. If it had been a woman Levi had met at a bar, would he be wrestling so badly with how last night had gone down?

Unfortunately, that wasn't the case, leaving him to try and face several unpleasant truths all at once. He was bisexual. He'd fucked his very first client. And he'd done it in a way that got pretty kinky.

He screwed up his fists and spat out the water that ran into his mouth. There was no good way out of this. The only solution he could see for the short term was to make sure it wouldn't happen again. The next time Raiden got anywhere near tequila, Levi would take three steps back.

He washed his hair and switched off the water. He was a disciplined man. He could refrain from having sex with someone. He did it all the time. Admittedly, not when the other person was flaunting themselves unashamedly in front of him, but it wasn't anything he couldn't handle.

It wasn't like he had feelings for Raiden, after all. He knew what it was like to be dazzled by a girl. When she made his heart sing and bamboozled his brain so he couldn't stop thinking about her. Raiden was like a splinter under the skin, irritating and festering. But eventually, it would grow out.

Once Raiden was out of sight, he'd be out of mind too. Levi just needed to persevere through this lust haze and he'd be in the clear.

As for admitting that he might indeed be bisexual…well, no one else needed to know that, did they? No sense running around telling people when it didn't have any real bearing on his day-to-day life. He could have sex with dudes if he wanted to, it might even be fun. But it wasn't like he was going to start dating a guy that he'd need to bring home to his mom or introduce as his boyfriend to anyone.

That calmed him somewhat. It felt kind of freeing, actually, to admit this about himself. But only to himself. He didn't need the stress of coming out to anyone. So if he could just move past this thing with Raiden, he might even be more comfortable in his own skin in the future.

He dried off and grabbed his clean clothes. A smile tugged at the corner of his mouth. He was bi. That was kind of cool.

Another guy entered the locker room and Levi immediately straightened his face. Fine, that was one crisis dealt with. And if he could deal with that, he could deal with admitting he'd enjoyed dominating in the bedroom last night. It hadn't got too wild. He didn't think he was about to start tying his partners up and cracking the whip. But the simple pleasure of calling the shots with someone who had really wanted the control out of their hands – there was nothing wrong with that, if that's what they'd both wanted.

So that just left the obvious problem of Raiden.

Of course it did.

Raiden's mission in life seemed to be to make things awkward, to stir up trouble and cause friction. Like he was a bored kid with ADHD that needed constant entertainment. Levi tied his shoes and told himself firmly that he needed to stop treating it as flattering when Raiden gave him a stupid nickname or said controversial things purely because he knew it would get a rise out of Levi. It was just good observational skills that meant he knew that Levi got irritated at the implication he was a bad driver, or that the Patriots were better than the Green Bay Packers. It also meant Raiden was just good at tormenting people. It wasn't thoughtful.

Levi sighed and looked at himself in the mirror before heading back into the belly of the hotel. He really wished he hadn't given his room to Trent now. Otherwise he could have gone back there and hidden. As it was, he was an ex-*Marine*, so he didn't hide, ever, and he'd just have to deal with going back to Raiden's room and facing him.

It was just past oh-eight-hundred when he slid the key card into the door handle and walked back into the suite. He was greeted by several voices all calling out greetings.

"Morning!" Elion said with a wave.

"How's the head?" Gabe asked with a sympathetic wince.

"Shush," Joey begged, cradling a mug of coffee like it was his lifeline.

They were all sitting on the sofas around the table which was towering with a dangerous number of plates. Pancakes and fruit platters and croissants and bacon and waffles all competed for space as the men around the table attacked the food with fervor.

Levi's eyes automatically darted to Raiden's as he closed the door behind him. He tried not to feel guilty for being gone when Raiden had woken up, but in his defense, he had imagined he would sleep in.

Levi had hardly slept at all on the couch. He was extremely glad he didn't have to drive anywhere today, but he would need his wits about him for attending the concert tonight. He thought if he hit the gym as soon as it opened he could tire himself out. Then he might be able to grab a nap when he got back. That would have to wait until later now.

Raiden grinned at him as if nothing was wrong. Levi suspected it was a form of challenge. "Muffin?" he asked, offering the basket out and inviting Levi to sit with them. "I ordered the entire breakfast menu, but at this rate, we still might need more."

"Not a bad idea," Blake agreed as he delved into what might have been an entire carton of scrambled eggs. Elion rubbed his back.

Levi sat himself carefully by Trent, perching on the sofa arm so he was a little removed from everyone. He needed to maintain his authority now that he'd fucked his client senseless.

"Good night?" he asked Trent as he sipped extremely creamy-looking coffee.

Trent winked at him. "Might want to ask the maid to switch those sheets out before you use the bed," he said brazenly.

Levi schooled his reactions carefully so he didn't glance towards Raiden's bedroom or the equally defiled sheets contained within. But he felt Raiden look pointedly at him, as if hoping for a reaction.

Levi was happy to disappoint.

"How about you?" Trent asked.

Levi looked at Trent and found him smirking. Before his heart could explode out of his chest, he reminded himself that Trent could have no way of knowing what Levi and Raiden had gotten up to. Unless Raiden had told them.

But a quick glance at the other guys indicated nothing out of the ordinary. Trent was either just messing with him or making an educated guess. Either way, Levi wasn't going to give him anything.

"The couch was fine," he said, pouring himself black coffee. "But Raiden snores."

"He does," Joey cried, slapping Raiden's knee affectionately. "I don't miss that from touring," he added with a laugh.

"Good thing you'll be back to your own bed tonight, then," Trent said, eyeing Levi as he slowly took a bite of a banana.

Levi almost corrected him. He obviously meant 'room,' not 'bed.' But that might sound defensive. So he ignored the comment, instead reaching for an iced Danish. After the workout he'd just put himself through, he could afford some extra calories.

Talk turned to their plans for the day, which mostly involved everyone else traveling back to their respective home states, leaving Raiden and Levi alone. After a while, Levi couldn't ignore the gaze burning a hole in the side of his head, so he turned and met Raiden's eye.

*Later,* Levi tried to silently communicate. They would discuss what happened when Raiden's friends were gone.

Raiden might not like what Levi had to say. But he would hear it nonetheless.

# CHAPTER
## *Sixteen*

### RAIDEN

IF LEVI WANTED TO PLAY GAMES, RAIDEN COULD PLAY games too.

He kept the guys there as long as possible, feeding them and reminiscing over old times. When TJ fell asleep on the sofa, even better. All the while, Raiden persisted in catching Levi's eye, asking him questions, touching him ever so subtly any chance he got.

He was not going to ignore what happened.

In the cold light of day, he understood how it put Levi in a bit of an awkward position. He could see that if Levi's uncle found out he was messing around with a client, his *first* client, it might look bad. But Kurt need never find out, and even if he did, Raiden had no problem taking the blame for everything in the slightest.

Not if it meant he got fucked like that again.

He'd been undoubtedly sore this morning. The first thing he'd done before calling the boys over was to have a long, hot shower. His ass had been tender, but Raiden had gently fingered himself regardless, closing his eyes and remembering Levi's touch. Then he'd jerked off hard and fast, whispering his name.

It was difficult to miss something you didn't know you were lacking, but now it was as if the door had been opened and Raiden now knew what kind of sex he'd been missing out on. Not that he hadn't enjoyed most of the encounters he'd had in the past. Several had been downright spectacular.

But he kept coming back to that bliss-like state he'd experienced in surrendering his control as he'd bent to Levi's will.

He'd never once felt uncomfortable or out of his depth. If he'd asked, he was sure he could have stepped out of it any time he'd liked. What did people normally do? Red, yellow and green traffic lights, he was pretty sure. Next time he'd mention something to that effect before they went at it again.

He had no doubt it would happen again. He could see in Levi's eyes he was going to fight him on this. But there was only so much you could deny that kind of chemistry. It was like they set each other on fire. It was blinding, fierce, and consumed everything in its path.

He enjoyed the morning trying to make Levi as uncomfortable as possible. Eventually, though, his friends began to head off in their own directions. Elion was driving himself and Blake back to Cincinnati, and Gabe and Joey had a flight to catch back to Connecticut. TJ woke from a forty-five-minute nap as fresh as a daisy, announcing he had people to see, and made his departure.

Raiden took his time over saying goodbye with everyone, giving lots of hugs. Much to his amusement, the guys also turned automatically to Levi for hugs as well, which he dutifully gave. Raiden imagined he wasn't normally one for cuddling, though, and he smirked at the awkwardness of it all.

Once they were all gone, the suite fell quiet again.

Raiden draped himself over one of the sofas in a provocative manner and gave Levi his best smoldering look. "Alone at last," he drawled, arching an eyebrow.

Levi raised a finger. "No," he said dispassionately, then stalked into the bedroom.

"No – no what?" Raiden asked with mirth, not moving from the couch. He'd expected Levi to be nothing less than icy with him and wasn't even remotely intimidated.

"Last night was a mistake," Levi's voice drifted from the bedroom. "There won't be a repeat."

Raiden snorted. "That's what you said in Knoxville," he said in a singsong voice. He was dressed in a t-shirt and sweatpants, and entertained himself swinging the drawstring from the pants back and forth. Levi was making an unnecessary amount of noise crashing about in the room. His temper only added to Raiden's enjoyment.

Eventually, Levi re-emerged, scowling. "I don't care what I said before," he said, his blue eyes blazing. "I won't be drinking with you again for the rest of this trip. It was unprofessional, as was my lapse in judgment."

Raiden rolled his eyes. "As if you were that drunk you didn't know what you were doing. Come on, man. Why are you making such a big deal of this? We had amazing sex. We're going to be traveling and staying together for the next several days. Who's it going to hurt if we have a little more fun?"

"Who says I had fun?" Levi asked coldly.

"Me," said Raiden, not rising to the bait. Levi could try and psych him out of this all he wanted, but Raiden hadn't been that drunk either. He remembered perfectly well how remarkable it had been, just how much they had both been into it. "And when you get that stick out of your ass and admit that too, you can come back. For now, get out of my fucking room."

Levi narrowed his eyes at him, his fingers tightening

around the handle of his bag, making the knuckles go white. He ground his teeth, then turned on his heel.

"I'll be next door, once room service has freshened it up. Until then," he paused at the door and flashed a sneer Raiden's way, "try not to get yourself shot."

He slammed the door behind him.

Raiden sighed. He'd have rather they just hopped back to it once more. He doubted his ass could take another pounding so soon, but they could have at least blown one another. It was fun to bicker too, but only for so long. Hopefully, they would get back to fucking again before long.

In the meantime, Raiden ate more bacon and pancakes doused in maple syrup, even though it made him feel slightly queasy. It tasted too good to let it go to waste, and although he'd been sober enough by the time he and Levi had stumbled into bed, he had still drunk a fair bit of alcohol yesterday. Extra carbs would only help get him through the day.

His phone dinged as he downed a tall glass of orange juice. It was Pearl. She and the band were staying at a more reasonably priced hotel across town, and she was wondering if Raiden wanted to meet up and work for a couple of hours.

He sighed with relief. *Hell yeah,* he texted back immediately. He felt wrong if he went too many days without writing. His fingers itched and he got moody if he wasn't careful. With a laugh, he realized that was probably one of the reasons why he was being such a shit to Levi. He needed to release his pent-up energy somewhere else.

Raiden tidied up as best he could, left a good tip for the room service team, then put some clothes on better suited to facing the outside world. No doubt Pearl would be her usual polished, glittery self, so he went for a more adventurous mesh vest and buckled some leather cuffs around his wrists. Sometimes it was fun to play up a role, and today, he was certainly feeling like a rock star.

He texted Levi to tell him that he was going to meet Pearl. He didn't give him the address because as much as he was having fun, he also wanted to ensure Levi understood Raiden was kind of pissed at him. If he really wanted to follow Raiden, he could do some detective work. Until then, Raiden was going to enjoy some time apart.

The front desk got Raiden a cab and he was on his way to the other hotel in no time. Pearl had told him her room number, so he crossed the small lobby and rode the elevator straight to her floor.

"Come in," her voice floated through the door when he knocked.

It was a small room, basically furnished, but Pearl seemed comfortable enough sitting cross-legged on the bed. She looked up at Raiden as he closed the door and gave him a smile. She had her lilac hair in pigtails with skulls on the bands tying together each end.

"Excellent," she said, picking up one of the sheets of paper in front of her. "I'm stuck on the chorus of that one we were doing about feeling like a shadow. It's bothering me it doesn't have a title."

"We could do something crazy and just call it Shadow?"

It was typical of Pearl to jump into things without even a hello, Raiden had learned, especially when it came to music. Which was generally all she ever talked about. So he pulled over the chair from the desk to perch beside the bed and look at her notes.

"Hmm. There is something to be said for keeping things simple." She tapped the chewed pen in her hand on her lip, then wrote something down. "You can sit here, you know." She pointed to the spot next to her by the second set of pillows. "I know you're not interested in me in a sexual way. I don't feel threatened by your presence."

Raiden chuckled. "True, but sometimes I like to prove I

can be a gentleman." He glanced at the door. "If someone came in, I'd hate for them to get the wrong impression."

Pearl was a lot younger than him after all, and this industry was full of some real dirtbags. After all the shit he'd gone through with his hacked emails, he didn't want to give anyone the chance to spin a story about him being in bed with a teenage girl.

She considered his words, then nodded. "Whatever makes you feel most comfortable. As long as you can see the notes okay."

Raiden assured her he could before picking up one of the other bits of paper. He'd been scribbling ideas down on this one last time. This song was just dangling out of their reach at the moment. They just needed a bit of inspiration to make it really awesome.

"I think we could go really dark and epic with this one," he said as he read. "Get some strings on it, maybe slow the tempo down and go a bit sinister."

"Where's Levi?"

He blinked and looked up at her. "Well," he said slowly, rubbing his chin. "He was a naughty boy, so I put him in time-out."

Pearl narrowed her eyes and stared at him for a moment. "But he's supposed to be protecting you. After the GPS incident, why wouldn't you want him by your side?"

Raiden focused back on the music. Pearl had a portable keyboard and guitar with her, but he'd need to get back to his studio to produce this the way he wanted.

"Even if you're annoyed with him," Pearl continued, "your safety is important."

"He just needs some time to cool off," Raiden said. He held up the paper in his hands. "What do you think about an instrumental interlude before a short sung one? I've got a couple of ideas. We could work backwards to create the chorus from that."

"Sure," she said with a shrug. "We don't have to talk about Levi if you don't want to. I'm sorry."

Raiden frowned at her and tried to temper his irritation. "I just want to move on with the song," he said.

Pearl chewed on the end of her pen. "Tell me more about the interlude."

Raiden fetched the keyboard to place on the bed to try and flesh out some of the concepts he had in his head. Unfortunately, they weren't the only thoughts bouncing around up there.

"He's just kind of an ass, and we've been traveling together for a few days," he said as he fiddled around with some chords. "I needed a break."

Pearl smirked at him. "I see."

"See what?" he asked nervously. What was that smile supposed to mean?

A knock on the door interrupted before Pearl could answer. Raiden threw her a glance, but she was already looking back at the composition notes, uninterested by whoever was at the door. So with a sigh, Raiden went to go answer it.

Of course it was Levi.

"What did we say about ditching me?" Levi growled, his icy blue eyes fixed on Raiden.

"Not to?" he guessed. He couldn't remember, not with those eyes boring holes through his own pupils. "That was fast work, finding me."

"It's almost like I was a trained Marine," Levi said, pushing his way into the room. "Pearl," he added, nodding to her.

She looked up, her gaze shifting between him and Raiden as he once again shut the door. "Hello," she replied. The corner of her mouth curled up. "We were just talking about you."

"Not really," said Raiden. He breezed past Levi and took his seat again. "More like a passing mention. Shall we continue with that interlude?" He did not want Levi thinking he'd been gossiping about him to Pearl. That would be mortifying.

"As you wish," Pearl said. "Let Levi have the chair. You can sit on the bed." She flashed Levi a grin as he turned away from inspecting the hotel room window. "Don't worry, he's not interested in me sexually."

"Uh, yeah, he can vouch for us," Raiden mumbled.

Because that's why Levi would be worried. About ensuring it didn't look like they were up to any funny business.

Not like he cared about who Raiden was attracted to.

Right?

# Seventeen

LEVI

THE REX THEATER IN PITTSBURGH WAS A SMALL MUSIC VENUE that was currently packed to the rafters. Straining at its six-hundred-person capacity, Glittergasm were in the process of whipping the crowd of kids in their teens and twenties into a sweaty frenzy.

Levi had never been one much for gigs. He had always been the kind of person to take note of emergency exits and the behavior of the people around him with dedication bordering on obsession. After his training with the Marines, an environment like this completely oversaturated his senses.

There were too many possibilities to contend with, especially when it came to protecting a client. He'd liaised with the theater security team who regularly covered events there and knew the venue inside and out. But he was only happy with Raiden immediately by his side at all times as they watched the show from the wings.

Unfortunately, that complicated matters.

The last place he really should have been was in touching distance of Raiden's body. Levi's cock was getting far too excited every time their skin brushed or he caught wind of

Raiden's distinct scent. Even amid such an onslaught of smells, Levi was still able to discern Raiden's unique spicy, musky blend. That was a bad sign.

He had no right to be pining over Raiden. Every logical part of Levi's brain had already agreed that he was to be completely off limits from now on. Unfortunately, the instinctual caveman parts of him were begging for Levi to pick Raiden up, throw him over his shoulder, and make love back at the hotel until they were both wrecked men once again.

Make love? Have sex. Good god, even his idle thoughts were working against him. Making love was something you did with girlfriends. It was tender and emotional. This was simply his body screaming out for more fucking. It had been a long time since he'd had anything more than a blow job, after all.

Raiden was watching the band intently. Sometimes he mouthed along with the lyrics. Other songs he bobbed his head or tapped his heel. He was always tuned in to the beat, constantly moving, so full of life. He'd brush into Levi hovering behind him and appear not to even notice.

Levi doubted that, though. He was clearly trying to aggravate Levi from that little stunt he'd pulled earlier. Perhaps he truly believed he could ditch Levi for a while and push him into reacting. But Levi had a constant tracker running on the GPS in Raiden's phone, so he was never going to get far.

Levi couldn't let it get to him. He could still salvage this job, so long as he kept things professional for the duration of the tour. He absolutely did not trust Raiden not to deliberately let their transgression slip to Levi's uncle and get him in trouble. The little shit would get a kick out of watching Levi get berated, he was sure.

"How much do you hate this?" Raiden shouted over his

shoulder, giving Levi a wink. "Girly punk pop probably isn't your thing, I'm guessing."

Levi arched an eyebrow at him. "Just because a song is sung by a young woman doesn't make the music inherently 'girly,'" he said. There was so much noise it was natural for them to both tilt their heads to hear each other's words. It brought their faces too close together, so Levi pulled back.

Raiden eyed him skeptically. "Well, yeah," he agreed. "I thought a Marine such as yourself wouldn't be caught dead enjoying anything that could be interpreted as girlish, though?"

"Ex-Marine," Levi corrected, keeping his gaze on Pearl as she enraptured the crowd. They lapped her up, with her dazzling, colorful outfit and shimmering purple hair. She looked like a doll and had the audience eating out of her hand. He could feel Raiden's stare on him, and he couldn't help the smile that tugged at one corner of his mouth. "And my gunnery sergeant had a thing for singing Avril Lavigne when we were on the move."

"No way," said Raiden in delight. Levi tried to ignore how much he enjoyed defying Raiden's expectations.

"Yes way."

They both focused on the stage as Pearl chugged from a bottle of water. Her energy was still radiating all through the room, keeping the band and the crowd engaged, but Levi could tell she was suffering a bit. Sweat was running down her back and she took a couple of deep breaths before speaking into the mic, announcing the last song for the night.

"I hope this keeps you fuckers happy," she growled with a smirk, causing the room to scream with joy.

There were so many flashes from cameras and reflections from phone screens in the throng, Levi strained to make out anything unusual. But he could make out a guy near the front in a hoodie that didn't seem to be enjoying himself, from what little Levi could see of his face. He was just standing there, not dancing or singing or taking pictures.

Something crawled up Levi's spine and instinct told him to move away. It was probably nothing, but after the incident with the GPS the day before last, he wasn't willing to take any risks.

Levi leaned down to talk against Raiden's ear. "We should leave now."

"What?" said Raiden. His head whipped around and his dark eyes narrowed at Levi.

"It'll be much easier to extract you before everyone starts moving," Levi explained.

Raiden didn't need to know about the shady-looking guy under the hood. He'd be quite right to argue that Levi was being ridiculous. But the fact of the matter was, someone *had* targeted Raiden again, and they didn't have any further facts yet. Levi had learned long ago to listen when his gut told him to be cautious.

But Raiden shook his head. "No, I want to stay and see the band. I can't ditch them. Besides, I promised we could go for a drink."

There was no fighting it. Sometimes, Levi just had to be the bad guy. "Until we know more about who hacked your GPS and what that means for your threat level, I need to restrict the number of locations you visit. Especially without prior investigation."

He didn't want to tell Raiden about the guy because it was Levi's responsibility to assess and monitor threats. If he shared that information with Raiden, he might react in an unpredictable manner and bolt. Better if Levi could just get him out of the theatre quietly and quickly.

Of course, Raiden wasn't going to make this easy though. He stared at Levi in disbelief. "So I'm under house arrest?" he asked.

"Don't be dramatic," Levi said. "If you want to go out after the next show, tell me and we can scout a bar beforehand. Or you can go to the hotel bar."

"Oh yeah," Raiden scoffed with a scowl. "I'm sure that'll be rocking." He folded his arms. "No, this is stupid. I want to take the band out. They've earned it. I'll let you come along, but we're going."

Levi should have known Raiden would dig his heels in. He wasn't going to apologize for spoiling his fun, though. Raiden was a brat and he needed to learn that sometimes, he couldn't always get his way.

"Not until we understand what happened to us better," he said. His gaze was unflinching. "Need I remind you that this is for your protection, Mr. Jones. If I say you need to do something, you do it, without question."

Raiden squared his jaw and looked furious. "So you're just going to boss me around now?"

As Levi recalled, he rather liked being bossed around the night before. He refused to let that memory surface, though, as blood would undoubtedly rush to his cheeks...and other places.

He could tell Glittergasm were wrapping up the song. There might be another encore, or the crowd might just keep them there for a while, but he and Raiden needed to move now.

Levi took hold of Raiden's elbow. "I'm sorry," he said, despite promising himself he wouldn't apologize. "But we have to go. Now. You can make it up to them. They'll understand."

There must have been something in his tone of voice that caught Raiden's attention. Because he narrowed his eyes at Levi and snarled, but he still nodded.

"Fine. Let's go."

He stormed off, pulling his phone out as he did and

tapping furiously on it with both thumbs. Levi rolled his eyes and escorted him back through the building and out into the alleyway where their car was waiting.

"You need to grow up," he said as he opened the door for Raiden.

Rain was falling lightly, illuminated in the dark by the streetlights. Ideal conditions for someone to lurk. A quick scan of the alley made Levi confident they weren't being watched, but he was still happy to get Raiden inside the Jeep with its bulletproof windows.

"It's just drinks. If I was being a real hard ass, I'd have stopped you going to the gig at all."

Raiden scoffed as Levi shut the door. Levi kept his face neutral as he stalked around the front then slipped into the driver's seat.

"You don't get it, do you?" Raiden said. Levi could see him glowering at him from the corner of his eye as he started the engine. "This isn't me bitching that I didn't get a few beers. It's all networking. These guys need to meet people in the industry. There are certain connections you can only make late at night in the corner of a club."

Levi knew connections like that, but he doubted that was what Raiden was referring too. He debated telling him about the sketchy guy he had seen at the front of the crowd, but he couldn't be sure it had been anything at all, and he didn't want Raiden ripping into him. Besides, he didn't have to explain himself. He was in charge here.

"If it's so important to you," Levi said, merging into the traffic around the theatre, "then it's up to you to explain. I told you, we can make it happen next time. By then we should have more info and can be better prepared."

Raiden crossed his arms. "Fine. If I can't socialize with these guys, there's no point in me being on this tour. Not for them, not for me. This is our careers on the line."

Levi didn't say anything in response to that. He understood Raiden's argument, but it was Levi's job to protect him. This was his career too, and he'd already fucked up too many times as it was.

They made the rest of the drive back to the hotel in silence.

Raiden refused to talk all the way back to their rooms. Not that Levi spoke either, but Raiden's silence was somehow deafening. He fumed next to Levi as they rode the elevator upwards and walked down the hall. They reached Raiden's room first, and he jammed his keycard into the handle to unlock the door.

"Night," he said stiffly, shoving his way inside. He made to yank the door after him, but Levi grabbed it just in time. "Oh for fuck's sake," Raiden muttered. He didn't try to pull it closed again, though, just walked into the room, rubbing his face.

Levi followed, shutting the door quietly behind him. Room service had done a good job cleaning up after the party. He purposefully didn't look towards the bedroom or wonder if the maid had switched the sheets after their adventure last night.

"We can't keep fighting," he said calmly. He placed his car keys down on the table and removed his jacket and gun. Raiden watched him from where he was sprawled on the couch, beer from the minibar already in hand. "You need to stop resisting me, or you're going to need a new bodyguard."

Raiden scoffed and took a swig of his drink. "You're the one creating issues," he said, not looking at Levi.

Levi decided to be straight with him, seeing as they were now back to the safety of the hotel.

"It was probably nothing," he said, walking towards the other sofa, "but I saw someone I didn't like the look of in the crowd. I wanted to get you to safety."

Raiden turned his gaze on Levi as he sat down. One of Raiden's feet was on the couch, the other on the table, his legs open just enough that it could be misconstrued as an invitation.

"I'm not a child," he said slowly.

His lower lip was just touching the rim of the bottleneck. He regarded Levi through his long, black eyelashes. Room service had left just a couple of lamps on to illuminate the room.

"I know that," said Levi. He willed his heart rate to stay steady.

"Then don't treat me like one," Raiden shot back. "If you'd told me there was an issue, rather than making me feel like a fucking diva for wanting to do my job, we'd get along much better."

"I apologize," Levi said. Raiden was right after all. "I didn't want to spook you."

"I'm not the one that's spooked." Raiden sipped his beer, his Adam's apple bobbing as he swallowed. He didn't take his eyes off of Levi. "I think you just didn't want me going out and having fun. I think you wanted to come back here. Just the two of us."

"Don't be ridiculous," Levi replied, not moving his gaze away from Raiden's, no matter how much he wanted to. He wouldn't back down. "If I can trust you to behave, I'll go back to my own room. But understand, if you leave the hotel without my permission, I'll know right away."

Raiden licked his lips and smirked. "I think the safest way to ensure I stay put, then, is for you to stay right here with me. Otherwise, I might be a bad boy. I'm feeling pretty rebellious, I must say."

Levi ground his teeth, willing himself not to rise to the bait. "I told you, last night was a mistake. I don't have feelings for you, so I'm sorry if you think there's something more between us than there really is."

Raiden laughed and took a long gulp of beer. "Okay, Kevin."

Levi shook his head. "Can I trust you or not?" he demanded. He felt the strong urge to get away from this situation. If he could just get to his own room and put a movie on, he could distance himself and forget about the way watching Raiden's wet lips were making his pants feel too tight.

"Probably not," Raiden said. "You're the one who lured me away under false pretenses. If you're not going to entertain me, then I'll just head back out and show the band a good time. That drummer girl is pretty into me, you know?"

Levi *absolutely* ignored the spike of jealousy that lanced through his chest. "You can entertain her after the next show," he said calmly. "Although that doesn't seem very professional to me."

Raiden placed his bottle down and stood up in one swift motion. "Turns out I'm not very professional, I guess," he said.

Levi told himself he didn't have time to get up before Raiden swung his leg over and straddled his lap. Levi was pretty sure if it had been an insurgent with a knife, he could have moved a lot fucking faster. But as it was, he just stared up as Raiden crowded into his personal space.

"What are you doing?"

Raiden smiled, like a shark. "Tell me to get off you, and I will." He had his hands on Levi's shoulders, his knees either side of his hips. Levi's heart was like a jackhammer in his chest. "Tell me to get you *off*," Raiden added in little more than a whisper, "and I will."

Levi's hands itched to move up and settle on Raiden's waist. He balled them into fists instead. He had been prepared to fight. Not to fuck.

"We shouldn't do this," Levi said.

"But you want to," Raiden retorted. He looked down at Levi, his hair falling in a dark curtain around his face. Levi wanted to grab it. "It's just fucking. Stop overthinking so we can both enjoy this already. I'm tired of fighting."

So was Levi, desperately. It felt like he'd been at some sort of war ever since he'd been a teenager. He was exhausted. He was disciplined. He could restrain himself and continue with this struggle. He had the strength to do that.

He no longer had the will.

One hand flew to Raiden's hair, the other to his waist, just like he had wanted. His lips crashed against Raiden's mouth, sucking the moan from it as it escaped his throat. Raiden's limbs tightened around him, latching on as if he might stop Levi from ever letting go.

Levi gave up. They were both adults, they both wanted the other. As long as Levi continued to do his job and protect Raiden from harm to the very best of his ability, it was nobody else's business what they did behind closed doors.

He seized Raiden's hips, easily twisting the smaller man and depositing him on his back along the sofa. Raiden gasped for air, his eyes sparkling in the dim light. "Yes," he hissed. "Get over here, you Neanderthal."

Levi should have been insulted by that, but unfortunately his mind did appear to have regressed to that of a prehistoric man. He all but pounced on top of Raiden, scooping him up and devouring his mouth, his tongue and lips savoring every drop of beer that Raiden had left lingering there.

Raiden's hands made short work of yanking Levi's shirt from his pants and slipping under the material to find his abs. It felt so good to have his fingers skimming over Levi's skin. He shuddered, needing more.

His shirt was over his head and on the floor in a matter of seconds. Raiden's gaze roamed over his chest, followed by his hands. It was like he was in awe.

A strange rush of pride flushed through Levi. He wanted Raiden to appreciate his body. It was what he'd worked hardest on, after all. His most prized instrument. Just as Raiden worked on a composition, Levi had honed his body to be as perfect as it could be, ready to help him do his job.

But in that moment, all his hard work was being appreciated in pleasure, not business. Plenty of girls had seen him naked, had enjoyed his body meeting with theirs. However, none of them had draped their hands over their heads and gone compliant quite the way Raiden did just then. It was like he became human putty in Levi's hands.

"What do you want to do?" Raiden asked.

Levi huffed. "So now I have to do all the work?" he demanded, tugging at Raiden's buckle and pulling his belt free from the loops on his jeans.

Raiden smirked. "I had to do all the work to get us back here," he teased, shifting his hips obediently as Levi yanked at his pants and briefs. "Now it's your turn."

"So, you'll just do as I say?" he asked dubiously. "Because I have been thinking about a gag."

Raiden didn't seem to care he'd now been stripped naked. He just squirmed underneath Levi and batted his eyelashes. "I knew you'd been thinking about fucking me again," he whispered triumphantly.

Levi loomed over him, but he didn't fight the grin that crept onto his mouth. "You really want that gag, don't you?"

"Kiss me," Raiden said breathlessly. "That'll do the same thing."

Levi dipped his head, claiming Raiden's lips. But he was softer this time, less punishing. He wanted Raiden to offer up his mouth, his breath, his words, all willingly. And he did.

Levi shifted his weight. His cock was straining in his pants, but it would have to wait. For now, he wanted to enjoy running his hands up and down Raiden's hips, flanks and arms. With one hand, he crossed Raiden's wrists and pinned them into the sofa cushion. With the other, he explored Raiden's body. He cupped his jaw, played with his hard nipples, then finally took pity and stroked his hard, dripping cock.

"Oh, fuck," Raiden cried into Levi's mouth, bucking his hips. "Jesus, yes, thank you."

Levi chuckled. Even if this was an unwise course of action, now he'd given up resisting, he was having a lot of fun.

He kissed his way down Raiden's chest, letting go of his hands. Raiden gripped the arm of the couch instead. "Good boy," Levi murmured against his skin. He looked up and met Raiden's gaze, their eyes locked as he inched his lips closer to Raiden's cock.

Raiden had ordered him to suck it the night before. Levi had complied, despite having reservations. Sometimes, it was best to tackle anything that scared you head on. Quite literally, in this case. But it was just a dick, hardly anything to be afraid of.

On his previous attempt he had merely swallowed the damn thing a couple of times. But now he felt responsible for Raiden's pleasure. He was running this show, and he wasn't going to go into any aspect of it with half-hearted effort. He was going to own this cock.

He brought everything to mind he had liked Collins doing to him. He was the most recent guy to go down on him and the most frequent. Levi wanted to blow Raiden's mind.

He nuzzled his nose into his pubic hair, taking a freaky enjoyment in the strong, intimate scent. He rolled Raiden's heavy balls in his hand and licked up the length of the veiny shaft a few times, like it was a melting ice cream.

"We ought to get you a cock ring," he said as Raiden moaned and writhed. Collins had been fond of using his fingers to that effect, prolonging Levi's climax. He did the same to Raiden now, wrapping his thumb and index finger in a circle under his balls and around his dick. "That way, you'd have to wait to come until I say."

Raiden gasped and clenched his teeth. "You don't think I can do that?" He gave him a shaky laugh. "I made a career out of performing on cue. The question is, what's in it for me?"

"You get to come," Levi said, licking and sucking at Raiden's tip. "If you do it before I say, then next time you won't be so lucky. If there is a next time."

"Oh," Raiden scoffed. "There'll be a next t-*oof!*"

Levi swallowed him down, sheathing his teeth with his lips and using his tongue to massage Raiden's length as he worked up and down. He honestly wasn't sure why the idea of controlling Raiden's orgasm was such a turn-on. Would either of them really get a kick out of it if he wasn't allowed to come? Wasn't that the whole point of sex?

He recalled this morning, though, and his thoughts on punishing Raiden if he couldn't keep him quiet. He didn't want to actually hurt him, of course. But maybe it was an extension of being in control of another person's body? Not necessarily having power over them...but earning trust from them. Like the group exercises he and the guys used to do in training. There was certainly an exhilaration that came from knowing your buddy had your back, no matter what.

Perhaps that was the kick Raiden felt? He could give up his control and let Levi take charge, knowing he'd make it good for both of them. It was a lot of responsibility, but Levi felt like a challenge.

Raiden was babbling a string of incredibly colorful profanities, some of which weren't even in English as far as Levi could tell. He popped off Raiden's cock. "Quiet," he said.

Raiden looked down at him, his breathing ragged through his nose. He nodded in understanding. That was three things now. He had to keep his hands in place, his mouth shut and wait until Levi allowed him to come.

Now what the hell did Levi do with him?

He desperately wanted to fuck him senseless again, but it hadn't even been twenty-four hours yet. After the pounding Levi had given him the night before, it would be unfair to expect his inexperienced ass to take him again. He'd just have to improvise.

He went back to sucking him, using the excess spit and precum to moisten his finger enough to make Raiden's hole wet. He played with the rim until his jaw started to ache and he decided to shake things up a bit.

"Sit up," he said.

Levi moved back, wiping his face and fixing Raiden with a firm stare. Raiden was panting, but he managed to push himself up so he was sitting next to Levi. His cock was shiny and stiff as a rod, sticking up from between his thighs.

"Can I kiss you again?"

Levi quirked an eyebrow. "What did I say about talking?"

Raiden bit his lip and dropped his eyes. He looked so adorable Levi took pity on him. He leaned in and captured Raiden's mouth for a lazy kiss.

"Don't do it again," he warned. Raiden nodded, a smile playing on those swollen, dusty pink lips.

Levi was all out of creativity, so he fell back into old habits.

"On your knees," he murmured as he ran his thumb over Raiden's lower lip. He glanced towards the carpet so Raiden would understand his meaning clearly. "I think it's time you did some work too."

Raiden may have been obedient, but he didn't exactly hop to it. He appeared to have recovered from his previous misstep, his confidence returned. Thus, he slid off the sofa like a silk scarf, taking his time to arrange himself in a kneeling position at Levi's feet, his hands resting lightly on Levi's knees.

Levi ran his fingers through Raiden's thick hair, brushing his cheeks then gently wrapping his hand around the back of Raiden's neck. Levi's other arm was slung over one of the sofa's throw pillows. He kept swinging between feeling like a king on a throne and a nervous wreck. But he had to trust in himself. It was just sex. As long as they were feeling good, then it was going all right.

It occurred to him to check. "Is this all right?" he asked. Raiden arched an eyebrow, then looked down as he made a show of biting his tongue between his teeth. Levi chuckled. "Okay, you can talk."

"We should use traffic lights," Raiden said, straight to the point. "Green for good, yellow for unsure, red for stop."

"We should, should we?" Levi asked, amused.

Raiden grinned up at him. "You're not the only one who's been thinking about this all day."

Levi felt like swatting Raiden's ass like he had last night. But he couldn't reach it, so he settled for rolling his eyes.

"Okay then, Mr. Expert. Color?"

Raiden licked his lips. "Green."

Levi took his time, enjoying petting his hair a little longer. Raiden's eyes drifted closed and Levi got him to suck his thumb decadently. "I want to watch you blow me," he rasped. "I want you to touch yourself, too. But you can only come after I do."

Raiden's eyes fluttered open, Levi's thumb popping from his lips. He nodded, automatically reaching forward to finally release Levi's cock from his pants.

Levi leaned back and let Raiden take care of him. He made short work of freeing him from his underwear and was soon sucking down on his cock, massaging the head with his tongue.

"Less teeth," Levi instructed, trying to keep his composure when he wanted to drop his head back and moan. Raiden raised an eyebrow, then did his best to wrap his lips around his pearly whites. "Better," said Levi with a nod. He had his fingers in Levi's hair again, guiding him as he pleasured Levi. "Touch yourself."

Raiden was definitely not shy. He angled himself so Levi could get a good look at him stroking his cock as he sucked Levi off, giving him loud, throaty moans and fluttering his eyelashes.

Levi tried to cling to his orgasm, but his climax built faster than he could anticipate. "Going to come," he warned. He was thrusting into Raiden's mouth now, fucking him unabashedly. He was going to ask Raiden if he wanted to swallow. As the one in charge, he should probably have just told Raiden that's what he wanted him to do. But Raiden used both hands to grip onto Levi's hips, working harder, milking his orgasm from him. He was obviously fine to continue, so Levi let him.

Within seconds, he was spilling down Raiden's gullet. He managed to keep his eyes open just enough to watch him swallowing, gulping him down with enthusiasm. His breathing was heavy as he struggled to blink the stars back from behind his eyes. As his wits came back, he was able to see Raiden was gripping tightly onto his own cock, holding back his orgasm.

"You can come," Levi said thickly. He stroked the side of Raiden's face, encouraging him to release his softening cock from his mouth. "Want to watch you."

Raiden nodded, his whole body shuddering as he jerked off vigorously. It was a matter of moments before he was spraying over the front of the sofa and Levi's pants. He slumped against Levi's right leg, gasping for air.

Levi continued to caress his cheek. "Good boy," he whispered. "Good boy."

# CHAPTER

## Nineteen

### RAIDEN

Raiden felt like jelly after his orgasm. Sex normally made him sleepy, but there was something about doing it with Levi that hit him like a truck. He was aware of Levi zipping himself up again, not bothering about cleaning up the mess, and easing Raiden to his feet.

"You all right there, kid?" he asked as he gently steered him towards the bathroom.

"Not a kid," Raiden mumbled.

He flicked the light switch on, bringing the bathroom into sharp relief. Levi stopped in front of him, looking him up and down. Raiden wasn't one to be that self-conscious about nudity, so he didn't shy away. There was no need to, though. Even in his bleary state, Raiden could see the affection in Levi's eyes.

Levi could protest this all he liked, but there was something real between them. Even if it was only an appreciation for great sex. He cupped Raiden's jaw and rubbed his cheekbone with his thumb. That was becoming a habit.

"No, you're not a kid," Levi said in response to Raiden's

protest. It was like he was only just realizing it. "Are you feeling okay, though?"

Raiden gave him a weak smile. "Green," he said honestly.

He didn't regret what they'd just done. He hadn't regretted it last night.

Levi nodded, a hint of a smile twitching at the corner of his lips. It was gone before Raiden could fully register it was there. He leaned over and turned the shower on, getting the water good and hot so the room started steaming up.

"Join me?" Raiden asked. He was going for sexy, but his sleepy slur ruined that somewhat. Levi smirked and eased him under the stream.

"Hurry up now," he said, his voice a low rumbled under the splattering of the water on the tiles. Raiden sighed and washed his body. He left his hair so he wouldn't have to dry it before collapsing into bed. He could do that in the morning.

Levi made no attempt to hide the fact that he was watching Raiden, so Raiden made sure to soap up every inch of his skin, lathering the suds over his chest and giving his sensitive, heavy cock a generous clean. His reward was a chuckle from Levi.

Raiden was disappointed Levi hadn't got in the water with him, but he was grateful when he was cleaned up in only a couple of minutes. He didn't think he could go for round two even if he tried. But he liked the idea of playing around with Levi like that. Even though what they were doing was a little kinkier than Raiden's usual tastes, he didn't feel intimidated by Levi in that sense.

But maybe Levi wasn't ready yet. He obviously cared, otherwise why would he stand and watch Raiden dry himself with the big, fluffy towel he had handed him. Or pull back the bed covers for Raiden to flop under. However, there was something that stopped Raiden asking what he really wanted to.

*Stay with me.*

It was ridiculous. Levi clearly wasn't going to be someone who cuddled after sex, especially not with Raiden. But Raiden couldn't deny it would have been nice.

"See you in the morning," he mumbled. His eyes were closed, but he braced himself for a second, just in case Levi decided to give him a kiss goodnight.

He didn't. Raiden forced himself not to be disappointed.

"Sleep well," Levi said from across the room. Through his closed eyelids, Raiden could tell Levi was switching the lights off one by one, leaving him in the darkness.

It wasn't long before sleep claimed him.

———

Raiden hadn't thought to set an alarm before going to bed. He'd fallen asleep before he could do much of anything. But luckily the front desk rang him at seven-thirty, no doubt on Levi's instruction. That gave him an hour to get his shit together before Levi wanted to set off for their drive to Philadelphia.

Raiden couldn't seem to shake his grumpy mood, no matter how much he tried to remind himself how great the previous night had been. How much he had been desperate for it. He showered again, washing his hair this time, feeling empty and hollow.

"Get a grip," he said out loud to himself as he shaved in the mirror afterwards. What the hell more did he want? Was he really that upset that Levi had gone back to his own room after they'd fucked? He had cleaned him up and put him to bed, for heaven's sake. For Raiden to want anything further was delusional.

He was packed up in plenty of time, so he sat at the desk and did some work on one of Glittergasm's tracks until Levi came to fetch him. Their album was shaping up nicely. Hopefully, by the time they got to New York to open for Dyrnoir they might even have a track good enough to release as their next single. It would be ideal to capitalize on the momentum they were achieving from the tour.

Raiden was proud every time he looked at their social media gaining traction. Thanks to their appearances so far, they'd amassed a decent rise in YouTube hits, Twitter and Instagram followers, and sign-ups to their newsletter.

It was good to feel useful. Raiden hated being idle, but he hated the pointless work he'd done on all those mediocre album tracks more. That kind of music wasn't going to be remembered by hardly anyone. But what he and Glittergasm were working on now could inspire countless people.

He smiled to himself, his funk lifted slightly for the first time since he'd woken up. There was more to life than Levi Patterson, after all.

A knock at the door stirred him back to his senses. He tried not to be nervous as he walked across the room, but he still needed to brush his damp palms on his jeans before he opened the door.

"Hi," he said as casually as he could manage.

Levi's packed bag was by his feet. He nodded at Raiden. "Good morning," he said in that low rumble of his that was really just his normal voice, but to Raiden had morphed irreversibly into a direct line to his groin. "Ready to go?"

"Uh, yeah," Raiden replied. "Just let me shut down my laptop."

He was aware of Levi watching him as he got his last few bits in order. How was it more comfortable to be watched while he was naked and vulnerable than right now? Raiden shook his head. He needed to sort himself out.

How many times had he assured Levi it was just sex? If he couldn't keep himself together now, he was just going to make Levi think he was clingy and pathetic.

They stood in the elevator in silence, although it was an entirely different silence to the one in which they'd spent the ride up in the night before. Raiden had been furious at Levi for mollycoddling him. At least when he had explained, Raiden could understand where he'd been coming from, even though he was still a little mad about it.

Surely it had to have been nothing and Levi was overreacting. Raiden was far more convinced it was this business between them that had motivated him more than anything. He'd been angry at Raiden for tempting him into sex then goading him about it afterwards.

But someone *had* fucked around with their GPS remotely. What if this shady figure Levi had described was the hacker?

Or, what if it was an older guy ashamed to be seen at a concert perving on a young singer, hiding under a hoodie for safety? That was the far more likely scenario.

Raiden glanced at Levi as the elevator dinged and they stepped out into the lobby. He felt like they had made progress the night before, but there was no guarantee Levi wouldn't try and roll that back. That seemed to be his M.O. when he could assess what they'd done in the cold light of day. So far, at least, he hadn't been a jackass about it.

He wasn't exactly friendly either, but Raiden had been smart enough not to expect a kiss good morning or an affectionate cuddle.

The guy at the desk distracted him as he and Levi approached. It was the same one that had checked them in a couple of days ago, the one who had allowed the rest of the band to sneak into Raiden's room and almost give Levi a heart attack.

"Be nice," Raiden growled at him out of the corner of his mouth. "He's just a sweet kid with a crush."

"Who could have gotten you killed," said Levi smoothly. He kept his eyes on the receptionist as they approached, the poor boy losing color in his face with every step they took.

Raiden scowled at Levi, giving him a warning not to pull any stunts. One of the biggest parts of being famous was being gracious to your fans, within reason. This young guy was clearly just excited at having met four out of five members of his favorite band. The idea that Below Zero was anyone's favorite anything these days made Raiden feel generous.

"Hey, man," he said. "We'd like to check out of our rooms."

The guy nodded, scrabbling to bring up the right screen on his computer. "I trust you had a good stay, Mr. Jones?"

Raiden purposefully did not look at Levi, nor did he allow himself to blush. "It was wonderful catching up with old friends. Speaking of which."

He retrieved a hotel room service menu from his bag. He had been inspired by the girls from the restaurant on the drive over and got the boys to all sign it for the clerk on the off-chance Raiden would see him on the way out.

The guy's eyes filled with tears as Raiden handed it over. "Oh," he said a little breathlessly. "Thank you."

Raiden just winked and got his credit card out. "I'll be paying for both rooms, thank you."

The guy took a breath to compose himself, tucking the signed menu safely away, then tapping on the keyboard to bring up the final bill. Raiden idly looked around at the few people milling about in the lobby as the desk clerk ran his card. He and Levi faced another long drive across state today, but hopefully it wouldn't be awkward.

Then there was another hotel waiting for them after that. Another two nights with rooms side by side ahead of the next gig tomorrow night, where Levi had promised they could go out with the band afterwards this time.

So many opportunities to continue with their fun. Raiden repressed a shudder just thinking about what they might get up to.

"Um," said the clerk nervously. "Mr. Jones?"

Raiden brought his attention back to the guy. He could feel Levi inching just a fraction closer to his side. "Yes?" he replied in a friendly manner. But the guy looked stricken.

"I'm so sorry," he whispered. "But your card has been declined. It says there's insufficient funds."

Coldness washed through Raiden, but he refused to let it rattle him just yet. "Have you tried running it again?" he asked. He knew full well there should have been more than enough left on that card to be able to charge the two room bills to it, even with all the booze TJ had ordered.

The clerk licked his lips. "I've run it three times," he said sympathetically. His voice was low, and he glanced around to make sure no one else could hear them. It was a thoughtful gesture, but Raiden would prefer it if the damn card would just work.

"It must be a glitch or something," he said with a smile, not letting his panic show. He took the card back and offered the guy his savings account card. There was absolutely no way that card would be declined.

But the look on the guy's face told Raiden all he needed to know before he even opened his mouth.

"No," stammered Raiden. He pulled his phone out with a shaking hand, unlocking it and loading up his banking app. With a few security checks, he was looking at his account.

His completely empty account.

"No," he cried. "No, no, *no.*"

"Raiden, calm down," Levi said. He grabbed Raiden's elbow and made him stare into his blue eyes.

But Raiden was rapidly losing his mind. "All my savings. *All* my accounts. They're empty. My credit card's been canceled. Look – *look.*"

He thrust the phone in Levi's face, who inspected the screen carefully.

"Okay," was all he said. He handed the phone back then turned to the anxious clerk. "I trust you won't mention this little hiccup to anyone," he said as he fished out his own wallet. "There's just been a bit of a mistake made with Mr. Jones's funds. You know how these things are. He'd hate for anyone to get the wrong idea."

He offered out his own credit card in exchange for Raiden's, which the clerk took immediately. "Of course, sir," he said. He sounded mortified at the idea that he would betray Raiden, which was of small comfort to him. The clerk scanned the card and was visibly relieved when the charge went through. "There we go, all sorted."

Levi smiled at the guy. It was sincere, warming up his face. It made Raiden feel marginally better just to see.

"Mr. Jones has had a bit of a shock, and I need to attend to a couple of things to set it all right. Is there somewhere we could sit for a few minutes, perhaps a conference or meeting room?"

The clerk perked up at the prospect of being able to help further. "Certainly. Gentlemen, if you'd like to follow me, I can take you to a suitable room right away. Would you like us to look after your luggage in the meantime?"

"No, thank you," said Levi. "We'll keep it with us."

Raiden guessed that was a security measure, just in case. It was obvious to him that the hacker had struck again, and the idea of keeping his possessions close by was deeply comforting.

"Thank you," he managed to stammer as the guy showed them into a medium-sized conference room. There was a long table, a dozen chairs and a flat screen TV mounted on the wall. From the corner of his eye, he registered Levi tipping the clerk a hundred-dollar bill.

"Oh, um, thank you, sir," he said, holding it in his hands. "But I promise I won't breathe a word about this. Below Zero are the reason I came out in high school. I just wouldn't hurt Raiden like that."

Raiden smiled at him and tried to calm himself down. He usually loved hearing stories of people's lives like that.

"I want you to have it," he said kindly, "I really appreciate what you've done for me." He looked at Levi. "I'll pay you back."

They both nodded at Raiden, then the clerk left them to it, quietly shutting the door as he left.

Raiden managed to slump into a chair before he began shaking too violently. "Fuck," he whispered, unable to stop the tears falling from his eyes. "Fuck, I'll fucking kill them, fucking bastards, fuck, *fuck!*"

Levi sat in the chair beside him and took his hands. Raiden was so shocked he stopped crying for a second.

"I promise you," Levi said. "Your bank's insurance will cover this. You'll have the money back in twenty-four hours."

"But what's to stop them stealing it all again!" Raiden cried.

He wasn't mad at Levi. But there was no one else here to shout at, and his logic only seemed to make him feel more desperate.

"That's *my* money, Levi, *mine!* I worked so fucking hard to stand on my own two feet, all those shitty projects I had to work on to build up my name, to be independent of my family and the fucking record label after they dropped us without warning. I never wanted to be in that position again, I wanted to stand on my own and these *fuckers* have taken that from me! It's not money, it's independence. It's my hard work and they've just taken it in the blink of an eye, and-"

Levi's lips on his stopped his rant.

It wasn't an aggressive kiss. It was probably the gentlest Levi had given him so far. Just the touching of lips as he cradled Raiden's face.

"I've got you," Levi murmured. He pulled Raiden into a hug, allowing Raiden to tuck his damp face into Levi's neck. "And I'll also promise you that we'll get these assholes, whoever they are. If I have to personally track them down, I will."

Raiden clung to Levi's jacket, feeling the tension ebb away from him. His embrace felt so good, like it alone was able to wash away his fear and rage, calming him. "I'm sorry," he said. "I overreacted."

To his surprise, Levi shook his head. "This is an invasion of your privacy. Their goal here isn't to rob you, that's a bonus. It's to rattle you."

"You think so?"

"I know so." Levi stroked his hair, his cheek resting on the top of Raiden's head. "Trust me."

Raiden nodded. He didn't have to think about that. He already trusted Levi. "Okay," he whispered back.

LEVI COULD FEEL RAIDEN'S HEART BEATING. IT WAS A RAPID, painfully loud *thump thump thump* that made Levi want to wince.

It was true that people got targeted like this every day. Identity theft and fraud were sadly a commonplace occurrence. But not when coupled with the email leak and GSP hack.

"Hello, is this Glenn?" Levi said as the phone call finally connected. He didn't want to leave Raiden's side, but he needed a clear head. So he stood up and moved a few feet away, concentrating on one of the paintings on the walls.

He hadn't felt anything that strong in years as his urge to comfort his lover when he'd broken down. Levi wasn't an idiot. Maybe if this hadn't happened he could have fooled himself in a few more days that the sex was all there was to it. But everything in him was screaming to protect Raiden. It was borderline desperate. Levi needed to acknowledge there were more feelings at play here than just lust, or he was going to fuck up.

"Yes, this is Glenn Browne," said the voice on the other end of the phone. "How can I help?"

Levi wasted no time in explaining who he was and why he was calling. After Raiden had phoned his bank, Levi had spoken to his uncle Kurt to inform him of the developments. He had then insisted Levi contact Glenn, the IT guy Raiden's dad had used before, the one working for the family lawyer friend that they'd met the day of the barbecue.

It made Levi a little nervous, this friend-of-a-friend-of-a-friend business. But his uncle had assured him that Glenn had worked for Eric and Raiden's dad for years and he really was a genius. If anyone could investigate Raiden's cyber issues fast, and on the down low, his uncle assured him it was Glenn.

"Oh shit, I'm sorry, man," he said once Levi had detailed everything he could. "Of course, I'll get right on it. You want to put Raiden on the line for a minute so I can grab some security details from him too?"

Levi watched Raiden talking. He'd calmed down a little in the last half an hour or so, most of which he'd spent in Levi's arms.

Not making out. They hadn't even kissed again since Levi had bizarrely thought that would be the best way to stop Raiden's escalating panic attack. But strangely enough, it *had* worked. Raiden had been able to catch his breath again.

Then Levi had continued to just hold him. Raiden had practically been in his lap. They hadn't really spoken a lot. Instead, Levi had rubbed Raiden's back and stroked his hair.

A lot of guys that Levi had served with would have seen a man getting upset like that and called him any number of misogynistic or homophobic names. However, in his time as a sergeant, Levi had come to understand there was no weakness in showing fear or distress, especially in times of a genuine threat.

Raiden wasn't a trained soldier or Marine. He was an average guy who was starting to realize that his whole life was being menaced by persons unknown. He had every right to lose his shit.

What was unreasonable was the lengths Levi wanted to go to to make it stop.

Seeing Raiden like this upset him. Normal Raiden wasn't fazed by anything. He joked and teased and fought. To see him trembling was wholly unnatural. Levi wanted to hurt whoever was doing this to him.

After several minutes, Raiden ended the call with Glenn and seemed a little reassured that things were going to be okay. Levi totally understood what he'd said about this being more than someone stealing his money, as awful as that was. But the bank would compensate him for that. He hadn't lost it for good. Once he took time to get over the shock of someone violating him in this manner, he'd stop being upset and start feeling angry.

Levi could work with anger much better than fear.

"Are you ready to head out?" he asked.

Raiden rubbed his hands over his face and nodded. "Sure," he said, then took a deep breath in and out. "Glenn's working things on his end, and the bank reckoned the money could be back in my account as soon as a few hours."

"That's good," Levi assured him.

Raiden nodded, getting to his feet. "Yeah. Fuck those assholes. They won't keep me down."

There was that anger. Levi smiled and picked up several bags. "Let's go then."

It was only about five hours to Philly, mostly along I-76. Levi took the drive easy and they stopped every hour or so to stretch their legs, use a restroom, grab some food, whatever they fancied. The next gig wasn't until tomorrow night, so they weren't in a rush, and Levi wanted Raiden to take his time and relax again.

Not that they didn't have reason to be alarmed. It was just that was Levi's job to fix it now, his and his uncle's company. If necessary, they would get the authorities involved. But he didn't want Raiden stressing any more than he had to.

"How's the writing going?" Levi asked as they left Harrisburg, where they had stopped for lunch. Levi could tell it irritated Raiden to have Levi pay for him, not because he wanted to be the big man. Levi was pretty certain that Raiden knew how lucky he was to be as well off as he was and took pride in taking care of others. It was a very attractive quality.

Levi was struggling now to deny there were lots of attractive qualities about Raiden. Not just his body.

"The writing?" Raiden repeated.

Levi shrugged. "The record you and Pearl have been slaving away over. Like, how do these things work? Is it progressing like you hoped?" After a few beats filled only by the music from the radio station they'd been listening to, Levi turned to look at Raiden. "What?" he asked, confused by the expression on his face.

"Nothing," said Raiden. A lopsided grin crept onto his mouth. "It's just...well, thank you for asking. It's going well, actually. Slower than if we were in a studio all week, but faster than I would expect on the road. More importantly, though, the songs are *great*. I think they could really make it."

"And that would make you happy?" Levi asked.

Raiden frowned. "Why wouldn't it?"

"I mean," said Levi, rubbing his chin. "You wouldn't be jealous?"

Raiden grinned fully. "Nah, man. I did the fame thing. That back there, at the hotel? That's the nice side of it. This hacking shit is definitely the downside. That and the never-ceasing assault on you and your music and your look. I don't miss the polls ranking the five of us from hottest to ugliest, or whole blogs dedicated to catching every dumb thing we said only to spin it to make us look like monsters." He stretched and ruffled his hair. "I wish Glittergasm the best, I truly do. But leave me on the sidelines from now on."

Levi didn't say it, but he felt like Raiden was the kind of guy who could never be fully relegated to the sidelines. He was too full of life.

It was nice, just talking in the car together. When Raiden started calling Levi 'Kevin' and 'Betty' again, Levi knew he was feeling better.

But a dangerous thought kept creeping into Levi's mind as they neared Philadelphia. He had gone from being resolutely determined to keep Raiden at arm's length, to having sex for a third time and, technically worse, comforting him like he was his boyfriend.

Hadn't he decided this bi thing was just going to be for sex? If he could date women and enjoy it, why put himself through the pain of picking a man to be with? The world was full of homophobic fucktards, and Levi really didn't want to deal with that.

But the dangerous thought was maybe that was exactly it. He couldn't choose who his heart reached out to. He'd been fighting against his feelings for Raiden for weeks, if he was truly honest. Now that he had given in, the floodgates had opened, and he was afraid by what he had unleashed.

He liked Raiden's company. He found him funny and cute and passionate. It wasn't just about a warm mouth sucking Levi's cock. It was about someone who made him feel alive.

He was falling for Raiden.

But that couldn't happen. Or, if it did, it would have to be long after Levi had stopped working for Raiden. Levi might have accepted there was no more fighting how he felt, but his uncle wouldn't see it like that. It was a gross abuse of his position as Raiden's protector, and he was putting his client at risk by allowing these feelings to develop.

It hurt his head to try and unravel all his thoughts, so he took the coward's way out and decided not to. Besides, there he was worrying about his heart messing things up, when for all he knew this was still purely about sex for Raiden.

That made Levi's stomach roll. Fuck. Was he really hoping that Raiden liked him for more than his body too?

Before he could stop himself, he reached over and squeezed Raiden's knee. He felt Raiden go still beneath his touch. Before it could get weird, Levi brought his hand back to the wheel.

The radio and meaningless chit-chat kept them company until they reached the city that afternoon. Levi was glad for the breather. Not because he wanted to get some space between him and Raiden, but because he needed to.

Once they were checked in to yet another hotel (they were all starting to look the same now) Levi made sure Raiden was okay to stay put before he hit the gym. Pearl was going to come over to work for a few hours, leaving Levi free to work off some of his pent-up energy.

He made sure to keep his phone in view while he was on the treadmill, but Raiden's little dot didn't move the whole time.

The workout helped clear his head. He needed to stop overthinking things, like Raiden had said. Better to just take things one step at a time and deal with any issues that occurred. But the truth was, he did care about Raiden. He wanted him to be happy, not sad. So that was how he found himself standing outside his door an hour later, having showered and picked out a reasonable t-shirt.

"This is no big deal," he muttered to himself, then knocked.

Raiden answered a few seconds later, his face lighting up when he saw it was Levi. Levi tried to ignore the butterflies that apparently took flight in his stomach at that.

"Hey, you still working?"

Raiden shook his head. "Pearl left about ten minutes ago. What's up?"

Levi shrugged, hoping to convey that this wasn't anything to get excited about. "I felt bad about not letting you stay out last night," he said. "Did you want to maybe scout a bar tonight? Somewhere you could take the band tomorrow? We could grab dinner on the way if you wanted."

Raiden's eyes went wide. "Give me five minutes," he said. He hopped on his feet like the morning Levi had allowed him to go running with him.

Levi agreed to wait in his room, ignoring the implication that Raiden wanted to freshen up and get dressed for any reason other than the fact they'd been traveling for most of the day. This wasn't a *date*.

And if Levi repeated it enough times, he might actually start to believe it.

# CHAPTER
## *Twenty~One*
### RAIDEN

RAIDEN SIPPED HIS RIDICULOUS COCKTAIL, VERY GLAD THAT HIS bank balance had been restored. He would have felt hideous if Levi had insisted they come to this place and then paid for everything as well.

He was still trying to wrap his head around the fact that Levi would pick a bar like this in the first place. As excited as he was about their date, Raiden had fully expected to end up at a sports bar with baseball playing on every available flat screen.

There was no doubt in his mind that this was a date. Levi was wearing a t-shirt and jeans for one thing, not a shirt and pants. They'd gone for dinner at a Thai place, and now they were at a quirky bar with overpriced drinks and low-level lighting.

So far, Levi had kept his hands to himself. As two guys not used to dating other dudes, that was hardly surprising, but Raiden was sort of longing for him to touch his knee again like he had in the car.

What the fuck had that been about anyway? Surely Levi was just in this for the sex. Except he had comforted Raiden without hesitation when the shit had hit the fan earlier. And then it had been his idea to come out tonight. Raiden chewed on his straw.

"Are you all right?"

He leaned back in his seat and smiled at Levi. The bar was packed, but they had somehow managed to get a table for two. The walls were deep red and had big, artful cracks in them to reveal naked brickwork underneath. Paintings of dogs in hats and photos from the twenties and spotted mirrors all hung in fat, gilded frames. Along the top where wall met ceiling was a bookshelf that contained leather-bound volumes. Raiden loved it.

He smiled at Levi. "Sorry, just tired," he lied. "I was thinking, this place is great, but might be a bit upmarket for the band and their groupies." He laughed and nodded back out to the street. "I think I spotted a dive bar on the way here where the floor looked good and sticky. Maybe we could check that place on the way back for tomorrow?"

"You don't like this," Levi said evenly, glancing around.

Raiden shook his head and put his drink down. He made to reach for Levi's hand, but thought better of it and retracted it back. But not before Levi saw. "I love it. For us."

Levi chewed on his lip. "I wanted to take you someplace nice. But well, I've never done this with, uh…"

"A guy," Raiden finished for him, smiling sympathetically. "Neither have I. We're just trying this out together. But, honestly, this place is awesome."

He would have been happy with some cheap beers back at the hotel bar if it meant Levi wanted to hang with him. So the fact that he'd put some effort in made it even better.

God, he couldn't get his head around this. He wished they could just talk plainly, but he was too chicken to do that, he knew. So that left him guessing and second-guessing and-

Levi's hand slipped over his knee. The tablecloth meant

no one else could see, but that only made it better. Raiden looked up at him.

"You know," said Levi. "If you don't talk, that leaves it up to me." He smiled ruefully. "And I'm not great at that."

Raiden laughed and rubbed the back of his neck. *I like you,* he wanted to blurt out. *I want this to be a real thing. I think I want to be your boyfriend.*

He wasn't going to act like the concept didn't terrify him. But that was precisely why he was tongue-tied and paying far too much attention to almost everything that wasn't Levi. Except now Levi had Raiden's hand on his knee, and that wasn't as easy to ignore.

"I am tired," Raiden began. "But I guess, well, I just think this place it really cool and was absorbing the atmosphere. I'll be better company from now on," he added with a grin.

Levi looked down like he was embarrassed. "You're, um, always good company."

Raiden barked out a laugh, some of his tension leaving him. "No, I'm damn well not. I'm pissy and bratty and wind you up for kicks."

He grinned at Levi and was pleased when he finally grinned back. "You're right. What the hell am I even doing here with you?"

Raiden sipped his drink, making sure to use his tongue to hook the straw to his mouth. "Having fun, I hope?"

Levi squeezed his knee. "I am." He didn't have to stretch or lean to keep his hand there, so he did. They both slowly drank some more, watching the crowd bustling around them.

"Damn," Raiden mused. "I wish I could Instagram this. But that would kind of screw up security for tomorrow night if seven million people knew where I was, huh?"

"You have seven million followers?" Levi asked, incredulously.

Raiden nodded and brought up the app on his phone. "It was ten, before…well, you know." He started scrolling through his pictures. They were mostly selfies or photos of food or other dumb stuff. "I'd thought you'd know that, from your research?"

Levi shrugged. "I knew it was a lot. But seven million?" He frowned and took a pull on his straw. His cocktail was less silly than Raiden's, but the fact it wasn't beer was impressive enough on its own. "Don't take this the wrong way, but…why?"

"Why do they follow me?" Raiden asked. He wasn't hurt. It was a fair question.

"I guess," said Levi. "But also, why would you want them to? Isn't that opening you up to all the scrutiny you hate?"

"True," said Raiden. He swished his straw around the glass, playing with the ice floating in his drink. "It's a double-edged sword, I suppose. Because it's also an essential marketing tool. You have to keep reminding people that you still exist. If I post a picture of me collaborating with a certain artist, that's potentially seven million people who might be that more inclined to listen or buy the record when it comes out."

Levi rubbed his thumb absently on Raiden's knee. "I can sort of see that. But isn't it kind of superficial?"

Raiden scoffed. "Massively. But that's human nature. It would be lovely to think people will become fans of Glitter-gasm because their music rocks, but the truth is, it will most likely be because of Pearl's lilac hair. She won't be able to change that color for years."

"You're serious?" said Levi.

"Perfectly," Raiden replied, swallowing down another mouthful of sticky cocktail. "It's all branding."

Levi cast his gaze out over the bar for a moment. "I don't get it," he admitted.

Raiden thought how he could explain it. "Okay, so did you ever have a teacher you really liked? Or coach, or drill sergeant or anything? Someone who was popular with your peers."

At the mention of a drill sergeant, Raiden felt Levi bristle. He hoped he hadn't put his foot in it. But then a hint of a smile twitched at the corner of Levi's mouth.

"Mrs. White. Rose White," he said, nodding. "She taught English at my middle school. Enormous woman, ginger hair, kept stuffed cats on her desk. You'd think a bunch of cocky teenagers would eat her alive."

"But they didn't?"

Levi shook his head. "She wasn't strict…she was *fair*. Let you get away with a lot of stupid stuff, so long as your work was done and you at least tried. If you crossed her, though…" He whistled. "Man, you were fucked."

"So, she had a reputation?" Raiden asked. "A brand. You didn't just remember her teaching methods. You told me about her fluffy cat toys first. What she looked like."

Levi raised his eyebrows, then glanced back over at Raiden. "That's true," he said.

Raiden smiled, pleased he'd understood. "Half of success in the creative arts – heck, any job – is about branding. Marketing. *That's* why I got obnoxious last night when you wouldn't let me go out. I post photos of me and Pearl at some bar, people are interested in me, her, the bar. Everyone wins."

Levi nodded. "All right," he said. "That's pretty cool."

Raiden watched him for a while as they drank some more and played footsie under the table. Of course, there was a chance someone *else* could sneak a photo of him, of them together, that would find its way onto Instagram or Twitter or Snapchat. But he couldn't help but think, even if it was childish, that as long as he was with Levi, he'd be okay.

He wanted to ask more about Levi's time in the Marines.

He'd hardly mentioned it at all, least of all why he had left. Once or twice he'd implied it was just the right time to move on, but Raiden hadn't imagined the way his whole body had tensed earlier at his mention of it.

But they were having a good time and he didn't want to sour that. Besides, despite his promise to perk up, he was struggling with exhaustion still. He stifled a yawn and gulped down the last of his cocktail.

"Do you want another drink?"

Levi rubbed his thumb along the edge of Raiden's knee. "We can do that," he said. "Or I can take you back to the hotel. I'm pretty bushed too. It's been a lot of driving over the past few days."

Raiden bit his lip. There was only so much he could beat around things. "That depends," he said over the bar's music. "I'm not done with you yet. So which will keep me in your company longer?"

Levi regarded him carefully. "Either," he said. "You've got me all night."

Raiden's mouth went dry. "Let's go back to the hotel then," he managed to say.

Levi nodded once, then stood and slipped on his jacket.

A couple pounced on their table before Raiden and Levi had even fully stepped away, but Raiden barely noticed. He just felt Levi's hand on his lower back, guiding him out of the bar into the night once more.

They hailed a taxi, even though the hotel was only a couple of blocks away. Raiden deliberately stayed on his side of the seat in the back for the few minutes' drive, his hands under his thighs.

This was quite different to either of them jumping the others' bones after a drink or seven. This was them calculatedly going back to somewhere private with the specific intention of having sex. Raiden did his best to slow his heart rate, but suddenly he felt a little sick with both excitement and nerves.

Levi kept his distance as they paid the driver and left the car to re-enter the hotel. It was like Raiden could feel the space between them, as if it was charged with electricity, waiting for a spark to ignite the air around them.

Levi appeared calm as they took the elevator up to their floor. From habit, Raiden got his card out and led them to his room. Levi walked by his side, standing behind him as he unlocked the door.

Raiden walked into the dimly lit room with his heart in his mouth, turning to close the door only to find Levi already doing so.

It was like two wrecking balls colliding.

Levi lunged for Raiden in the same moment Raiden threw himself into Levi's arms. Their mouths were frantic and moans possibly too loud considering there might be people still awake in the rooms around them, but Raiden didn't care. He grabbed at Levi's dirty blond hair and the back of his neck, thrusting his already hardening cock against Levi's thigh.

"Fuck," Levi breathed into his mouth. He grappled with Raiden's belt buckle as he pushed him back against the wall. "Been wanting to kiss you for hours."

Raiden melted into him, their chests heaving and legs entwined. "Going out is overrated," he said as Levi kissed down his throat. "Let's order room service next time."

"Okay," Levi agreed, sucking on his throat.

'Okay?' Raiden's heart fluttered. It seemed that Levi had stopped trying to deny that this was going to keep happening.

Levi won the battle with Raiden's jeans, shoving them to his thighs along with his briefs and wrapping his hand around Raiden's cock. He cried out, banging his head on the hotel room wall. Levi stopped nibbling on his collarbone to claim his mouth again.

Raiden reached for Levi's zipper, wanting to free his obvious erection. Between them, they managed to push his pants down as well. Then he was crowding against Raiden, pressing him against the wall like their first time together, their cocks rubbing against each other and wrapped in Levi's big hand.

"Jesus, fuck," Raiden whimpered. "Can I talk? Am I allowed to talk?"

Levi laughed and kissed him again. "I want to hear every filthy thing that pops into your brain."

Raiden moaned. "Christ, yes, just like that. Oh my god I love your cock, Levi. *Levi.* Don't stop."

Their precum helped lubricate their dicks and Levi's hand, but if he was honest, Raiden didn't mind the roughness of it. He was close, embarrassingly so.

He couldn't help but worry that the number of encounters he'd get with Levi was limited. He wanted to make the most of every single one of them. But right then he just needed them to come together. No games, just a pure climax as one.

He got his wish. It only took a few more tugs before he was spilling up himself and Levi, but then so was he, their cum mixing and hitting their shirts equally. Levi sagged with one hand on the wall, the other on Raiden's waist, pulling him close.

"Fuck," he said with a tired laugh. "Sorry, that was quicker than I'd anticipated."

Raiden clung to him and hummed. "S'oaky," he mumbled. Shit, he didn't want to pass out again, that was what he always did.

Levi stepped back enough to strip his soiled clothes, keeping his boxers on. He pulled Raiden's shirt off too, but

Raiden managed to kick his own jeans off and pull his unmarked underwear back up over his softened cock.

Levi wrapped his arm around Raiden's waist again, leaving their clothes behind as he steered them towards the bedroom that Raiden hadn't even unpacked in yet. Levi pulled back the covers and Raiden prepared himself to be put to bed again.

Except Levi crawled in after him, yanking the comforter up over them both. Then he hauled Raiden back over to him so they were spooning. Raiden was too afraid to breathe, let alone speak, in case he shattered this magic moment.

Levi kissed the back of his neck and hugged him tightly. "Sleep," he said simply.

Raiden complied, a contentment seeping through his skin he hadn't felt in years.

# CHAPTER
## Twenty-Two
### RAIDEN

RAIDEN awoke to an empty bed. He reached out to find the sheets were cold. His heart sped up. When had Levi left? Had he even slept here at all? Had Raiden imagined him cuddling up to him last night?

He curled his knees to his chest. It was completely irrational to allow someone else to make him feel so insecure, but damn it he wanted Levi to stop making him jump through hoops. He took a long breath in and out, then reached for his phone.

Sure enough, there was a text waiting for him.

*Gone to the gym. Meet me for breakfast at 9?*

Raiden smiled. See, everything was fine. Working out was obviously something that centered Levi, and he'd just hoped to get it in before Raiden woke. That was kind of sweet in its own way.

Raiden replied that would be great and stretched his arms over his head. He should probably go for a run too. But he really wasn't keen on treadmills. He much preferred the fresh air, and seeing as they were in the middle of an unfamiliar city it didn't really feel appealing.

Besides, what if Levi was right? He thought he'd maybe seen someone sketchy at the gig back in Pittsburgh. What if this wasn't just a cyber attack and there was someone lurking in person? Raiden couldn't know either way, but it certainly dampened his enthusiasm for a run. Levi would kill him if he went outside without him, anyway.

Looking at his watch told him it was just before eight, so he had plenty of time before he needed to head downstairs. He retrieved his laptop from his bag, planning on checking his emails and maybe listening to his current work in progress a few times before grabbing a shower.

Levi wanted to meet for breakfast. He didn't mind being seen out, just the two of them. For someone who had obviously been closeted until now, he was making a remarkable effort. Again, Raiden couldn't help that whisper of hope at the back of his mind that this was more than just fucking.

Could he and Levi really work as a couple? They were both based near Williams Pike now, so location wasn't really an issue. But would Levi want to date a guy? Would Raiden?

His laptop distracted him as it pinged up with multiple notifications at once. Raiden rubbed sleep from his eyes and yawned, picking through the various apps and websites to catch up on his messages.

An email caught his eye as soon as he opened his mail program. There was no sender listed. The space where the person's name should have been was blank, and when he clicked on the body of the message, the slot for the address was blank too.

Odd. Raiden looked at the brief written note.

*I'm sorry Raiden, I've not been very nice to you lately, have I? How about I make it up to you. There's a little present attached here, just for you. Enjoy ;)*

Raiden frowned. He wasn't an idiot. He knew not to click on attachments from unknown sources. That was the easiest way to get a virus. But the email had mentioned him by name, and his curiosity was blazing.

Could this be the hacker? Surely they weren't about to give him something he actually wanted? What could they offer, after all?

But Raiden was sick of this cat-and-mouse game. If it was from them, then maybe this would tell him *why* he had been targeted, or what they wanted from him?

In a reckless move, he clicked on the zip file before he could talk himself out of it. All his work was backed up externally. If they wanted to steal his money again the bank's insurance would cover him, and he could change all his passwords again if he felt there was anything corrupt about what he had just opened.

So far, it just seemed to be a collection of written documents and pictures. They were all labeled by dates which stretched back over the last couple of years. Raiden frowned. There were perhaps a dozen items in the zip file, so he figured if he was going to do this, he might as well look at them in chronological order.

His first assumption was that this was more blackmail on him. Maybe more nude photos?

It turned out, it had nothing to do with Raiden.

Slowly, he opened each document, one at a time. With each new click he felt sicker and sicker. This couldn't really be happening.

When he checked the time again, twenty minutes had passed. He fumbled for his phone and managed to tap out a text to Levi.

*Meet back in my room instead.*

Somehow, he managed to get himself in a scalding hot shower which went some way to clearing his head, then put some decent clothes on. Then he just sat on his bed, waiting for the knock at the door, thinking too many things and nothing really at all.

How could he have been so stupid?

The knock came before nine o'clock, and Raiden wasn't surprised to find Levi still in his workout gear when he opened the door for him. "Hey," he said a little breathlessly. He cracked half a grin and gave Raiden a seductive flick of his eyes. Raiden's stomach rolled. "Can I come in?"

Raiden nodded and stepped back so Levi could follow him. He walked back to the bed and sat crossed-legged, watching Levi close the door. Levi stopped at the foot of the bed and rubbed the back of his neck absently with the hand towel he'd evidently brought from the gym.

"What's going on?" Levi asked. There was a note of caution to his voice, obviously having caught on to Raiden's mood.

"I don't know," said Raiden stiffly. He turned his open laptop around and pushed it towards Levi. "Why don't you tell me?"

Frowning, Levi pulled the computer to him and held it in his hands so he could stand and flick through the documents Raiden had left open. His face suddenly dropped, his complexion going ashen.

"This is classified information," he said, his voice barely a rasp.

"I don't care if it's classified," Raiden spat out. "Is it *true?*"

Levi looked up at him, then back at the screen. "It's complicated."

Rage erupted in Raiden like a volcano. "Complicated!" he cried, jumping from the bed. He jabbed his finger at the laptop and advanced on Levi, who didn't budge. "That's not complicated, that's a lot of *fucking dead people!*"

Levi snapped the laptop shut and dropped it on the bed.

"What did you imagine happened in Iraq?" he asked. "It was war."

"But that's you, right?" Raiden demanded. "That's you in those photos, in front of those villages blown to smithereens. By those dead teenage boys lined up neatly on the ground. Walking around calmly with your fucking big gun while women ran for their *lives?*"

Levi's jaw flexed. His eyes were barely slits. Raiden couldn't believe he thought they were beautiful before.

"Did you look at the reports?"

Raiden scoffed. "Yes, of course," he said. "Pretty fucking horrifying bedtime reading there, Sergeant Patterson. No wonder you left the Marines in such a hurry. You probably only had a matter of time before you were dishonorably discharged."

Levi took a step forward, his whole body tensed into a menacing hulk. Raiden instinctively flinched backwards. Levi stopped and took a breath through his nose. "You don't know all the facts."

"I don't need to," Raiden shot back. "You're not denying these things happened, are you?"

"It's not what you think," Levi began.

"I think I'll be having nightmares for weeks," Raiden said. He could feel himself shaking. "You can tell me that's war, but I'm pretty sure war is fighting other soldiers. Not obliterating whole villages while they sleep."

Levi looked the most furious Raiden had ever seen him. His cheeks were blotchy but the rest of his face was gray. His fists were clenched and his shoulders hunched. He looked like a monster.

"I can't believe I let you into my bed," Raiden choked out, distraught when his voice cracked. He felt utterly sick and ashamed, but he managed to blink back the tears that pricked behind his eyes. He was not going to let this sick bastard see him cry.

His father would never have done anything like this. Levi should be in prison for what he'd done.

"Did you ever stop to think that this is the hacker messing with you?" Levi asked.

Raiden laughed. It was a bitter, hollow sound. "Who gives a shit? They said it was a present. They're obviously doing me a favor!"

"They're *fucking* with you!" Levi shouted. "Again! If you calm down, I can explain!"

"Explain?" Raiden hissed. "I don't want you to explain. I want you gone. Now. I want a new bodyguard, and if your uncle wants to know why, I'll tell him."

Something diminished in Levi's posture. His shoulders dropped a fraction, his frown lessened a millimeter. "Okay," he said. The fight had gone from his voice. "I'll handle it. You can't tell anyone about this, though. It's classified information. You could get in serious trouble. But…I respect your wishes. We'll get someone new out here as soon as possible."

Raiden refused to be moved by the hurt in his voice. So what Levi might have really liked him? Raiden didn't want that. He needed another shower.

Levi turned and took a step towards the door. He paused, then glanced over his shoulder. "I'm sorry," he said.

Raiden pointed at his laptop. "Tell them that."

Levi hung his head and left the room without another word.

Once the door clicked shut, Raiden marched over and turned the lock. Then he walked back on the bed and collapsed onto it. He hugged a pillow to his chest and finally let himself cry. He was disgusted and horrified and so very hurt.

How could Levi be that person?

Raiden wasn't ignorant. He knew sometimes bad things happened to the wrong people in times of war. But he would never have thought Levi would be someone like that. Raiden would never be able to unread the things he had seen in some of those reports.

All he could do was distance himself from it now. That wasn't his world. He didn't know about war zones. He and Levi were obviously not meant to be together.

He rubbed his chest as his tears made the sheets damp. It was like he could feel his heart breaking.

How could he have ever thought he was falling in love with someone like that?

# CHAPTER
## Twenty~Three

LEVI

HOW COULD LEVI HAVE BEEN SO FUCKING STUPID? HE SHOULD have known this would catch up to him sooner rather than later. He'd just hoped it wouldn't be so soon.

That Raiden would have never found out at all.

If things had gotten serious between them, then who knew? Maybe he would have confessed someday, risked Raiden rejecting him with the disgust he had just shown in his room. Or maybe he might have listened, understood?

But now, Levi would never know.

He should have insisted on explaining, telling his side of the story. But what did it really matter? Like Raiden had said, those people were all still dead.

To make matters worse, his uncle was pissed at him. Kurt didn't know the full details, only that Raiden needed a new bodyguard immediately.

Levi had left the military on an honorable discharge. As far as everyone, including his uncle, knew, it was just because he'd had enough of being away from home. He'd served his country like his father had before him, like his uncle and cousins and grandfathers. No way he was going to dishonor his dad or any of them by running his mouth on the things he'd seen.

But that now meant Raiden had seen just the one side of what his last tour had been like, and all Levi had was his word against the official reports. Not that Raiden wanted to hear it. Why should he?

What was more troubling when Levi calmed down to think about it, was *why* the hacker had done this. Was it simply to try and scare Raiden away from his protection?

Or to split him from the lover bringing him happiness?

It would be much, much worse if someone had figured out they were an item, because they had hardly even worked that out themselves. Did that mean someone was closer than Levi had anticipated? Or had they been able to suss it out from scurrying around online?

Levi wasn't sure how he could get any answers, though, so for now, he just had to sit with that uneasy knowledge.

Unfortunately, there was no one else available at the security firm for at least a couple of weeks. That, combined with the fact that Raiden was demanding a change in personnel in the first place, made the company look bad all around.

"So I don't care what you've done," Kurt had told him down the phone. "But you *fix* this."

Levi didn't know how.

He knew how to storm a building full of insurgents. He knew how to talk his men through an ambush. He knew how to navigate a minefield. But in that moment, he didn't know how to knock on Raiden Jones's door.

There was no alternative, though. If Raiden wanted to attend tonight's performance and support Glittergasm as intended, he needed protection. Levi was his only option unless he wanted to hire a completely unknown service here in Philadelphia.

Levi had texted him with that possibility a couple of hours ago and received no response. So therefore, he steeled himself, and rapped smartly on the hotel room door once.

Raiden opened after a minute and regarded him silently. "I told you your choices," Levi said, keeping his voice even. "If you haven't hired anyone else, I'm all you've got."

Raiden shut the door in his face. But the rummaging around beyond the door told Levi that Raiden was getting his shit together.

They made the journey to the venue entirely in silence. It couldn't have been a more different trip to their ride home from the bar the night before. Levi turned his face towards the window, the busy city street passing by in the afternoon sunshine. He screwed his eyes shut and allowed himself a moment of grief.

Was this really it? If Raiden never let him explain, he'd probably hate him forever. Levi would never get to be with him again. And fuck, he didn't just mean sexually. He loved their stupid drives talking about nothing. He loved how hard Raiden had tried to help him love his music. He loved his awful jokes and inappropriate teasing and...

Was he falling in love with another guy? With Raiden?

The likelihood of that happening had seemed so improbable two months ago. But now, Levi's heartache was telling him that maybe it wasn't so insane to imagine.

It was also entirely pointless. Raiden had seen what he'd seen. He was never going to look at Levi with anything but disgust, so Levi needed to make his peace with that.

They walked backstage and Levi became a shadow, like he was supposed to be. He watched on as Raiden came to life, greeting the band, offering words of encouragement to the crew, even talking to a couple of bloggers who had shown up. Glittergasm were gaining traction in the right circles, and people were starting to pay attention, or so it seemed. Levi didn't really know about these things. He just paid attention to what other people said.

Once again, he and Raiden watched from the wings. But unlike last time, Levi didn't hover with that delicious sexual tension lingering between them. He stood like a rock, acutely aware of Raiden's every move, but they might as well have been a mile apart.

This was torture. Levi couldn't manage the anger bubbling within him. There were so many people he wanted to lash out at and, infuriatingly, none of them were Raiden. He had every right to be hurt and pissed off and repulsed. Levi just wished he knew how to make it right.

A third of the way through the set, Pearl stopped for her customary water break. These small venues always liked to step in at some point to promo their own services, events, whatever drinks were on offer, that sort of thing. So Pearl sauntered over, downing a full bottle of water before she even reached Raiden and Levi on the side of the small stage.

She dropped the bottle in the recycling bin and flicked her eyes between the two of them. Levi remained still while Raiden crossed his arms. Pearl frowned.

"What?" Raiden asked, clearly uncomfortable.

Pearl shook her head. The host was calling her back on stage. She considered him and Levi a little longer, then sauntered back on stage, waving like the queen of England.

Levi refused to react, but Raiden shifted from foot to foot. Levi wanted to say something, anything. This was all his fault. But instead, he said nothing. He let the baseline drown out his thoughts and the beat of the drum dictate his heartbeat.

Raiden deserved better than him, of that he had no doubt. So until his uncle could find a replacement for the tour, or even back at the ranch, Levi would do his duties as if made of granite. Observe, but not interact.

The band finished the song, but movement near the doors caught Levi's eye. Underground Arts wasn't a large venue, so he could see almost all the emergency exits from this vantage point. He straightened. Security guards didn't run for no good reason.

"Get back," he said, automatically pulling Raiden away from the stage. Raiden swatted him away, but Levi had a fistful of his shirt and wasn't letting go. There was panic spreading through the air.

The band faltered on stage. They could sense something was wrong.

"Just a second, folks," Pearl said with a smile, looking over to the wings for someone to give her a cue.

It came.

A young guy dressed in black with a walkie-talkie from the crew skidded to a halt in front of Levi and Raiden.

"Bomb!" he shouted. "There's a bomb in the building!"

# CHAPTER

## Twenty~Four

RAIDEN

RAIDEN DIDN'T EVEN HAVE A CHANCE TO PROCESS THE WORD before Levi was a blur before him, scooping Pearl up from center stage. "There is a bomb in the building," he said confidently into the microphone. "Everyone is to calmly and quickly evacuate the premises *immediately.*" The room burst into a frenzy of screams and people panicking as they ran for the emergency exits. Levi turned to the band. "GO!"

His arm was around Pearl as they ran from the stage, the other four members of Glittergasm right behind him. It was all over in a matter of three, maybe four seconds, until Raiden found himself swept up in Levi's other arm.

Levi let go of Pearl, who was already sprinting hand in hand with the bassist for the backstage exit. But Levi had Raiden glued to his side like they were running a three-legged race.

The street outside was pandemonium, people running everywhere, the sound of sirens in the air. Raiden was still trying to wrap his head around what was happening. There couldn't really be a *bomb* in the building, could there? That was *insane.*

But before he knew it Levi was bundling them into the Jeep and pulling away from the theatre. "Wait," said Raiden, his voice catching up to him. "Pearl, the band, where did they go?"

"Venue security has them," Levi said, squealing around a corner, not looking at Raiden. "The authorities will already be on the scene."

Raiden realized he was shaking. "Was there really a bomb?" he stammered.

Levi licked his lips and tore the Jeep down another street, ignoring the people blaring their horns at him. "It doesn't matter. We treat it as real until the bomb squad have combed every single square inch of that place."

Raiden blinked and pulled his phone from his pocket. He wasn't sure why. It wasn't like he should really be checking Twitter right then. Except...

He cried out, a snarl and a wail all in one. There was a text message from nobody. No number or caller ID It was completely blank, aside from the single word in the body of the text message.

*Boom.*

"What?" Levi demanded.

A little too late, Raiden realized they weren't going back to the hotel. They were halfway out of town already. He looked around in confusion, his head spinning. "Can we stop? Levi – *stop!*"

In a split second, they swung around ninety degrees and reversed down an alleyway. Raiden gulped down breaths of air, then handed the phone over, the text message clearly on display.

"Fuck," Levi growled.

"Is it real?" Raiden whispered. "Are they going to bomb a whole building just to get to me?"

Levi handed the phone back and killed the car ignition.

Silently, he looked out into the night, not that they could see anything much beyond the alley. But Raiden guessed it was the direction of the venue.

"No," said Levi slowly. "I don't think there's a device. I'd bet any money they were just after attention."

Raiden let out a sob. "I'm so sick of this. I'm *so sick!* Why are they doing this? What the hell did I ever do to these people?" He hadn't buckled up, so he was able to turn easily and shove Levi in the chest. "What do they *want?* A ransom? To kill me? *What the fuck is going on?*"

He didn't even realize he was beating Levi's chest until Levi grabbed his wrists and pulled Raiden to him, wrapping his arms around him as he cried and trembled. He'd never felt more pathetic in his life.

"Shh, shh," Levi said, stroking his hair. Raiden was ashamed that he let him. All the anger from that morning's revelations melted away in the face of needing someone to comfort him, to stop him spinning out of control.

"I hate you," Raiden whispered, clinging on tighter.

"I know," Levi said.

Raiden screwed his eyes shut, the tears leaking over his lashes. "Why did you have to ruin everything?" he asked.

Levi continued to hold him for a few more minutes. Raiden realized with another sob that this was what he wanted. He wanted Levi to be the person he turned to in times of crisis. He wanted to be there for Levi when trouble darkened his door. But knowing what he did now, surely there was no way that could happen. He couldn't be attracted to someone who had been a part of something so heinous.

Except Levi just didn't seem like he would do that. Raiden couldn't know him inside and out. They had only been working together for a couple of months. But did Raiden really believe he was the cold-blooded killer those photos had made him out to be?

Maybe Raiden should have listened when Levi said it was more complicated than it appeared? Instead of being horrified that he had fallen for a monster, Raiden should have at least given the man a chance to tell his side.

As his heart rate slowed, a flicker of hope burned in Raiden's chest. He didn't want to be duped by Levi, but he did desperately want to be proved wrong in his assumptions if at all possible. He wanted Levi to be the hero he just showed himself to be.

After a while, Levi stirred. "I want to get off the street," he said in his no-nonsense voice. Obediently, Raiden sat up, wiping his eyes as Levi brought the Jeep back to life.

They drove for another fifteen minutes until they came across a basic chain hotel where they could park close. They had nothing on them but their phones and wallets, but Levi still guided them inside and towards the front desk.

Raiden did his best not to fall apart, not hearing a single word Levi said to the woman behind the desk as he paid in cash. Pearl had already texted several times to let him know they were okay and emergency services were looking after them all.

Initial reports seemed to agree that, yes. This was a hoax.

Raiden pressed the corner of his phone to his forehead. Why was this happening to him? What had he ever done to offend someone so badly that they'd go to these lengths?

He wrote back to her that he was okay and agreed to stay in touch. Before he knew it, Levi was escorting him towards the elevator. Once again, they rode in silence.

Raiden was crashing hard. After the emotional turmoil of trying to process everything he had learned about Levi that morning, he wasn't able to cope with evacuating the gig for a bomb scare too. He stumbled out of the elevator and followed Levi, trusting he would lead him to his room.

He got out a key card and opened a door, as expected.

Raiden looked left and right. "Which one's yours?" he asked. "I wasn't paying attention."

Levi shook his head. "I don't have one," he said. "Come on."

Raiden opened his mouth to question what the hell he was talking about. But before he knew it, he was ushered inside, and the door was shut behind him.

Then Levi was hugging him like he'd come back from the dead.

"I know I have no right," Levi growled, his breaths ragged. "But for a second there I thought you were going to die and I can't…I won't…*please*. Raiden. Hate me all you want, I promise I'll let you go if that's what you need. But I have to at least try and explain."

Raiden allowed himself to be hugged.

He hadn't really thought about losing Levi. He'd been so blindsided by the notion of an actual *bomb*, he hadn't stopped to think they could have died without ever speaking again. Touching again.

But by all accounts, Levi had taken part in *war crimes*. Raiden didn't want to be anywhere near that. On the other hand…could there really be an alternative explanation?

Raiden used every scrap of strength he had and pushed himself gently free. He felt Levi watch as he moved over and sat on the edge of the solitary double bed occupying the basic hotel room.

"I'm not promising it will change anything," Raiden said, scrubbing his face. He looked up into Levi's icy blue eyes. Who was he kidding? Of course they were beautiful. "But, if you have something to say, I think I owe you to at least hear it."

Levi nodded. He removed his jacket and gun the same methodical way he always did. Then he pulled out the chair by the desk and sat, his hands clasped between his knees. He looked up at Raiden, a ghost of a smile on his lips.

"Thank you."

# CHAPTER
## Twenty-Five

### LEVI

LEVI WRUNG HIS HANDS FOR A MINUTE, CONSIDERING WHAT HE had to say. He absolutely could not fuck this up. This was his one chance to keep Raiden. He wanted that so badly, but only if it was genuinely what Raiden wanted too. Levi wasn't going to trick him into staying in this relationship they had found themselves in.

"It has been the proudest honor of my life to serve my country," Levi began. "I have a big military family. I wanted to follow in their footsteps."

He licked his lips and glanced at Raiden. His dad had been a Marine too, but Raiden obviously hadn't felt that urge to sign up that Levi had. He was so creative, he was meant for a more beautiful world than that of war.

"I have served in both Iraq and Afghanistan, as well as a couple of peacekeeping missions. My last tour, the one you saw the documents for, was Iraq."

Raiden dropped his gaze and swallowed. Levi would have done anything to take away the distress seeing those files had caused him.

"In the military, the chain of command is absolute," Levi

continued. "If orders aren't followed when they are given, without pause, the whole operation could come crashing down. When your superiors are competent and have earned their position as well as your trust, this works just fine. It saves lives and wins battles." He licked his lips, the pain welling up inside him. "When your superior is incompetent, the situation can get FUBAR in the blink of an eye."

Raiden looked back up. His face was hard to read. He clasped his hands together, rested his elbows on his knees, then placed his chin on his fingers, watching Levi intently.

Levi took a slow breath in to steady himself. "I'm not trying to shift the blame," he said. "Just give context."

"I'm listening," Raiden murmured.

Levi rubbed his thumb against his chin, stalling for time. "My lieutenant was a guy named Meyrick. He…had issues."

Levi shifted in his seat. Nausea rolled through his stomach. He had done his best not to think about this at all the past few months.

"Issues?" Raiden repeated.

"He was a fucking gung-ho cowboy," Levi growled, unable to look at Raiden. He stared at the threadbare carpet instead. "He only got the position because he had an uncle in high places."

The irony that Levi had only got his current job – that he was screwing up – was thanks to his own uncle was not lost on him.

"He was borderline unhinged most of the time. Thought the enemy was hiding around every corner, just waiting to take us out. A glint of a mirror through a window became the barrel of a machine gun. Kids playing in the street were suicide bombers. Guys who couldn't speak English were Iraqi special forces trying to infiltrate our camp." Levi swallowed, but he couldn't dislodge the lump that had risen in his throat. "I wasn't the only sergeant that tried to question

Meyrick, that reported his actions to higher powers. But ultimately, it was his command, and what he said, went."

Raiden's gaze on him was unflinching. "So, you were just following orders?"

Levi suppressed the flare of rage that filled him. "No," he managed to grind out. "I refused his orders on more than one occasion. As you said, I was very close at times to a dishonorable discharge. Some of the other guys weren't so lucky and took the blame for his shit when they were simply helpless bystanders to his hysteria."

He looked back at the carpet again, afraid of Raiden's reaction. "I should have done more. I should have fought harder after the third hamlet he accidentally leveled. But…" Shame threatened to overwhelm him. "Do you know how my dad died?"

He shifted his gaze to see Raiden frown at the apparent non-sequitur. "Um, no I'm sorry, I don't. I assumed he died on duty?"

Levi sighed. "He was killed by an idiot kid texting on his phone while driving. He didn't see the red light, so he ran straight into my dad's pickup. The kid walked away."

He refused to let the tears fall. But that would always be the greatest regret of his life. He had been on the other side of the world, and one day, his dad was just gone. After everything Dad had faced in the service of his country, he had to go in such a pointless way.

He hadn't seen Raiden move. But his sneakers appeared in Levi's view of the carpet. When he looked up, Raiden cradled his face, letting his head lean on his stomach as he stroked Levi's hair. Levi let out the breath he had been holding and rested his hands tentatively on Raiden's narrow waist. He thought he was never going to be able to touch him like this again.

"I'm so sorry," Raiden whispered.

Levi hugged him closer. "No, I'm sorry," he said. "For everything." He closed his eyes and let Raiden hold him. "The Marines were everything to my dad, and betraying them felt like betraying him. So, when I couldn't make the higher-ups see sense about Meyrick, I knew I had to go. I couldn't stand to work for an institution that would rather blindly follow the word of a maniac than protect people."

"Weren't the Marines everything to you, too?" Raiden asked quietly.

Levi dug his fingers into Raiden's skin, not enough to hurt him, but enough to anchor Raiden to him. "Yes," he said, so grateful Raiden understood. "They were my family too, my brothers. I'm proud of my career and the good I did in the world. But it ended in a tower of flames, and I'll never be able to set it right."

Raiden cupped his hands either side of Levi's face, getting him to look up at him. They stayed like that for what felt like forever but was probably only a minute. Levi allowed Raiden to look into his eyes and didn't flinch away.

"I believe you," Raiden said.

Levi gritted his teeth and couldn't help but look down. He hadn't cried since his father passed away, but he was damn close to it now.

"I wish you didn't have to," Levi said, unable to look up. "I wish I could be better for you. I…I want that. To be good. For you."

Raiden lowered himself to his knees so they were at the same level. It was more difficult for Levi to avert his gaze like that. "You want to be with me?" Raiden asked. His eyes were glassy with what Levi dared to believe was hope.

He swallowed, afraid. But he had almost lost Raiden with this mess already. He could have lost him for real at the gig earlier. He was done being a coward. It was time to do the right thing.

"Yes," he said. "I want to be partners. Officially. I under-stand if that's not-"

Raiden stopped him with a kiss. "It is," he said, the tears escaping his eyes that Levi wouldn't allow himself to indulge in. "I'm sorry I jumped to conclusions. I should have believed you when you said there was more to it."

"Why would you, though?" Levi said. His relief may have been strong, but he was still deeply ashamed. "The evidence is pretty damning."

"Because I should have known the man I love wouldn't do that."

Levi's breath disappeared from his lungs. He and Raiden looked at each other as the seconds ticked by. Love. He had almost convinced himself that was what it was between them, but for Raiden to name it was terrifying.

He ran his hands through the black hair he adored. "How can you love me?" he asked, skirting the issue. "I've been such a dick to you. And now this..."

Raiden didn't look away from him. "Because I do," he said. "That's why this hurt so much. But...I'm starting to think that's what the hacker wanted. They've tried to take my reputation, my career, my safety. Why not take my partner too, in the cruelest of ways?"

That was what Levi had thought before. This was more than just trying to separate Raiden from his bodyguard. He rubbed the back of Raiden's neck. "I won't let them do that again," he promised. "If I can. You're very important to me. I..." He couldn't say it. It was too much.

Raiden saved him by pulling him close for a hug. Levi rested his head on Raiden's shoulder and splayed his hands over his back, holding him tightly.

"I need you," he managed to say instead.

"Partners?" Raiden asked, hope naked in the single word.

Levi nodded. He preferred that so much more than

boyfriends. He'd never been keen on the word, even when dating women. "Partners," he agreed. It made it sound like they were both working together towards the same goal. "To hell with the consequences. We'll work something out."

Raiden chuckled. "Oh god, I thought I'd lost you," he said. "You big, grumpy ogre."

Levi laughed and kissed the side of Raiden's neck, making him squirm. "It'll take more than that to get rid of me, I'm afraid."

They stayed embraced until Raiden protested his knees were starting to ache. Then he led Levi by the hand over to the bed, where they laid down, side by side, Raiden snuggled up to Levi's flank, his head resting on his chest. Levi continued to stroke his silky hair.

"I think," Raiden said slowly, "I need to quit the tour. It's not fair at all to the band if they're going to get caught up in the fallout of my shit with this hacker. We can work over email until it goes away."

Levi sighed. He knew how much being on the road again had meant to Raiden, and it had been almost entirely ruined every step of the way by whoever was behind these attacks.

"Are you sure?" he asked. "I won't stop doing what I can to make it safer for you." He wanted to offer to bring in a team, but his uncle didn't have anyone else to spare right now.

Raiden nodded against his chest. "Let's just go home. We can try and figure out who this asshole is, and…" He paused and bit his lip, looking shyly up at Levi. "We can figure out how to do us as well?"

Levi smiled, leaning down the inch or two to bring their lips together for a chaste kiss. "As long as I'm with you," he said, feeling like an idiot but saying it anyway, "I'll go anywhere."

RAIDEN WASN'T SURE WHAT HE WAS SURPRISED BY MORE. THE fact that they had slept in the same bed together just cuddling, no wandering hands at all. Or that when he had woken several hours later, Levi was still there.

Raiden blinked in the sunlight streaming through the cheap curtains. Levi was snoring lightly, his arms slung possessively over Raiden's belly. Raiden felt his heart contract, a fullness there that he suspected had been missing from their previous encounters.

He didn't want Levi just for the things he could do to his body or the way he could make him come. He wanted him for sweet cuddles and idle chatter. Raiden wanted to share his heart and time with him, not just his flesh.

Stroking Levi's hair carefully from his face, Raiden felt perversely thankful to the hacker. If they hadn't targeted Raiden in the first place, he wouldn't have needed Levi's protection. If they hadn't called in the bomb scare last night, they might never have made up.

Of course, Raiden also would never have known about what had happened in Iraq in the first place. But he was glad he did. This had pushed Levi to share one of the darkest times of his life with Raiden, trusted him with that knowledge. It had brought them closer together, maybe giving them the push they needed to acknowledge their true feelings.

He loved Levi Patterson. This cranky, uptight *man*. Raiden felt like he didn't see his gender, though, he just saw the person who made him feel whole. Maybe Joey would know if there was a word to describe that. In the meantime, Raiden reveled in the acceptance that he was a bit queer, and that was sort of wonderful. The more love in the world, the better, as far as he was concerned. It didn't matter how it manifested itself.

Levi roused and Raiden stilled his hand on his hair. He held his breath, anxious in case he spoiled the moment.

But Levi simply blinked a couple of times, absorbing his surroundings. Then he closed his eyes again with a sleepy smile, pulling Raiden closer to him. "Morning," he said.

Relief flooded Raiden. "Morning," he said. He lightly kissed Levi's shoulder. It was the closest part of his skin he could reach with his lips. Before going to bed they had stripped to their underwear, and Raiden was vaguely aware of his half-hard dick now. But he wasn't feeling the desperate need to get fucked senseless. His time with Levi no longer felt finite.

Instead, he shifted his weight so he could trace a few kisses along his partner's neck and jaw, finding his mouth for a couple of sweet kisses.

"I wish I had my toothbrush," Raiden said with a laugh, certain he had morning breath.

Levi smiled at him. "Still gorgeous," he said with a wink. "But how about we head back to the hotel. I'm sure it'll be safe now. We can pack up and start the drive home?"

Raiden sighed. He knew it was the right thing to do while

the threat was still looming. There was no telling what the hacker might try next. But damn it, he didn't want to leave the tour. Despite all the hiccups, this was the most alive he had felt in years.

"Sure," he said to Levi, though. At least if he had to ditch, he got to spend the next couple of days traveling with Levi. That meant sharing more hotel rooms, after all…

He got up before his morning wood could get fully erect. While he searched for his jeans, he thought about what it might be like once they got back to Apple Blossom Ranch. If Levi continued to be his bodyguard, would he stay at the farmhouse with them again? Raiden liked the idea of having him that close by.

Even afterwards, Levi didn't live that far away. Raiden guessed Levi would have to travel depending on who his other clients were. But maybe he might be based in nearby cities like Lexington.

As he pulled his t-shirt back over his head, he realized he was seriously considering their future together. He was excited about it.

"What are you smiling about?" Levi asked as they walked to the door.

Raiden shrugged. "Nothing," he said, not quite ready to confess how mushy he was getting already.

They took the drive slowly across Philly back to their original hotel. Despite his preference for the outdoors, Raiden thought he might go for a run and workout in the gym before they got back in the car. Otherwise, his muscles were going to murder him.

He checked his phone again. He'd told Pearl that Levi had looked after him the night before, and for the sake of everyone's safety, he was going to go home and leave them to the rest of the tour.

*Okay,* was her initial reply. Then a second text followed. *So you and Levi made up?*

Raiden smiled but also huffed in exasperation.

"What?" Levi asked.

Raiden felt a little guilty, even though he hadn't done anything wrong. "I guess Pearl picked up that something was going on between us and that we'd fallen out," he said. "She wants to know if we're okay now."

He had no idea how Levi felt about this. He may want to be together, but how public did he want to make it?

"What did you tell her?" Levi asked, looking over and raising an eyebrow.

Raiden bit his lip. "What do you want to say?"

Levi slowed to take a corner, then glanced back over at Raiden. "Tell her your dumbass partner apologized and everything's okay again?"

Raiden tried not to show how pleased he was. "Okay," he said quietly, then tapped out the message.

Pearl and the rest of the band were already on their way to New York for the final leg of their tour. They would play a couple of smaller gigs before their biggest show to date, opening for Dyrnoir. Raiden was sad not to have said good-bye, but he would hopefully see them soon enough.

In the meantime, that meant there was no one for them to bump into at the hotel. But Raiden still felt like people were looking at them. Like they could tell something seismic had shifted between them just by looking their way.

He allowed Levi to guide him towards the elevator, the silence as they rode it up subtly different once again. Raiden's body was turned slightly towards Levi's, their hands brushing. Raiden bit his lip and he smiled, his gaze shyly on the floor. Levi leaned over and placed a quick kiss on his temple.

They managed to make it to their floor without anyone

joining them in the car. Raiden had his key card out before the doors even opened. His heart was beating in his throat as he walked down the corridor. He almost missed his room, such was his anticipation.

"You, um, want to come in?"

Levi gave him a smirk and leaned casually against the door frame. "Sure, why not?"

Raiden slid the card in and out of the slot, letting them inside.

Once the door was closed, Raiden's heart rate picked up even more. "So, I'm just going to…"

He pointed towards the bathroom and made to go inside. But Levi grabbed his wrist, spinning him into his arms, kissing him hungrily. Raiden melted into the embrace, grabbing either side of Levi's face. But then he pulled his mouth back with a laugh.

"I need to brush my teeth," he whined.

Levi picked him up. Raiden automatically wrapped his legs around his waist. "No, you don't," Levi said. "You need to take all your clothes off for me."

Raiden moaned, kissing him harder. His cock had gone from cautiously excited to rock hard in mere seconds and was now poking Levi in his equally hard abs. "But I'm gross."

Levi shook his head. "You're perfect. Please, Raiden."

Raiden was pretty sure he'd be a lot nicer after a shower. But then, if he and Levi were on the same page, they were probably going to get good and messy right now. They could shower later. Maybe this time, Levi would join him.

Raiden lifted his shirt over his head and dropped it to the floor. Levi started kissing him again as he walked them towards the bed. "Why didn't we do this back in the other hotel?" Raiden asked as he bounced on the mattress, looking up at Levi.

Levi looked around for Raiden's overnight bag, then

fished out the condoms and lube Raiden had purposefully left within reach of the bed, rather than in the bathroom with the rest of his toiletries. "This is why," he said, placing them on the nightstand and crawling onto the bed. "Now, Mr. Jones. I do believe I told you to take your clothes off?"

Levi knelt back on his heels, watching Raiden with his arms crossed. Raiden did his best not to blush as he slowly lowered the zip on his jeans.

"Just the pants," Lev instructed.

So Raiden lifted his hips and slid the jeans over his ass, his cock straining in his briefs. Luckily, he was wearing his favorite old sneakers, so was able to kick them and his socks off as he shimmied free of the denim.

"Good," said Levi. "Hands above your head."

Raiden did so, wantonly. He arched his back a little and squirmed, loving being the subject of Levi's gaze. "Like that?" he asked, crossed them over the pillow.

"Yes." Levi crawled across, looming over Raiden as he ran his large hand over Raiden's chest. "Keep them there."

"You could secure them?" Raiden suggested, thinking of the tie on the bathrobe hanging on the back of the bathroom door. A spike of exhilaration shot through him at the thought of it.

But Levi shook his head, a lazy, lop-sided smile gracing his features. "Trusting you to be good is part of the fun," he said. He rolled one of Raiden's nipples between his fingers, making it hard. Raiden groaned and bit his lower lip. "You'll be good, won't you, Raiden?"

He nodded. "Yes, Levi." Saying each other's names felt like a vow, a promise that connected them deeper than anything before.

"Excellent," Levi murmured. He palmed Raiden's aching cock through his underwear, making Raiden gasp. "Good boys get rewards."

"I'll be so good for you," Raiden said, panting and writhing. He wanted to grab his briefs and yank them off so Levi could get his coarse fingers directly on his shaft. But he couldn't move his hands, so he had to trust that Levi would strip him when he wanted to. "I promise."

"Is that so?"

Levi let go of his cock and ran his finger under the waistband of Raiden's briefs. Then he stood and stretched his impressive arms before slowly popping free each button on his shirt. Raiden drank in the expanse of muscles as he exposed his chest.

"Can I talk?" he asked.

He didn't really mind either way. He just liked showing Levi he could do as he was told when it really mattered. Still, he liked the way Levi's eyes darkened as he peeled off his shirt.

"I think you can talk today," he said, a glint in his eye.

"Holy fuck, I want you to come back over here and decimate me," Raiden said. "I want that body to just *crush* me. Please, Levi. Please."

Levi laughed. His face was breathtakingly beautiful when it was fully relaxed and full of joy. Raiden was doing that. Whatever he had done to incur the hacker's wrath, it was balanced out by whatever he had done to earn such a magnificent sight.

"Okay, baby," Levi said. He flicked open his belt buckle, dropping his head back and giving Raiden a scintillating look through his eyelashes. "If you think that tight little hole of yours can take it?"

Raiden rolled his body. He would have loved to touch himself, but he settled for thrusting his hips up and making his junk bob in his underwear. "Damn right. Only cock I've had in this ass. It's made to measure."

"You're a filthy little fuck," Levi said. He had to yank his shoes off before he could ditch the pants, but he did so swiftly. Then he was walking back over to Raiden, his big dick standing fat and proud in his boxers. "I said you would be."

Raiden looked up at him fondly. "You did," he said. Even then, Levi had known him. It was fucked up that he found that romantic, but it was already pretty obvious that they weren't a run-of-the-mill couple.

Levi looked down at his underwear. "I think you should take these off for me. See what's in store for that tight ass." Raiden sat up eagerly and reached out. "Nah ah," said Levi, shaking his head. Raiden stilled. "Who said you could use your hands?"

Raiden looked down at them, then grinned and clasped them behind his back.

Levi caressed his cheek. "Good boy," he said. His voice was thick with lust. The fact that it was all directed at Raiden made him even harder.

Carefully, he leaned over and used his teeth to grasp the elastic band on Levi's boxers and tugged them down. Getting them over the tip of his erection brought Raiden face to face with it. He had loved sucking Levi off on the couch back in Pittsburgh while he'd jerked off. Once a show-off, always a show-off, Raiden figured.

He managed to yank the underwear down to Levi's balls, then couldn't resist slipping his lips over the crown, lapping up the bead of precum already leaking free. Levi moaned and carded his fingers through Raiden's hair. "Yes, baby boy."

Raiden wasn't sure he'd like pet names like that from anyone else. But on Levi's lips, it made his whole body shudder.

He worked Levi's cock until his jaw began to ache. Suddenly, Levi pushed him back down on the bed. Raiden gasped in surprise, flinging his hands back over his head, breathing heavily as he waited for Levi to come to him.

He slipped his boxers the whole way off, then climbed naked over Raiden, his cock pointed upwards like it was accusing Raiden of some nefarious deed. "You're gorgeous," Levi said, running one hand along Raiden's flank. The other gripped his ass cheek through his briefs. "Can I have you?"

"Always," Raiden rasped.

Levi moved up to kiss him tenderly, his hands entwining with Raiden's above them. For a moment, Levi's face hovered just above Raiden's, his eyes flicking back and forth fractionally as he studied Raiden's expression.

"Levi?" he asked.

Levi swallowed, his Adam's apple bobbing, making his throat look oddly exposed.

"I love you, too," Levi whispered.

Raiden could have sworn his heart stopped beating. He felt his eyes grow wide. "Really?" He knew he sounded pathetic, but he had to ask.

Levi nodded. "I'm sorry I couldn't say it earlier. But I know it's true, and you deserve all my truths from now on."

Raiden wasn't sure what to say. He felt like his mouth had gone too dry to speak. But he had to say something. He knew how huge this was for Levi to confess. "You can have my truths too," he said. "And my love. I – I'm glad there wasn't another guy before you. You'll always have that part of me."

He almost expected Levi to be crude and grab his ass, take him literally. But instead, he placed a hand over Raiden's heart, understanding him completely.

Levi moved his hands and disposed of Raiden's briefs, then scooped him up against him so their bodies were pressed entirely together in a tender embrace. Levi undulated slowly, rolling his body so their cocks tortured one another in mind-dazzling pleasure.

"You can move your hands," he said, kissing Raiden's neck and capturing his earlobe with his lips. "I want you to hold me again."

Raiden brought his arms down, wrapping them around Levi's back like a drowning man clinging to driftwood. He wasn't sure how long they lay like that, kissing, skin to skin as their throbbing erections teased each other. But soon, Raiden felt his desperation growing.

"I want you inside me," he said, running his hands over Levi's biceps and shoulders before holding either side of his neck. "Claim me. I'm all yours. I'll do anything you want."

Levi kissed his mouth, his breaths coming out in needy puffs. "I want you to lie back and enjoy yourself," he said, sucking on his collarbone. "I want you to take what I give you and tell me how much you like it."

"Yeah, I think," Raided gasped, "I think I can do that."

Levi made short work of slicking up his fingers and soon he was entering Raiden, getting him ready for his cock.

Raiden squirmed and pawed at Levi as much as he liked, loving the hungry way Levi watched him. "Fuck, yes," Raiden said. "You're like my own fucking Viking. God, I want you to plunder me already. If you weren't so huge you'd fit by now."

"Is that so?" Levi said, a dangerous note to his voice. He arched an eyebrow and shoved a third digit inside. Raiden cursed and bucked, but he was harder than ever.

"Yeah, you freak. How many people have you destroyed with that thing?"

"So many," Levi growled. "But now its only mission is to impale you, for as long as I like. Do you want that?"

"Fucking Christ, Jesus almighty, *yes.*"

Raiden could cry. He clawed at Levi's back and ground his ass on his fingers, stretching himself as quickly as he could. He was drenched with sweat and his cock was leaking more precum, throbbing with the need to be touched again.

So of course Levi ignored it, sucking on one of Raiden's nipples instead.

"You bastard," Raiden said, laughing breathlessly. "Can you just fuck me already?"

"Keep that up and you won't get fucked at all," Levi threatened.

But Raiden knew he was full of shit. His pupils were blown with lust and his own cock was dripping. He wanted Raiden just as much as Raiden wanted him. He pulsed his fingers a few more times, then snatched up the condom, ripping the foil off with his teeth to free the rubber inside.

Raiden panted and dropped his hands back over his head again as he watched Levi suit up and coat his cock with more lube, drizzling more over his hand to slather over Raiden's entrance for good measure.

When he positioned himself on all fours over Raiden, he used one hand to help guide his dick inside Raiden's stretched hole, the other to grip the back of Raiden's neck to steady him as they kissed with fervor. "Let me in, baby," he whispered between kisses. "Raiden, sweetheart. I've got you."

Raiden nodded, trying not to cry out. He could do this for Levi. He could relax and allow him to enter. "Levi," he mumbled, not able to say much else. "Levi."

Slowly, with much grunting and kissing and sweat dripping onto the bedsheets, Levi managed to bottom out. Raiden sunk his teeth into Levi's shoulder, whimpering as he urged himself to adjust to the burn.

Levi gave him all the time he needed, though, touching his lips to Raiden's eyelids and the tip of his nose as he played with his hair. "If I call you pretty," he asked, "will you hit me?"

"Boys can be pretty," Raiden replied, not sure if he was laughing or crying. "I'm *so* damn pretty."

It got better surprisingly quickly. He should have remembered from last time, as impossibly full as he seemed at first, it did eventually improve.

"Can I try to move?" Levi asked.

"Only if you find my sweet spot again," Raiden said.

Levi thrust gently in and out. "You just lie there and be a good boy. I'll take care of you. I promise."

Raiden nodded, unable to do much else.

Levi took his time building up a rhythm, but once he hit his stride it was all Raiden could do to hang on and enjoy the ride. He was practically wailing, not even conscious of the profanities slipping from his mouth as he gasped and moaned, begging for release.

"Come whenever you like, baby," Levi breathed into his ear. "I won't be long."

He reached between them and jerked Raiden's cock. Within seconds, Raiden's vision blacked out and he screamed, digging his nails into Levi's back. His orgasm tore through him, lifting him up like he was three feet above the bed.

As he floated back down, he was aware of Levi pounding into him with fervor. Then he stiffened, shouting out Raiden's name as he came. Raiden lay there, boneless, until Levi's wits came back to him enough to hug and kiss him.

"That was amazing."

Raiden nodded in agreement. He was going to be sore after this. He wasn't sure he could face a long drive right now. But it would be worth it. Every time he winced from his tender ass, he'd remember the way Levi had yelled his name, totally undone.

But for now, he was barely able to reach for some tissues. Levi helped him and they both mopped up a little before Levi was back to his usual role of fussing around him, pushing him around until they were able to get under the covers. Next time, Raiden was going to pull the damn comforter back *first,* then he'd be free to pass out to his heart's content after.

"Get over here," he grumbled, pawing at Levi, hardly able to keep his eyes open in spite of the sunshine streaming through the windows.

Levi was happy to cuddle close, the big spoon like before. He brushed Raiden's damp hair back and kissed his neck. "Sleep, baby. I've got you."

Raiden was happy to do as he was told.

# CHAPTER
## Twenty-Seven
### RAIDEN

By the time Raiden and Levi finally left the hotel room, it was several hours later. After a post-coital nap, Raiden had achieved his goal and managed to coax Levi into the shower with him. Between the kisses and shared hand-jobs, they did eventually get themselves cleaned up and ready to hit the road.

Their plan was to just drive the most direct route home back to Lexington, stopping whenever they liked for food and a hotel. Levi seemed keen on keeping everything spontaneous, so if the hacker did feel like striking again, it would make their job a whole lot harder. It had probably been really easy to strike when Glittergasm's tour schedule was so well publicized.

Raiden hoped the hacker would leave him alone now. They had run him off the tour and attacked almost every other aspect of his life. What more could they want? But he agreed with Levi in that the more unpredictable they could be, the better.

Thanks to their shenanigans, they were leaving late afternoon. Much later than was ideal. Levi wasn't stressed, but he did have his game face on. "How about I pack the car while you check us out?" he asked as they entered the lobby.

Raiden felt a mild flare of panic. What if his card didn't work again? But it had been fine since leaving Pittsburgh. He couldn't freak out every time he had to pay for something. Otherwise he would drive himself nuts. Besides, if there was an issue, he would just call Levi. The signal was surprisingly good down in the underground parking lot.

"Sure, see you in a sec," he said.

They paused, both of them looking at the other in a moment of uncertainty. Then Raiden leaned over and kissed Levi on the cheek.

It was such a simple thing. Raiden wouldn't have hesitated if it was a girl he was now officially dating. But doing it with Levi felt like a monumental act of defiance, even though it seemed like no one around them particularly noticed.

Levi noticed well enough. He gave Raiden a smoldering look and took his bag from his hand, their fingers brushing.

"See you down there, baby," he murmured so quietly Raiden wouldn't have heard if he wasn't already paying full attention to Levi and his delectable mouth.

Raiden winked and turned to cross the lobby and join the line at the front desk.

A chirpy redheaded woman processed his checkout with no problems at all. "Thank you so much for staying with us, Mr. Jones," she said with a big smile. "We do hope you and your friend will come back soon."

For a moment he paused, concerned she had seen them kiss and was subtly taunting him. But a quick glance at her wrist showed a rainbow bangle just visible below her shirt cuff. When he looked back up, she smiled even broader.

Raiden relaxed, warmth flooding through him. Was this how Joey always felt? And now Blake? On edge, wondering if people were going to judge you or, worse, deny you service because of who you loved? Sadly, he realized that yes, it was probably exactly like that. But he would deal with it every single day if it meant being with Levi.

He felt impossibly grateful toward the redhead and beamed his best smile at her. "We will come back, I'm sure," he said with a wink.

He left the line and made for the door to the right that would take him down to the parking lot. But his phone rang, and rather than risk losing signal in the stairwell, he stopped to answer the call in the lobby.

When he checked the screen, there was no caller I.D.

His blood ran cold. He should go down to Levi and let the damn thing go to voicemail. But he wanted to talk to this asshole, no matter how stupid it was. He wanted to know why they were doing this to him.

"Hello," he said, keeping his voice as steady as he could.

"Raiden," said an unfamiliar voice. "My little cockroach. I've been waiting for some time for you to ditch that Marine of yours. I see my present did little to keep you two apart."

"You. Where are you?" Raiden demanded, looking around. Could this dickhead see him?

The voice, a man as far as he could tell, laughed. "Don't bother spinning around like that. I'm not there. But I can see you."

Raiden stopped, then looked up until he found a security camera on the ceiling.

"Clever boy," said the hacker. "Why don't you give me a nice little salute?"

"Fuck you," Raiden spat. "Who are you, and why are you doing this to me?"

The hacker laughed again, but this time it was more of a sneer, filled with loathing. "Are you fucking kidding me? You don't recognize me? Fine. You'll work it out soon enough. In the meantime, give me a goddamned salute, or you won't like what happens next."

"What the hell is that supposed to mean?" Raiden demanded, but he got no reply.

At least, not for a few seconds. Then he heard ragged breathing down the phone. "Say hello, sweetheart," the hacker's voice came faintly.

"Raiden?"

Icy cold fear flooded Raiden's body in a second. "Pearl?" he spluttered. She sounded hoarse, scared. "Pearl, is that you? What's happening?"

"Raiden, you *fuck this asshole!*" she screamed, even as the phone was obviously moved away from her mouth. "He's insane! Don't you-"

She cut off with a crack that sounded liked a hand slapping her face.

Raiden was trembling with fury and terror. "If you've hurt her, you sick *fuck,*" he began, but the hacker interrupted.

"I won't hurt her if you do as I say. Which means starting with that fucking *salute.*"

Raiden's heart was like a jackhammer in his chest. He wasn't sure if he wanted to throw up or scream. This couldn't be happening. Pearl had texted him only a few hours ago to say she and the rest of the band were on the road to NYC. But now he thought about it, they were all split between different cars. Pearl drove alone.

Slowly, Raiden turned back to the camera, then touched his fingers to his temple in a salute.

"Thank you," said the hacker. "Right, here's what's going to happen. You are going to go out the front of the building and walk to the blue Honda Fit parked on the curb. You will get inside and follow the GPS instructions. You're good at doing what you're told, if I remember correctly." Raiden glowered at the camera and the hacker chuckled. "Oh yes.

Did you know your phone can be turned quite easily into a microphone? I've heard the most *repulsive* things over the past few days. You really enjoy letting that soldier-boy degrade you, don't you?"

"Fuck you," Raiden snarled, feeling his face heat up.

"No thank you, knowing what you're into," the hacker shot back. "Speaking of which, under no circumstances are you to contact that beast or anybody else. If you use your phone, I will know. If you alert the authorities, *I will know*. And pretty little Pearl here won't be happy if you do."

"Fuck you!" Pearl screamed, making Raiden's heart break. He'd never felt so helpless.

"Okay, all right," he hissed before the hacker could hit her again. Blood was pumping so loudly in his ears he could barely hear himself. "I'm going, look?" he glanced towards the camera, then headed towards the hotel's front door.

"Good boy," the hacker said, clearly mocking Levi. Raiden burned with fury and humiliation that *anyone*, let alone this fucker, had heard what they had done together. "I'll be in touch when you reach your destination. Don't take long."

The line went dead. Raiden clutched his phone in his hand so hard he thought it might crack. But he did as he was told and didn't contact anyone else. He desperately wanted Levi, though, and willed him to come back up looking for Raiden. *Please,* he willed the universe.

But he was on his own.

The small Honda was there, just like the hacker has said. As Raiden approached, the doors unlocked, sending a chill all the way down Raiden's spine. He slipped into the driver's seat, feeling rusty from lack of practice as he turned the key waiting in the ignition. He couldn't freak out about driving now, though. Pearl was depending on him.

Numbly, he followed the directions the GPS gave him. Was he driving to his death?

He tried to stay positive. But he had no idea what this maniac wanted. Was he bringing Raiden to him, or somewhere else entirely? Would he let Pearl go, or was she in just as much trouble as Raiden?

Was she already dead, now she'd been used to lure him away from Levi?

Raiden took a deep breath and blinked back tears. He couldn't think like that. He had to keep his head screwed on. He didn't know anything yet, and it would make no sense to panic before then.

Traffic wasn't that bad for a weekday afternoon in a city. Raiden couldn't have gone any faster, so he just hoped the hacker knew that and didn't do anything rash.

"I'm coming, Pearl," Raiden whispered to himself. "Just hang on."

His cell rang, making him jump. When he glanced at the display, it was Levi's face and number flashing back at him.

Raiden bellowed in frustration. He wanted Levi so badly it made him sick. He was so out of his depth, but Levi was trained for this sort of thing. He would know what to do. Raiden just had to let the damn call go to voicemail, and he bashed the Honda's steering wheel in bitter defeat.

After around fifteen minutes, he found himself in a slightly rundown neighborhood with the GPS telling him that his destination was three hundred feet up on the right. Raiden parked the car in front of a boarded-up office block covered in signs proclaiming it was under renovation and not to be entered without a hard hat. As soon as Raiden unclipped his belt, his cell rang again. This time, the screen was blank.

"Well done," the hacker said. "Now get out and go through the front door. It's open."

Raiden stayed silently on the line as he trotted up the

stairs and carefully pulled the door open. Like the hacker had said, it wasn't locked.

Inside was gloomy in spite of the summer sunshine beaming down outside, as all the windows were boarded up. Raiden swallowed as the door swung shut behind him. "Now what?"

"Walk over to the elevator and head to the fifth floor."

Raiden frowned, confused as how it would have power when the rest of the building looked gutted. He glanced at the dusty sign in front of him that pointed towards the stairwell.

"The steps are partially collapsed," the hacker said. He obviously had cameras somewhere here too. "A whole floor of them are gone. But don't worry, the elevator works just fine."

Raiden really didn't like the idea of trusting this guy not to drop him several floors once he was inside. But the door to the stairs was gone, leaving a gaping hole covered in warning tape where he could see big chunks of debris from a collapsed wall on the floor.

It looked like the hacker was telling the truth. Besides, if he was watching, he'd know if Raiden deviated from his instructions and might hurt Pearl. With an increasing sense of dread, Raiden called the elevator down from the fifth floor.

Sure enough, the display panel lit up, showing its progress from the upper level. When the doors opened, there was a light on inside too, even though there was dust and little bits of crap all over the floor. It looked like work had been abandoned on this building for the time being. It didn't leave Raiden with much hope that anyone would be able to hear if he and Pearl screamed for help.

His hand shaking, he pressed the button labeled with a

number five. He still had his phone pressed to his ear, but the hacker wasn't talking.

It seemed like forever until the doors opened again into a similar-looking corridor to the lobby he'd just left. To his right, the hall led to an open plan office, or what was once an office. Now there were only a dozen or so desks left where there probably had been fifty, and several wheeled chairs loitering around, most of them covered with old sheets. Cardboard boxes and shredded paper were scattered around everywhere.

The windows not facing the main street had had the wooden boards that had been nailed over them ripped off, letting in some natural light. The wood had been thrown haphazardly to the stained carpet with all the rest of the trash.

One of the tables in the middle of the floor had been cleaned and was currently holding several laptops, computers and other bits of technology that Raiden couldn't identify by sight. Next to that was one of the office chairs, where Pearl was tied up, gagged and struggling. By her stood a man Raiden took a good ten seconds to place.

*"Glenn?"* he cried. He cut the phone call off and dropped his cell into his pocket, stepping forward with complete confusion. The two of them were about twenty feet away from him. What the hell was his dad's IT guy doing there?

Glenn Browne curled his lip and dropped his own phone on the desk with the rest of the computers.

Then he picked up a handgun and pointed it at Pearl's head.

"Hello, Raiden," he said with an ugly smile.

# Twenty~Eight

## LEVI

LEVI HAD BEEN LOOKING AT THE ROADMAP FOR TEN MINUTES before he realized how much time had passed. Raiden should have been down to the garage by now. Unless there had been a problem?

Maybe his card had failed again. Belatedly, Levi realized he shouldn't really have let Raiden out of his sight. If he was lucky, it would just be his credit card. Or, even better, a long line at the checkout desk.

It was probably nothing, but Levi jumped out of the Jeep in any case and jogged back up to the hotel lobby. Grinding his teeth, he wondered if he wasn't really cut out for this private security business. He was used to taking orders, not always being the one calling the shots.

By the time he reached the first floor he'd begun to really worry. But what could have happened to Raiden in such a short amount of time in front of so many people?

The lobby had perhaps two or three dozen people milling around or queuing at the front desk. There was no sign of Raiden though.

Levi approached reception with an increasing sense of

unease. He held up his hand to the person next in line as he cut in front. "I'm sorry, ma'am," he said, wishing he had a badge to flash. "But this is a matter of security." He turned to one of the people serving at the desk. "Excuse me, sir, I'm looking for my friend. Asian-American man, mid-twenties, my height, smaller build."

The redheaded clerk next to the guy Levi was addressing perked up. "Mr. Jones?" she asked. "You're his friend." It wasn't a question.

Levi nodded and moved over, apologizing to the man she had been serving. "Yes, ma'am," he said. "It's urgent, did you see him?"

"I checked him out," she said, eyes wide.

"Did you see where he went after that?"

She nodded. "He took a phone call over there," she said, pointing to the middle of the lobby floor. "He looked upset. I was going to see if he needed any assistance once I'd finished with my next guest, but then he walked out."

"Which direction?" Levi asked, fear mounting. The hacker. It had to be. He'd proven he had Raiden's number the night before with the text after the bomb scare.

She pointed again. "Front door. I don't know where he went after that."

Not down to the parking lot, that was for damn sure. Levi nodded tensely. "Thank you, ma'am. You've been incredibly helpful."

"Of course," she said. "Let us know if there's anything else the hotel can do?"

He nodded again and moved away, phone in his hand already dialing Raiden. "Come on, come on," he muttered. "Pick up, baby."

The call rang out, though, taking him to voicemail. Levi cursed and hit the end call button. Next, he brought up his GPS to show him where Raiden was. He had to zoom the map out a fair bit until the little dot showed up. From the looks of it, Raiden was in a moving vehicle, going away from the hotel.

*"Fuck,"* Levi said, breaking into a sprint back down to the garage. This was really, really bad.

He jumped into the Jeep and brought the engine to life with a roar, slamming the pedal down and zig-zagging his way out of the lot. He had to wait for the barrier to scan his ticket before it would rise, all the while Raiden's dot was still moving away.

"Hold on, Raiden," he growled, tearing out onto the street. "Hold on. I'm coming for you."

Traffic wasn't great and Levi pissed off several other drivers by cutting them off. He scared the hell out of some pedestrians when he mounted a curb to get around a line by some roadworks. But there was no way he was letting Raiden and whoever was driving him get too far away from him.

If anything happened to him, Levi would never forgive himself. He could just about convince himself that all those terrible mistakes in Iraq were out of his control, but there would be no one else to blame but Levi if any harm came to Raiden. That simply couldn't happen.

Mercifully, the dot came to a halt. Levi picked up his speed. He risked taking one hand off the wheel to zoom his phone's display in to see if Raiden moved again. Sure enough, after a few moments, his dot slowly shifted from the road to the sidewalk and into whatever building was there.

"Please," Levi growled to no one in particular. "Please, please, just hold on, a few more minutes."

It was more like ten minutes before he finally caught up to the dot. He found an unremarkable blue Honda parked on the curb in a slightly rundown neighborhood. There was no one inside. The building directly to the left of it was an old, small office block of eight stories. Judging by Raiden's now stationary dot, that was where he had walked into.

Levi quietly closed the door to the Jeep and un-holstered his gun, clicking the safety back. No one was around close enough to especially pay attention to him. After a quick look around, he dashed up the few steps and made his way through the unlocked front door.

He really should have backup, but who could he call? The cops? He didn't necessarily know if Raiden was in trouble or not, let alone what the circumstances were. He could be bringing men and women into an extremely volatile situation if he involved them without knowing all the facts. For now, he just had to handle this on his own.

The lobby of the office block was as derelict as the outside suggested. Levi moved into the gloom inside with his gun raised, sticking to the walls and shadows. There was no movement inside, though. A glance to his left showed him a stairwell blocked off with warning tape. As Raiden wasn't in the lobby, he slipped under the tape and took a look beyond.

He barely made it to the second floor before the steps crumbled away and became extremely creaky and unsafe. Peering around the corner, Levi could see that between the first and third floor there were hardly any steps at all.

Raiden hadn't gone this way.

Levi quickly made his way back down and realized that if Raiden had indeed come inside here, his only option was the elevator. Surprisingly, the display was lit up, and when Levi pressed the call button, a car began to descend from the fifth floor.

What the hell was going on? Was the hacker here, or had they coerced Raiden here for some other reason? Who had picked Raiden up? How had they been able to convince Raiden to get into the car? Surely Raiden knew better than that after everything the hacker had already pulled.

When the doors opened, Levi saw no choice but to ride the elevator up. As the car had come from the fifth floor, that was the button Levi now pressed to take himself. He had no idea what would be waiting for him when the doors opened once again.

As the display telling him the floor number slowly crept upwards, Levi thought of all the elevator rides he and Raiden had taken together in the past few days. They had all been in silence. Some filled with anger, others filled with deep sexual longing. With love.

If anything happened to Raiden when Levi had only just worked up the courage to tell him how he truly felt, he was going to burn the world down.

He couldn't focus on that, not until he knew the facts. Instead, as the elevator pinged to announce as it passed the fourth floor, Levi inhaled slowly.

Calm filled his veins as he channeled his adrenaline like he had been trained to do. Perhaps he wasn't a natural body-guard. He'd made too many mistakes now for him to believe anything else. But combat was in his blood. This was his home. Whoever thought they could take him on in his own backyard was sorely fucking mistaken.

And when Levi got his hands on them, he wasn't going to show a shred of mercy.

Pearl cried out in fear as the gun barrel touched her temple. Tears ran down her face, tracing black mascara into the cloth gag in her mouth. For an awful second, Raiden thought Glenn had taken her pants off. But then he realized she was wearing short shorts with a hoodie and combat boots. Even though she was clearly terrified, she struggled her wrists and ankles against the cords securing her to the chair.

"You fucking bastard," Raiden whispered, holding his hands up in an effort to stop Glenn from hurting Pearl any further. Through her smeared makeup Raiden could see a black eye forming. "Let her go."

Glenn swallowed and shook his head. "You've been so spectacularly uncooperative so far. I think I'll keep her as a little insurance."

Raiden almost lost his temper, but he saw the fire in his friend's eyes and kept himself calm. He was going to get her out of this if it was the last thing he did.

"What do you want, Glenn?" he asked. He risked stepping closer so they didn't have to shout. Glenn watched him until he was only about ten feet away, then twitched the gun.

"That's close enough."

Raiden stopped and held his hands up higher. "I assume you're the one behind all these attacks." Raiden shook his head, trying to wrap his thoughts around it all. "Even the first doxing of all those celebrities?"

Glenn's breathing was shallow and rapid, but a look of pride flashed across his shiny face. The gun shook ever so slightly in his hand. "Of course. I had to give you a pool of literally thousands of suspects. You never once looked my way when I was supposedly fixing it all for you." He barked out a laugh. "All you were doing was giving me better access!"

"But *why?*" Raiden cried. "What have I ever done to you? You've worked for Eric for years, you know my family!"

Glenn laughed again, but it was more like a demented shriek. He pressed the gun closer to Pearl's skull, making her snarl and squirm. Her bloodshot eyes were wet but murderous.

"You don't even fucking remember, do you? That – *that's* why I'm doing this, you spoiled, privileged, selfish *brat!*"

He licked his lips and let go of the gun with one hand. Carefully, he fished out a packet of cigarettes, making Raiden remember that was what he always stank of, and removed one from the packet with his teeth. He put the rest away, then retrieved a lighter. It took him several clicks to get a flame as his hand was quivering so much, but eventually he managed it and took a long drag, visibly relaxing.

"I never wanted to do this," he said. He dropped the lighter into his breast pocket and took another deep pull from the cigarette. His lips were thin, framed by his scraggly goatee. "I'm not the kind of person to terrorize little girls. That would be your *boyfriend.*"

He spat the word out, but Raiden didn't flinch. If Glenn thought attacking his sexuality was going to insult him, rile him up, he was mistaken.

Raiden also knew the truth behind those sealed files from Iraq. He wasn't going to let Glenn unnerve him.

"You still have a gun to my friend's head," he said.

"Because you made me!" Glenn shrieked. As he jerked, so did the gun and the cigarette. "Because you left me no choice! I don't want to be here any more than she does, but someone needed to teach you a lesson!"

"For what?" Raiden said, trying not to shout, lest he spooked Glenn and his trigger finger. From this distance, Raiden couldn't tell if the safety was on or off. "What did I ever do to you that was so bad?"

Glenn glared, hatred clear in his eyes.

"Apple Blossom Farm."

Raiden blinked. "What?" What did his home, his dad's business, have to do with anything?

Glenn shook his head, taking another drag from his cigarette, the smoke escaping from his mouth and nose. "I can't believe you don't remember stealing my family's legacy from me. I should have worked harder to destroy yours."

Slowly, realization came over Raiden. He *did* remember that when his dad had taken over the ranch and all its horses, it was because the previous owner had gone bankrupt.

"Wait, that was you?" he said. "But, we didn't steal anything. Your dad had run the business into the ground. We bought him out in cash."

"It's not about the money!" Glenn yelled, knocking Pearl with the gun, making her flinch and whimper. Her hands were in fists, though, showing she still had fight in her. "That ranch was my home. Those horses meant everything to me! You don't even *ride*, you little prick. You just use them like a business, paying other people who don't care about them to muck out the stalls and feed them and-"

He broke off with a sob, and, despite everything, Raiden felt a pang of sympathy for him. "Glenn," he said as evenly as he could manage. "The ranch is my dad's pride and joy. But it's nothing to do with me."

"You'll inherit it!" Glenn cried. "It's in your family name now, but it should be mine!"

Raiden couldn't believe he was hearing this right. "So, buy it back from him? Or ask to work there? Jesus, there's no need for all this!"

Glenn shook his head, flicking the ash from his cigarette haphazardly. "No, no, I tried to talk to your dad, but he laughed at me. *Laughed!* Said I'd never be able to buy him out, and he didn't want to sell anyway. Told me my dad should have been more careful than to gamble our fortunes away."

Raiden did remember that now. His mom had once mentioned that Mr. Browne had made some seriously bad investments in the housing market. Right before it had all come tumbling down around everyone.

"He took my legacy away, so I took his away right back." He sneered, crushing out the cigarette with his boot and lighting another one, faster this time. "Unfortunately, his record was squeaky clean. But you." He shook his head and laughed without mirth. "G.I. Joe was right. You are filthy."

Raiden clenched his jaw but said nothing. He wasn't going to give Glenn the satisfaction.

"Not as bad as that homo you let fuck you, though," he said. "What a dream it was when I pulled up his service records. But of course, I heard him spin you that sob-story about his lieutenant. Which you swallowed, hook, line and sinker."

Raiden ignored the flicker of doubt that crept into his heart. He was not going to believe this asshole over Levi.

But Glenn scoffed, taking a long puff on the cigarette. "Meyrick doesn't have anything like that in his file. All his targets were approved for engagement. And yet you let that 'Viking' mount you like a dog. Fuck you like the little whore you are."

Raiden was shaking with anger, but he focused on Pearl instead. "It's okay," he said to her. "He doesn't know what he's talking about. Levi's a good man."

"He's not here now, though, is he?" Glenn snapped. He purposefully shoved the gun barrel roughly against Pearl's head. "So, you're going to do exactly what I say."

Raiden shook his hands, the palms still facing Glenn. "Okay, okay," he said.

He wasn't sure what scenario Glenn imagined would end this. But he was looking at charges of kidnapping and assault at the very least. That, combined with all the cyber attacks, meant he surely knew he would go to jail for a damned long time.

Raiden had also watched enough crime thrillers to know that if Glenn were sensible, he wouldn't want to let him and Pearl live as witnesses.

He was so scared he wasn't sure how he was still standing. But Pearl was depending on him, so he had to stay strong.

"What do you want?" he asked.

Glenn used his cigarette to point at Raiden's pocket. "Get your phone out. Call your dad. Call Eric – you're going to need a lawyer. You're going to get the ranch signed over to me by the end of the day, or they'll never find your body."

Pearl gnashed her teeth and screamed something from behind the gag. Raiden would bet any money it was an insult to Glenn's moral character to the highest degree. Glenn grabbed her lilac hair and pulled her head back.

"I don't want to hurt you," he hissed into her ear. "So don't give me a reason to." He looked back at Raiden. "Same goes to you. Behave, and I promise she'll walk away from this."

He wasn't offering the same promise to Raiden, but Pearl was the immediate priority. She was completely innocent in all this. Glenn was only using her purely to manipulate him. Raiden wanted to call him the worst kind of coward, but he couldn't risk any more harm coming to Pearl.

"Fine," he said. "I'm going to reach for my phone and make the calls. Okay?"

Glenn nodded, then pointed the gun towards Raiden.

A shot rang out, so loud Raiden dropped to his knees and covered his head. Pearl screamed. Glenn staggered back, blood spurting from his arm as he dropped his cigarette. But the hand with his gun was still vaguely pointed at Raiden.

"Don't. Move," Levi's voice growled from somewhere behind Raiden.

THE ELEVATOR DOOR OPENED AND THANKFULLY ONLY GAVE A quiet ping. Levi slipped into the empty corridor and immediately moved to the small amount of cover to his right. There was a short portion of wall jutting out next to the elevator before the hall opened out into the abandoned office space. It didn't give him much, but it was better than nothing.

A voice traveled through the air. Levi immediately recognized it as Raiden, and that he was about ten feet away.

"What do you want?"

The next voice was familiar to Levi, but he couldn't quite place it. "Get your phone out. Call your dad. Call Eric – you're going to need a lawyer."

*That* was it. The link to Eric Solomon and Sam Jones sparked his memory. That voice belonged to Glenn Browne, the IT expert. What the hell was he doing here? Levi risked glimpsing around the corner into the office. A split second was enough to show him the horror scene he was facing.

Raiden was standing with his hands up, his back to Levi. Then about twenty feet away stood Glenn. He had Pearl tied to a chair, a gun pointed to her head.

Very quickly, Levi pieced together that however he'd done it, Glenn must have lured Raiden to him by using Pearl as a hostage. Rage made Levi's focus laser sharp. But he still didn't understand why.

He got part of an answer as Glenn continued talking.

"You're going to get the ranch signed over to me by the end of the day," he told Raiden, "or they'll never find your body."

Levi almost lost control. No one was going to hurt Raiden. *No one.*

Pearl screamed and struggled in her chair. Levi wished he could look more than a fraction of a second each time. But he couldn't take the chance that Glenn would see him.

"I don't want to hurt you," he heard Glenn say, presumably to Pearl. "So don't give me a reason to. Same goes to you. Behave, and I promise she'll walk away from this."

"Fine," Raiden replied. "I'm going to reach for my phone and make the calls. Okay?"

Levi looked out just in time to see Glenn switch the target of his gun from Pearl to Raiden.

Levi didn't hesitate. His training told him that Glenn was far less likely to hit a target ten feet away than when he had his gun pressed to someone's head. So Levi fired as he stepped out, clipping Glenn on the arm not holding the weapon. Levi would have preferred a chest shot, but Raiden was slightly too close to his line of fire to risk that.

Raiden, god bless him, dropped to his knees. Glenn raised his gun again, but Levi had his own weapon trained on him now. "Don't. Move," he snarled.

"Levi?" Raiden cried.

"I'm here, baby," Levi said calmly, advancing into the room. "I've got you."

"You fucking *shot* me!" Glenn screeched, like he couldn't believe Levi's audacity.

"You pointed a gun at my partner's head and kidnapped my friend," Levi said. He reached Raiden and placed a reassuring hand on his shoulder. Raiden leaned into him. "You're very lucky I didn't blow your brains out."

Glenn gave an hysterical laugh. "Oh, because that's what you do, isn't it? You barbarian. You shoot innocent people and call it heroism."

"You're confusing me with someone else," Levi said. He was stalling for time. His concentration was entirely on Glenn, but he could have sworn he smelled smoke. "But how about you put that gun down and we can talk about it?"

Glenn was trembling quite badly. Blood was dripping down his arm from the flesh wound Levi had given him, and his forehead was beaded with sweat. He shuddered and scowled. "So you can shoot me in the head like you just promised? I don't think so."

Several things happened at once. The first of which being that one of the piles of shredded paper by Glenn inexplicably burst into flames. Pearl screamed, Raiden bucked backwards and Levi, stupidly, glanced to see the source of the fire.

So did Glenn, but he recovered quick enough to fire a shot.

Hitting Raiden in the leg.

Levi roared, grabbing Raiden and pulling him behind a desk. Glenn also threw himself down behind another table, leaving Pearl exposed in the open office. Raiden screamed in pain, then called her name.

"Pearl," he shouted, clutching his leg as tears streamed down his face. "Get Pearl!"

He'd been caught in the thigh, though. Levi had to prioritize him, already pulling his belt off to make a tourniquet. In seconds, he had it buckled as tightly as he could at the top of Raiden's thigh. Then he peeked back around the desk.

Pearl was shouting and thrashing her body around. The

flames had already moved at an alarming rate, catching not only the cardboard boxes littered near the shredded paper, but also one of the cloths thrown over a nearby desk. There was no sign of Glenn.

Gun raised, Levi sprinted the few feet over to Pearl, seized the back of her chair, and wheeled her to safety with Raiden. Glenn didn't show himself. He could have crawled anywhere in this small maze of office furniture by now.

To give her cover, Levi tipped Pearl and the chair backwards so they were all protected by the desk. Luckily, it was one of those ones with a panel at the front. It likely wouldn't stop a bullet, but it meant Glenn at least couldn't see them.

Raiden reached out and grabbed Pearl's still-bound hand with his own bloody one. "Shh, shh," he said, trying to smile. "We've got you now."

Levi undid her gag first and she gasped in several panicked breaths. "Sh-shoot that fucker," she stammered at Levi.

He smiled as he sliced the rope around her left wrist with the Ka-Bar knife he always carried with him. "Good girl," he said, freeing one hand, then the other. "Let's get out of here first, huh?"

His heart rate was too high, so Levi focused on calming himself as he released her feet and she crawled out of the chair to Raiden's side. But Raiden was still losing a fair amount of blood despite the tourniquet, and when Levi glanced around the desk again, he was dismayed to find the fire had already spread twice as far. Smoke was filling the room and there was obviously no working sprinkler system in place.

"Levi?" Raiden said. His voice sounded horribly weak.

Levi turned and grasped his hand, kissing his lips once. He knew Pearl wouldn't judge. "I'm here, baby. You're doing so well. But you're going to stay awake for me, aren't you? I know you can do it."

His heart swelled as Raiden nodded, his eyelids drooping. He reached up with crimson fingers and touched Levi's cheek.

"I promise."

Levi looked at Pearl. She was shaking and disheveled and rubbed raw from the rope that had been tied around her. But she looked mad as all hell and ready to fight.

"There are no stairs," Levi told her, not dancing around the problem. "We need to get to the elevator before the fire does."

To prove his point, she coughed from the smoke as she nodded. The heat in the room must have risen ten degrees already.

"Raiden, sweetheart," Levi said. He slipped his arm around Raiden's back. He was sluggish and shaking from the pain. "I'm going to help you get back to the elevator. Okay?"

Raiden nodded.

"Me too," said Pearl. She scooted around to his other side, this ninety-pound girl, and grabbed Raiden's other arm.

Before they stood, Levi took a good hard look for Glenn. But amid the billowing smoke and flames, he couldn't see him anywhere. The trash on the ground and cloth covers were being devoured by the flames. Levi was deeply concerned about using the elevator, but it was either that or jump from the fifth floor.

"Let's go," he said.

The three of them rose and moved as fast as possible towards the corridor. Raiden could hardly walk at all, and even though Levi was much bigger than him, he was still a fully-grown man made into a dead weight as his conscious-ness slipped away. "Raiden," Levi barked as Pearl struggled underneath his arm. "You stay with me, you promised. I-"

The gunshot missed them by inches. Levi pushed them all to the ground, his heart aching as Raiden screamed in agony. But Levi dragged him back behind a toppled bookcase despite his poor lover's protests. They were so close to the damn elevator. But so was the fire.

"He's not going anywhere!" Glenn screamed. Levi's heart sank. Even over the roaring flames, he could tell he wasn't that far away from them. "He's not leaving until he gives back my legacy!"

"He's insane," said Pearl as she applied pressure to Raiden's gun wound with both her hands.

"Glenn," Levi bellowed. "We're all going to die here unless we leave now."

Glenn spluttered, the smoke reaching his lungs. Levi's clothes were drenched with sweat and the flames danced around the edge of the room. Something groaned and crashed to the floor as the fire consumed it.

"No!" Glenn howled. "I was so close! *He owes me!*"

He fired off a volley of shots. Levi counted, waiting for the barrel to empty.

Then he stood and fired a single shot.

It clipped Glenn on the opposite shoulder to his first injury, forcing him to drop the empty gun as he jerked and slammed to the floor, catching his head on one of the desk corners. Levi only watched long enough to make sure he wasn't going to get back up, then turned back to pick up Raiden.

He'd lost consciousness and Levi clenched his jaw, not allowing his emotions to get the better of him. Instead, he scooped his arms under his back and knees, hugging Raiden to his chest and carrying him like a groom would his bride over the threshold.

To his horror, Pearl ran back into the room.

"We need to go!" Levi yelled. *"Now!"*

Pearl grabbed Glenn's shirt by his shoulders and began dragging him, unconscious, towards the elevator. "He is *not* getting out of jail time," she said, coughing.

Levi didn't have time to argue. He marched out into the hall, just managing to keep hold of Raiden's limp body, and pressed the call button with his knee. Relief flooded him as the doors opened immediately. The car must not have gone back down after he'd used it.

Carefully, he sat Raiden down in the corner of the car. A quick check of his pulse told Levi it was thready, but definitely still there. Satisfied, he jabbed the hold button, then ran back out into the hall to help Pearl drag Glenn's worthless ass inside the elevator as well. He was still breathing, so Levi had to admit she had done the right thing.

Once the four of them were inside, Levi pressed the button to close the doors and jabbed several times at the first-floor button. There was already too much smoke filling up the car and the flames were reaching out into the corridor. Most of the office was now a roaring inferno.

The fire had to have spread to other floors by now and it was absolutely not safe to use the elevator. But Levi knew they had no choice. As the doors finally closed, he crouched down to hug Raiden to him. "Hold on," he told Pearl.

He expected her to grab the railing. Instead, she latched on to his arm.

He held his breath, watching the numbers that glowed through the smoke as they ticked down too slowly. "Come on, come on."

The elevator lurched and he and Pearl both cried out. Levi hugged her and Raiden closer to him. He'd get them out, he would, they were so close…

The three turned into a two. Levi didn't dare blink. Surely, even if the car fell from this height, they'd still be okay?

He'd never know. Two flicked to one, and the doors opened.

"*Go!*" he roared at Pearl. He wouldn't let her stick around for Glenn this time.

She did as she was told and bolted out of the elevator, sprinting for the front door. Levi did Glenn the courtesy of pressing the hold door button again, but after that, he only cared about Raiden.

He cradled him to his chest, grateful for every puff of breath that touched his damp neck. "Nearly there, baby," he whispered. He managed to get to his feet and stumble into the lobby.

The whole building creaked and felt like it was swaying. Levi staggered towards the door, daylight streaming through the cracks between the boards on the walls, beckoning him forward.

Part of the ceiling gave way to his left and he almost tripped to steer clear of it. He could hear sirens wailing outside. Using his shoulder, he slammed into the door and broke into the fresh air.

Pearl was waiting at the bottom of the steps on the side-walk, her hands in her purple hair as she hopped anxiously from foot to foot. As soon as she saw them she cried out and ran forward, but Levi was already down the steps, laying Raiden on the ground.

The sirens were almost as deafening now as the blaze raging above.

The firefighters were the first to disembark at the scene, running to the three of them almost as soon as Levi placed Raiden on the ground. "Is there anyone else inside?" the first guy to them asked.

"One male adult, in the elevator," Levi said through his coughs. "He's injured but alive. He started the fire and shot my partner, so be careful. And the staircase is out."

The firefighter nodded and he and his colleagues disappeared into the building. Others were already aiming the hose from the truck at the flames, dousing them with a powerful blast of water.

Pearl sagged and wiped her face, smearing her makeup around further. Levi grabbed her hand.

"Will he be okay?" she asked with a sob.

Levi looked up towards the EMTs tearing towards them through the smoke. "Yes," he said simply.

Because it had to be true.

# CHAPTER
## *Thirty~One*
### RAIDEN

THE ROOM WAS MADE OF BEAUTIFUL COLORS.

Raiden hummed and swam in his contentment. Had he ever felt so wonderful?

"Baby?"

He knew that voice. He loved that voice. Even when he was being a Grumpy McGrumpypants. "Hmm, baby," he purred, wriggling in the crisp bedsheets.

Someone touched his face, stroking it. Raiden liked that. He leaned into the hand, feeling the coarse fingers and large palm. He loved that too. He was filled with so much love, he was so lucky.

"Raiden? Can you hear me?"

"Levi," Raiden mumbled. He smiled, then felt his lips crack. They must be dry. Did they hurt?

"Raiden, take a drink for me now, please." The voice was firm. Raiden liked doing what the voice said. It made him feel whole. He trusted that voice so much.

A plastic cup met his lips and he obediently swallowed as water trickled into his mouth. It tasted amazing.

"Raiden, I'm going to go get a nurse. You're in the hospital and had surgery on your leg. Do you remember getting shot?"

Raiden giggled and managed to blink his eyes open fully. The gorgeous, slightly scary face swam into view. He reached up, batting at the mouth on the face. "Love you," he said, knowing it to be true. "All mine. All yours. Promise…promise…"

The face laughed and rolled its eyes. "Do you remember all the drugs the nurses gave you?"

"Hmm, yummy," said Raiden, snuggling down under his comforter. "Grumpy baby. Love you, baby."

The face – Levi. Levi was the face. Levi leaned forward and kissed his forehead. "You're safe, Raiden. You're on the mend and everything's okay. Just sleep now."

"Yes," said Raiden very seriously. He liked doing what Levi told him. "Promise. Sleep."

"See you soon," Levi said as Raiden floated back into the lovely blackness.

"Soon," he said. And he meant it.

———

Raiden shifted in his wheelchair. "Oh, Levi," he moaned. "Can't I use the crutches, just for a bit?"

Levi ran his hand through Raiden's hair, then tugged just a bit too hard as he reached the crown. Raiden looked up and they shared a grin together.

"Doctor's orders were to stay in bed," Levi said with a raised eyebrow. "I let you come to Madison Square Garden. You'll sit in the damn chair."

Raiden wanted to kiss him so badly. But the backstage area was frantic and Raiden hated being confined to the chair. It was only the second time he'd tried to use it, to be fair. He'd probably get used to it if he had to. People did it every day, after all. But he didn't feel as confident as he usually did.

Levi stroked his neck instead, then let him go. Glittergasm were going to play their next song, and he probably knew that Raiden wanted to pay attention. This was the one he and Pearl had been slaving over for weeks.

The wings were a hub of activity. Dyrnoir's people were scrambling around trying to get everything ready for their big performance. But even if the seats were only half full, this was by far Glittergasm's largest show ever.

Pearl was strutting around on stage on platform boots with skin-tight jeans, a big, furry cape and glitter on everything as usual. "So," she drawled, filling the break while the guitarist changed his instrument over. "Last week I had a bit of a thing. It sucked."

She glanced over towards Raiden and Levi. They hadn't gone public with anything that had happened in Philadelphia, but Raiden had sworn to pay for any therapy she needed and help in any way possible after that fucked-up shit. She was doing okay for now, but he suspected after the tour, it would hit her like a steam train.

The bassist came over and the two girls held hands. Pearl smiled, but Raiden could see she was fighting back tears. "Do you guys have heroes?" she asked the crowd. They were the act on directly before Dyrnoir, so actually, the place was way more than half full. She laughed into the microphone. The bassist kissed her cheek, and Raiden wondered if he'd missed something there.

The crowd was screaming. It was deafening. As usual, Pearl had them eating out of her palm, and Raiden felt a surge of pride.

"Yeah," said Pearl, rubbing her nose and swinging her foot. "Heroes are pretty damned important, aren't they? I...I have a couple of my heroes here tonight. It doesn't matter what they did exactly. But how about we just scream our fucking lungs out for a couple of seconds for the heroes in our lives, huh? Wanna do that?"

She pointed the microphone out into the stadium, letting thousands of people just roar themselves hoarse. From the wings, Raiden watched as she inhaled deeply, then let out a battle cry that made his skin tingle.

She wiped her eyes then laughed into the mic. "See, isn't that awesome? Feelings are great, dudes. Don't bottle them up. Okay. This is our new single, Shadow. Go fucking nuts."

The drummer attacked her kit and the guitarist wailed as hard as his strings would let him. Raiden felt that unique, sick excitement that only came from hearing one of your compositions come to life. Man, he loved this song.

Amid the din, he realized he wasn't the only one singing along. Raiden stopped and looked incredulously up as Levi joined in with Pearl on the chorus.

"You're singing," Raiden said, utterly delighted.

Levi blinked, like he hadn't been aware of himself. "It's a good song," he said bashfully.

Warmth filled Raiden's heart. After all the time they had spent listening to the radio, the song that finally got Levi Patterson to sing for him was Raiden's own.

"Damn right it's a good song," he said. He looked back at the stage so Levi wouldn't see his eyes get glassy. But he might have spotted something anyway, as he reached down and took Raiden's hand, rubbing his fingers with his thumb.

A commotion to their right caught both their attention. They naturally let go of each other as they waited to see who was coming through.

"Hi! Yes, sorry, excuse me, yes, I'm looking for – RAIDEN!"

Joey pushed his way between a throng of people, still in his makeup from a day's filming. He spotted Raiden and his face crumbled at the sight of his bandaged leg.

"I'm fine," Raiden cried quickly, but Joey was already throwing himself at him for a hug. "Oh, careful," Raiden said with a laugh.

"Sorry, sorry," said Joey over the music. He pulled away and wiped his eyes, flapping his hands over the wheelchair. "Fuck, dude, I heard you were here and I came straight from the set." He turned to Levi and his lower lip wobbled again. *Bless beautiful Joey*, Raiden thought with a smile. His heart was permanently on his sleeve. "Oh my god, you saved him, didn't you?"

Levi looked bashful. "No," he mumbled, rubbing the back of his neck. "I was just doing my-"

Joey flung his arms around Levi's neck, tugging him down for a proper hug. "Thank you, thank you so much. He's so important. He means so much to us."

"I know," said Levi as they pulled apart. He looked at Raiden, who felt his love very keenly.

"Oh my god," said Joey. He stepped back and looked between the two of them. "Are you...is this...?"

Raiden bristled. "Don't make a big deal, okay? Blake isn't the only one who gets to be queer."

Joey broke into the biggest, happiest smile. "You are, aren't you? Well...fuck." He laughed again and covered his mouth.

Raiden glanced at Levi and arched an eyebrow. "Dude," he said as evenly as he could. "I thought you'd be cool about this."

Joey cackled behind his hand. "Oh, I'm ecstatic. I just owe TJ twenty bucks now," he added with an eye roll.

"TJ?" Raiden spluttered.

"Y'all bet on us?" Levi asked, incredulously.

"Hell yeah," Joey said. He grinned and slapped Levi on the shoulder. "So you're coming to the wedding, yeah? It's no problem at all. I'll just need to fudge the seating plan sooner rather than later."

Levi's mouth dropped open. "I…uh…"

"Yes," said Raiden, laughing. "Yes, he's coming." He took Levi's hand and kissed his knuckles. "Because I told him so."

Levi's expression softened. "In that case, I have no choice."

Joey made a gagging noise. "Okay, all right, knock it off."

Raiden laughed wholeheartedly. "See, it's not so fun when it's someone else being a bucket full of mush, is it?"

"Shut up," said Joey. But he swept down to kiss Raiden's cheek and squeeze his shoulder. "I'm so unbelievably happy for you, buddy."

Raiden squeezed his hand back. "Me too," he said honestly.

For a while, the three of them watched Glittergasm tear it up from the wings. Then Raiden tugged on Levi's hand to make him lean down so they could talk. "When will you know your next assignment?" he asked. He'd been dreading asking since Glenn had been caught and Raiden had been discharged from hospital. But he'd need to know if they were going to make the wedding together.

To his surprise, Levi beamed down at him like Christmas had come early. "Actually, I got a new job offer this morning. I wanted to talk to you about it."

"Oh?"

Levi played with a lock of Raiden's hair. "It's a training facility just outside of Lexington. About half an hour's drive from the ranch. They have day events where they train government agents or just do bonding exercises for corporate teams. You get paint guns and have to storm buildings, that sort of thing. They need someone to coordinate the events as well as work with the more serious clients, like the FBI and Homeland Security."

Raiden couldn't find the words. The band was so loud it was difficult to talk anyway, but right then, he had to swallow a couple of times. "A day job?" he clarified. Levi nodded. "No traveling?" Levi shook his head. "No one actually firing bullets at you?" Levi shook his head again.

Raiden pulled him down quite violently for a hug. "If it works out," Levi said into his shoulder, "I thought, maybe, we could think about getting our own place. Not that your folks don't have a lovely home-"

Raiden yanked Levi's ear to his mouth. "I want you to fuck me in every single room of our own home. Any time you feel like it."

Naturally, that was the moment Glittergasm finished their song. In the second of silence before the crown erupted into applause, Joey looked over at them in horror. "I do *not* need to hear that, buddy!"

Levi looked somewhat abashed, but Raiden cackled. He was still mildly loopy on painkillers, but he knew really it was the thrill of Levi's news that was making him high. It was as if the clouds had parted and the future seemed so much more certain all of a sudden. He and Levi were a real couple. They could get a place together, build a routine, a home.

A life.

They managed to keep their hands off each other for the rest of Glittergasm's set. Mostly. But finally, the band was done with their last gig of the tour, and Pearl walked off stage to immediately hug Raiden and Levi.

She picked up a bottle of water and downed half of it, not taking her eyes off of them both. When she finished, she wiped her mouth, careful of her lipstick, and smirked. "You sorted it out, didn't you?"

Raiden laughed and took Levi's hand. "Yes. Very much so."

She turned to Joey, her eyes narrowing. "You used to be in the band too. And you're gay."

Joey laughed. "Um, yes, that's correct."

Pearl looked back at Raiden. "So, you're all queer now?"

"Not TJ," Raiden said with a laugh.

"Or Reyse," said Joey a little too loudly.

Pearl met her gaze with Levi's, then laughed, sipping from her water bottle again. "Sure," she said. "Love you guys. See you later."

They watched her walk backstage with her band. "She's a funny one," said Raiden.

"Pretty much," said Joey.

"Hmm," said Levi skeptically, then refused to elaborate.

Before too long, Dyrnoir were taking the stage, and Levi moved Raiden back out of the way with Joey. "You want to see the show?" Levi asked.

But Joey was already making noises about getting back home to Connecticut and his family. As much as it would be cool to stay, Raiden was totally shattered.

"Take me home?" he asked, then realized what he'd said. "The hotel, I mean…"

Levi smiled and kissed him slowly. "Home soon. Hotel for now. I've been thinking about all the things I could have been doing to you the past week. I think we need to catch up."

"Yeah?" said Raiden.

Levi nodded but looked at his bandaged leg. "Of course, we'll start slow, but-"

Raiden rolled his eyes. "When have I ever liked slow?"

Levi licked his lips. "Okay, then. Whatever you want."

"I want you." Raiden didn't care how cheesy it sounded.

"You can have me," Levi replied.

Raiden entwined their fingers, staring into his icy blue eyes. "Promise?"

Levi kissed him once more. "Promise."

# Epilogue

## LEVI

"Keep still," Levi growled, pulling Raiden closer.

Raiden just grinned impishly over his shoulder at him. "I would, but it's a little difficult with that enormous cock in my ass."

Levi swatted his cheek and gave a particularly hard thrust. "Someone's being a bad boy today. In the mood for some punishment, are we?"

Raiden snorted and tried to dig his fingers into the cloakroom wall. "Dear lord, yes," he said, squirming back against Levi.

They didn't have long. Levi had locked the door, but he still didn't want to risk anyone walking in on them. Part of the thrill, though, was that they could be discovered at any second with their pants around their ankles.

"I'll forgive you," Levi said, nipping and sucking at Raiden's earlobe. "But only because you thought to put lube in your pocket."

Raiden pouted and gave Levi his puppy dog eyes. "But I want to be punished," he said, then grinned.

Levi was happy to oblige.

He bent him over and grabbed his hips, pounding his tight, perfect hole. After returning from the tour a couple of months ago, one of the first things they had done was to visit the clinic and get the all clear. Levi never wanted to have anything between him and his lover again, especially when Raiden was an utter minx for public sex.

Levi was still worried about Raiden's injured leg. But he'd made the mistake to fuss about it during sex only once, and Raiden had got so mad he never dared do it again. So instead, he did his best to hold Raiden up and take his weight as their orgasms crept closer.

Levi's other concern was keeping their clothes tidy. This was not the sort of event you could just nip away and switch outfits. Raiden's tux was rented, and it matched the other groomsmen.

But lucky for Levi, his partner was always prepared to get his brains fucked out. He'd have tissues and hand sanitizer stashed away somewhere on his person, Levi had no doubt.

"Are you going to make me come?" Raiden asked breathlessly. "Or am I going to have to do all the work myself?"

He winked over his shoulder, but Levi gave him a dark look. "I shouldn't let you come at all," he said, reaching forward to jerk Raiden's cock mercilessly. Raiden cried out, and Levi hoped no one was walking past their closet. "You're utterly spoiled." Any retort Raiden had was choked down as he dropped his head and moaned, coming all over Levi's hand. "Yes," Levi hissed, hammering faster inside him, coming deep within him with a satisfied gasp.

For a few moments, there was only their panting. But eventually, Levi pulled his softening cock free and they did their best to clean up. There had been a couple of times now where Levi had made Raiden wear a butt plug for the rest of their evening after a tryst. The idea that Raiden would have to walk around with his seed inside him, the plug reminding him of Levi every second, was extremely erotic.

But today wasn't about them, so he cut Raiden some slack. Within five minutes, they were all neat and tidy again, and hopefully no one that looked at them would be any the wiser. Levi captured Raiden's face for a slow, sweet kiss. "Ready, sweetheart?"

Raiden smiled back at him. "Absolutely, gorgeous."

Levi held his arm out for Raiden to take. He had refused to bring his crutches today, despite still really needing them. So Levi had to do the best he could without directly drawing attention to the injury.

He understood that Raiden had some way to go in his recovery, not just with his leg. He talked a lot about Pearl's therapy and how she was doing after the kidnapping, but he seemed to be struggling to acknowledge his own troubles.

It had helped somewhat that Glenn Browne had been charged immediately for his various crimes. Levi hoped once he was tried and convicted, Raiden would be able to forget all about him. But in the meantime, he had made up his mind to suggest that they go for counseling together.

While their relationship was flourishing right now, Levi knew what horrors PTSD could do to poison people if left unchecked. He might as well deal with some of his own issues from his time in combat, especially if it would help Raiden to cope with what had happened to him.

"What?" Raiden said as they walked slowly back to the wedding reception. Levi realized he had been staring.

"Nothing," he said, before leaning over for a quick kiss. "I love you."

"I love you too," said Raiden.

Joey and Gabe had tied the knot in a beautiful fall ceremony near their home in Connecticut. The barn was lavished with roses and fairy lights, and they'd even brought their damn dog Max to the evening party. He was currently being chased by the flower girls and having a ball of a time.

It had been a day brimming with joy. He and Raiden walked back into the main room to find the happy couple surrounded on the dance floor as everyone drank and made merry.

"Thanks to you I think I'm going to have to stay clear of the dance floor," Raiden groused, pulling Levi towards one of the tables. If he wanted to pretend he couldn't dance because of his sore ass, rather than his aching leg, Levi wouldn't say a word. Instead, he seated Raiden with a kiss on his cheek, then went to get them some Champagne from the bar.

"Cheers," he murmured, lightly tapping their glasses together.

They watched the frivolities for a while, sipping their drinks and making silly chit-chat. Raiden was always so easy to talk to. Levi found they never ran out of things to say thanks to him.

Blake owned the dance floor, naturally. Elion was generous, not minding at all that everyone in the party wanted to have their chance with the legendary Feet of Flames star. "I'm the one that gets to take him home," he whispered devilishly into Levi's ear at one point.

It was something of a revelation, being surrounded by so many queer people. Almost all of Joey and Gabe's friends were LGBT. So Levi didn't feel wary for once as he unabashedly held Raiden's hand all night.

"There you are," Joey cried, falling into the chair beside Raiden. "Are you having a good time?"

"Amazing," said Raiden genuinely. "But how about you? That's all that matters."

Joey bit his thumb and looked around at the room. "Best day of my life," he said.

Raiden leaned over and hugged him. "As it should be."

"All right, all right," Trent's voice rumbled over the music. He was dragging Elion into a seat with one hand and held a tray of shots in the other. "Enough with the lovey-dovey crap, time to get this party started."

Levi protested as loud as the others, but secretly he'd come to think of tequila as his and Raiden's drink. He didn't mind partaking in moderation.

Trent sent Elion off to wrangle his fiancé and Gabe off the dance floor to come join them, then began to divide up the shot glasses and lime wedges.

"No Reyse?" Raiden asked, despite already knowing the answer. Levi knew he missed the final member of Below Zero, even though he tried to be understanding.

Joey and Trent were the same. They shook their heads. "We've been talking more, though," said Joey, playing with a bit of confetti. "He really wanted to come, but he's in Japan this month."

"I'm sure he got you a decent gift to make up for it," said Raiden sympathetically.

Joey raised an eyebrow. "He got us a honeymoon. In Japan."

Raiden and Trent laughed. "Well, that's fair enough, then," said Trent as the others flocked toward the table. "Ah, there we go, come on boys."

They toasted to Gabe and Joey, wishing them a lifetime of happiness together. Levi didn't doubt it would come true.

The rest of the evening passed in a contented blur. Raiden insisted on getting up and mingling, but Levi was always there when he needed to come back. Blake dragged Levi up to dance a couple of times, but with the shots Trent kept slipping him, Levi found he didn't mind so much.

He thought he'd left behind most of his family when he quit the Marines. Especially with the loss of his dad. But looking around the room, Levi felt loved and accepted and whole.

Towards the very end of the night, Raiden dropped into his lap and hiccuped. "There he is," he cried in delight. "Hi, baby."

"Hi," said Levi, rubbing his back. "And just how many shots have you had now?"

Raiden frowned and began counting on his fingers. He seemed to lose track when he got to eight. "Lots," he answered firmly.

Levi laughed, glad that he'd got to have his way with him earlier. He'd be doing nothing but putting Raiden to bed once they got back to their hotel, he knew. "As long as you're having fun."

Raiden nodded and played with Levi's tie. "Wedding's are great," he said, then frowned. "Going to them, I mean. Not planning one. That must be a nightmare."

Levi raised his eyebrow. "You wouldn't want all this?" He tried to pretend the answer didn't matter to him for about two seconds.

Raiden scrunched up his nose. "*All* this. No. My ideal wedding would be eloping to some beach paradise. Have a couple of turtles as witnesses. Then just come back and have a big party, you know? Nothing formal or fancy. Just friends and love and fun."

He smiled dreamingly, then dropped his head onto Levi's shoulder. Suddenly, Levi felt very sober. "You know," he said, stroking Raiden's hair. "I was planning on taking you to Hawaii next year," he said truthfully.

"Ooh," said Raiden, squirming on his lap. "That sounds lovely."

Levi couldn't help but grin, despite the nerves in his belly. "They have pretty great beach paradises there," he hinted.

Raiden went very still. Then he raised his head and looked into Levi's eyes. "Are you…was that…a proposal?"

Levi bit his lip and continued rubbing Raiden's back. "It was a thought," he said, "that maybe we could consider if that's what we wanted."

He didn't want to be the one to make the decision. Dropping to one knee was extremely romantic, but it didn't feel right for him and Raiden. They were equal in all things. This needed to be something they both chose.

Raiden chewed his lip. "But I get to go with you to Hawaii, no matter what, right?"

Levi laughed and kissed him. "Yes, I promise we'll go to Hawaii next year."

"And," said Raiden, drawing out the word as he rubbed the silk of Levi's tie again. "If we happened to come back married, that would be nice, wouldn't it?"

Levi knew he should have been shocked he was even considering this. It had only been a couple of months. But they weren't formally getting engaged. They would spend the next year as they had been, enjoying their love and growing closer. It seemed natural to Levi that if Raiden didn't want any fuss, they could just tie the knot on a whim whenever he liked.

"Nothing fancy," he said. "Just friends and love and fun. If that's what you want?"

Raiden bit his lip and nodded. "So long as we're together."

Levi couldn't agree more. "Together."

# Bonus Epilogue

## RAIDEN

Tropical sunshine streamed through the gauzy, fluttering curtains. Raiden stretched and blinked his eyes. The sounds of the ocean lapping at the shore drifted through the open windows. This was the life.

Why didn't he go on vacation more often? Oh, he'd traveled far and wide. But actually going somewhere with the simple intention of lying on a beach and not doing anything aside from drinking cocktails and reading a trashy book? Yeah, Raiden could get used to this.

Especially now he had someone to go with.

He pushed his hair back and turned to look fondly at his lightly snoring companion. Raiden smiled to himself, then reached over to run his fingers gently over one of Levi's sculpted arms. He was on his belly with his hands under the pillow, half the sheets kicked off his body and his mouth hanging open as he slept peacefully.

He was disheveled and perfect and so completely unexpected. How had Raiden's life brought him here, to this man he loved so much?

Raiden had learned some time ago not to overthink

things too much. Unless it was one of his compositions, then he generally needed Levi to drag him away from whatever song he was obsessing over. But when it came to love, it really was that simple.

Levi made him whole.

"You're staring," Levi mumbled, his eyes still shut. Raiden jumped slightly, then grinned.

"It's your fault," he said. "You're gorgeous."

Levi made some grumbling noises as he slung one arm out and caught Raiden around the waist. Raiden squeaked as he was hauled against Levi's body, the bigger man cuddling up to him from behind. He sleepily kissed the back of Raiden's neck.

"Do I need to spank you?"

Raiden wriggled his ass provocatively against Levi's morning wood. "Oh, yes, please," he said. "That would be delightful."

"Too tired. Do it later," Levi muttered into Raiden's neck. His kisses were sending the most wonderful shivers down his spine.

"And whose fault is it you're tired?" Raiden teased. Then he gasped as Levi's large hand found his hardening cock and gave it a squeeze.

"Yours," Levi replied. He was sounding more awake as he stroked up and down Raiden's length. "If you didn't have such a pretty ass, I might get some sleep every now and again."

Raiden frowned and placed a finger to his chin. "Hmm, that doesn't sound like fun at all, though."

"No, it doesn't," Levi growled. He flipped Raiden onto his back and laid on top of him, their naked bodies pressed together from head to toe. His grin was feral. "Whatever shall I do with you now?"

Raiden was already panting. It was at times like this when

he wondered if their lust for one another would ever calm down. As it showed no signs of waning after a year, he figured he didn't need to worry about it.

"I can think of at least seven things you could be doing," Raiden said between kisses. "Eight if you feel like moving to get that banana over there."

Levi grabbed his wrists and pinned them to the bed. "No moving," he said, kissing down his throat. "No talking. Just lie there and take what I give you, like a good boy."

Raiden quivered. "Yes, Levi."

He surrendered his body. Levi trusted him enough to let him go, knowing he would stay put without being restrained. They had played around a bit with cuffs in the past, but they both found it more exhilarating for Raiden to just control himself and remain in place.

Levi didn't make it easy for him, however. He never did. He teased with his lips and his tongue and his fingertips, caressing and tickling his favorite parts of Raiden's body. Like he was worshiping at the altar of their love.

Raiden longed to scream in pleasure. To wail and beg and generally make the most of their secluded, private villa off the Hawaiian beach they had lived in for the past week. But he wanted to please Levi more than any of those other urges, so he restricted himself to simply gasping for air whenever Levi did something particularly sinful.

Levi was trailing kisses up the inside of his thigh as his strong fingers stroked the sensitive underside of Raiden's knee. "You taste so good," he said. "Sun drenched and salt washed. I could eat you all day."

Raiden bit his tongue and screwed up his eyes. That sounded like heaven.

Leisurely, Levi sucked on Raiden's swollen cock, running his tongue over the slit and along the veins and ridges. He rolled Raiden's heavy balls in his hand, rubbing the taint firmly. Raiden fisted the bedsheets and tried not to lose his mind.

With a pop, Levi's wet, reddened lips left Raiden's cock. "I'm still sleepy," he announced. He crawled back up the bed, running his hand up Raiden's flank as he did. "I want to watch you do some work, you spoiled little minx." He captured Raiden's mouth for a kiss, his tongue strong and invasive. Then he reached over to the nightstand where they'd left the lube. "Make yourself ready for me. I want a good show."

Raiden's skin tingled with anticipation. Levi had a thing for watching him jerk off, probably because he knew how much Raiden loved doing it for him. There was something utterly depraved and erotic about looking into the eyes of the person you loved while touching yourself in the most intimate ways possible.

Raiden's breaths were shallow and fluttery as he covered his hole and cock with the slippery, silky lube. Levi's usually icy blue eyes were black with blazing lust. He gently rubbed Raiden's chest with one hand as he drank in the sight of him. Raiden already had two fingers in his ass and his hand wrapped around his weeping prick.

"Slowly now," Levi rasped. "Take your time, baby. You look so pretty. I want to enjoy every inch of you."

Raiden nodded, eager to please. He bit his lip hard to stop himself from moaning or shouting. If Levi had let him talk, Raiden would be cussing him out now, telling him he was a fucking tease and could go screw himself. Levi would naturally pretend to get mad and take him roughly, maybe throw him to the floor and fuck him like an animal on all fours.

But today was a day for gentleness, and their eyes were locked as Raiden silently drove himself wild, pleading without words for Levi to come rescue him, come claim him.

Levi tortured him a little longer, though, petting his hair

and stimulating his nipples with featherlight touches. "You're so perfect. I love you, Raiden."

Raiden closed his eyes, overwhelmed. Levi kissed each lid, then slowly brought his lips down Raiden's body, capturing each inch of skin he passed with openmouthed kisses and licks of his tongue.

Without speaking, he loosely took each of Raiden's wrists in hand and placed them back by his hips. Raiden opened his eyes again to watch him. Then Levi used both his hands to spread Raiden's cheeks so he could bestow sweet kisses to his hole. His tongue lapped at the stretched ring of muscle, relaxing it further.

"This is mine," he murmured. "No one else has ever had it, and they never will." He looked up at Raiden, who nodded in response. His heart was pounding so fast and loud Raiden worried it might actually jump out of his chest. "You'll always be my little ass virgin."

Raiden nodded again, trembling as Levi loomed over him, kissing his mouth as he angled up his dick. He pressed the tip against Raiden's throbbing hole.

"You can hold me," Levi told him. Raiden immediately wrapped his arms and legs around Levi's body, forcing the hard cock deeper into his body. "Holy fuck, yes, baby. *Yes.*"

Raiden was well accustomed to Levi's length by now, enjoying the way it burned as it first went in. He was soon thrusting back against it, chasing the orgasm that Levi had made him work for.

"You want it so bad, don't you?" Levi laughed, his fingers digging into Raiden's back and hip as he ground into him. "That's it, good boy. You can take it, can't you?" Raiden didn't bother to reply, he just rutted faster, his vision blurring as his climax reached its peak. Levi gripped onto his hair, the sweat running from his naked body onto Raiden's. "Scream for me, baby," he whispered.

The bellow Raiden let loose as he came probably shocked any birds perched nearby into flight. His body went totally rigid before he flopped back on the mattress with Levi panting on top of him. Levi nuzzled his nose into Raiden's damp hair and kissed along his jaw.

Raiden allowed himself to be enveloped by Levi's big arms, melting into the embrace as he felt his eyelids droop. Sex with Levi always wiped him out, and he knew his partner wouldn't mind if he dozed off in his arms.

He was safe, sated and slick with the evidence of their passion. This really *was* the life.

———

Raiden woke up naturally an hour or so later. Levi had already showered and said he had a surprise waiting, so Raiden hurriedly made his way through the bathroom as well. Once dressed in board shorts and shirts, Levi led him by the hand out onto the beach. Palm trees flanked them on either side, reaching towards the waters of the Pacific Ocean.

Raiden blinked. There was a small table set up on the sand, a white tablecloth fluttering in the gentle breeze. Two chairs stood on opposite ends of the square table, and in between sat as many bowls and plates of food as could possibly fit on the table-top. Fingers of sticky fruit and iced pastries and crispy bacon were nestled among hot coffee and fresh juice. In the sand next to the table was a silver bucket on a stand, a Champagne bottle sticking out from the ice, glistening with condensation.

Raiden's heart rate picked up, just a fraction. "What's this?" he asked. He squeezed Levi's hand as he looked over at him.

Levi smiled and kissed his cheek. "Breakfast, dummy," he said affectionately.

Raiden allowed him to pull his seat out for him. He sat and nibbled on a strawberry as Levi popped the Champagne cork and made them mimosas with the orange juice. "It's a very *nice* breakfast, Kevin," Raiden said, deliberately using the old nickname to get a rise out of him. They normally went to the main complex to have breakfast there or strolled into town.

Levi remained unrattled, though. "I think you meant 'thank you, Levi.'"

"Thank you, Kevin," Raiden said. He grinned around another strawberry and squirmed in his seat. Levi would know that made his ass ache.

But he simply arched an eyebrow and handed Raiden his drink.

Raiden let the matter drop, but he couldn't deny his suspicions were raised. They hadn't explicitly talked about a certain something since that night at Joey and Gabe's wedding. How Raiden wasn't averse to the idea of eloping if they were to ever get married themselves. In fact, that had become his dream.

But, although they had booked the vacation to Hawaii as planned, neither of them had brought up marriage again. So Raiden simply sipped his drink and ate himself silly of all the delicious food Levi had organized for them.

"I thought we could go out today," Levi said casually. "Walk out to the botanical garden, maybe hike up the mountain a bit?"

To be fair, they had spent most of their first week on the island lounging on the beach, reading, drinking and fucking. *So* much fucking. So Raiden was quite keen to do some exploring. He tried to keep his curiosity low. This was just a nice day out, spent with his partner.

Levi assured him that the dishes would be taken care of,

so they walked back to the villa and put some sandals on to go exploring.

The botanical gardens were stunning. Raiden had never been much of a fan of the great outdoors, but he could certainly appreciate its beauty when he got the chance. They traversed the wooden paths and bridges through the gorgeous scenery. Small waterfalls spilled into lily ponds, and peacocks strutted around, flashing the visitors their enormous, colorful tailfeathers.

"Bit of a show-off, isn't he?" Raiden said playfully as they passed one of the birds.

Levi leaned into him. "I know someone like that," he murmured. He brushed his hand subtly over the top of Raiden's ass, making him blush.

They wandered happily for a few hours before Levi lead them to a little place along the shore that specialized in traditional pork laulau. The meat was so tender and juicy it practically melted in Raiden's mouth.

The third time Levi touched his pocket, Raiden decided he was justified in the butterflies that had come to life in his stomach. Levi was definitely up to something, but Raiden promised himself he would be patient and not jump to any conclusions. Instead, he made a spectacle of licking pineapple juice from his fingers, enjoying the faint blush that rose on Levi's cheeks.

Once the bill was paid, Levi checked his watch. Again. "Do you feel like a bit of a hike?" he asked. Raiden didn't miss the hopeful note to his words. "We could work off some of that food?"

Ordinarily, Raiden would tease him by suggesting they go back to their villa and work off their lunch in other ways. But today he just took Levi's hand and told him that was a great idea.

They were on the biggest island in Hawaii. The lush,

green mountain rose in the backdrop wherever they went, so it was exciting to finally venture inland and explore some more. They took a taxi to the start of the trail where Raiden held Levi's hand the whole way. That stopped Levi checking his watch and touching his shorts pocket every three seconds, so Raiden didn't have to pretend he didn't notice.

Excitement bubbled in his belly like a bottle of champagne waiting to explode.

The walk was tranquil. They passed other people as they navigated the twists and turns around the trees and boulders. But as far as Raiden was concerned, they were the only two people there.

When they reached the falls, Raiden gasped.

Where they stood overlooked a lagoon, twenty feet below. The waterfall dropped over on the opposite side to them, cascading in front of a cavern. All around the lagoon lush flora spilled over the edge, a riot of colorful flowers and bright green plants. But that wasn't what had stunned Raiden so completely.

Across the water, a large rainbow stretched from one side of the bay to the other. Its colors were vibrant and clearly defined. Raiden wasn't sure he'd ever seen anything more beautiful.

"It's called Rainbow Falls," Levi murmured into his ear from behind him. He slipped his arms around Raiden, hugging his back to his chest. Raiden traced his fingers along Levi's thick arms, his skin warm from the sunshine. "There isn't always a rainbow, but I hoped there would be today."

"It's amazing," Raiden agreed. It wasn't just beautiful. It filled his heart with hope. Like anything was possible.

"You're amazing," Levi told him.

Then he let go with one hand, reached into the pocket he had been fussing with all morning, and produced a box that he held in front of Raiden.

A ring box.

Raiden stared for a moment, but Levi continued to simply offer it to him. So he took it between his trembling fingers and pried the lid open. Nestled inside were two matching platinum bands.

"It's just an idea," Levi said. "I can easily put them away, and we can go back and get drunk, then go swimming with sharks tomorrow."

"And what if you don't put them away?" Raiden asked, heart in his throat.

He heard Levi chuckle. "I've got another surprise waiting for you on the beach. *Then* we get drunk and go swimming with sharks tomorrow."

This was it. Levi wasn't so much proposing as he was asking Raiden if he felt like getting married *right now*. As always, Levi offered him the choice. It was up to Raiden what they did next.

He knew in his heart what he wanted. What he had wanted for some time now. Levi was his other half. Together they were complete. He didn't yearn for all the traditions that came with a regular wedding because there was nothing traditional or regular about Levi Patterson.

People would be disappointed. His mom in particular would struggle to understand if they did this. She would want to fuss over him and invite everyone he had ever met and have people make speeches about how great they both were. That was too much. Raiden just wanted to make official what he knew in his heart to be true.

That Levi was the man he wanted to spend the rest of his life with.

They could celebrate when they returned. He'd let his mom plan whatever she wanted for a big party. But this moment was just about Raiden and Levi. The two of them standing united against the rest of the world, forever.

Raiden took one of Levi's hands in his own, guiding him so they both wrapped their fingers around the dual ring box, closing the lid. He turned to look into Levi's anxious eyes. He grinned.

"Let's go get married."

———

Raiden walked back down from Rainbow Falls in a daze. Levi held his hand firmly the whole way, which was good as Raiden would probably have slipped several times otherwise. They didn't speak, but every minute or two Raiden would lean into Levi's body, or Levi would kiss his cheek.

"Do I need to, um, do anything?" Raiden finally thought to ask when they were back in another taxi.

Levi shrugged. "A couple of things to sign," he said. He smiled, lifting Raiden's hand to kiss the knuckles. "No big deal."

"No big deal," Raiden repeated faintly. "You did all this?"

"Yes," said Levi. The look in his eyes told Raiden what he already knew. That Levi would do anything for him.

The taxi took them back to their villa. Raiden didn't really pay attention as Levi led him through the building, only pausing to place a Hawaiian lei over both their heads. "You dork," Raiden said, his nerves making him laugh. He fiddled with the flowers around his neck.

Levi just grinned and kissed him on the mouth. "You love it."

"I do," said Raiden without hesitation.

Levi rolled his eyes. "Not *yet*," he chided playfully. "You have to wait to say that."

To his surprise, Levi took Raiden's hand and led him out onto the beach where they had eaten breakfast that morning. The sun was beginning to set. The last traces of gold, orange, purple and blue were fading to black in the sky above them. The stars were starting to peek out, and farther along the beach people were lighting torches. Like the last embers of a fire, burning just for Raiden and Levi.

There was a minister waiting for them on the sand, standing between two more blazing torches in anticipation of their arrival.

"Um. Don't we need witnesses or something?" Raiden asked.

"It's funny you should mention that," Levi replied. He nudged Raiden with his elbow and looked to their right. By the palm trees, the table and chairs had been set up with more food and Champagne. But waiting in the seats were two familiar faces.

"Joey?" Raiden spluttered. "Gabe?"

He struggled to reconcile them being there as the two men jumped to their feet. They looked smart for the tropical climate. Dark cream chinos and white short-sleeve shirts. Almost like they were going to a wedding.

Joey, Raiden's former bandmate and one of his closest friends in the world, came bounding over the sand. "Ray!" he cried, throwing his arms around Raiden's neck. "I take it you said yes?"

"Looks that way," Raiden replied. He looked back over at the minister. She smiled and waved, apparently in no hurry.

Joey's husband, Gabe, came and joined them. He and Levi shook hands.

"What are you doing here?" Raiden asked, not quite believing it.

Gabe shrugged and gave Raiden a wink. "A little bird told us Hawaii might be a nice vacation spot this time of year."

Raiden shook his head at Levi. "No big deal," he grumbled, blinking back the tears from his eyes. As much as Raiden didn't want the fuss of a big white wedding, Levi had still known that sharing the simple ceremony with one of his best friends would be the thing to make it absolutely perfect. "Thank you," he whispered.

Joey danced from foot to foot. "Come on, then," he said, more giddy than either groom. "I can't believe you're really doing this!"

Raiden took Levi's hand, beaming at his soon-to-be husband. "I can."

The ceremony was simple, over and done within ten minutes. Raiden said 'I do' in the right place and the rings Levi had picked slipped easily onto both their fingers. Joey and Gabe held hands as they watched the happy couple kiss to make it official, then doused them in flower petals they'd had hidden away in their pockets. The minister shook all their hands as she offered them congratulations, then left them alone to celebrate.

Raiden couldn't stop staring at the ring on his left hand. He was sitting on Levi's lap, Joey on Gabe's, as they toasted around the small table with more Champagne and ate traditional Hawaiian poke. The sun was almost fully set above them, leaving red and orange trails in the inky black sky. Waves rolled onto the beach behind them, splashing against the sand to create the perfect soundtrack to their night.

"How do you feel, Mr. Patterson-Jones?" Levi asked, pulling Raiden's attention back from his swirling thoughts.

Raiden grinned and pecked a kiss on the tip of Levi's nose. "Perfect, Mr. Patterson-Jones."

"I think that might be our cue to leave," said Gabe with an arched eyebrow.

Joey's face dropped, pausing with a cube of marinated fish halfway to his mouth. "Already?"

"I think the happy couple might need some alone time." Raiden blushed as Gabe chuckled. "But how about we take you guys out to dinner tomorrow night?"

"That would be lovely," Levi said, stroking Raiden's back.

Joey insisted on another piece of fish before he downed the last of his bubbly. Gabe managed to bribe him away with the promise of pizza for dinner and, if the look in his eye was anything to go by, some alone time of their own.

Raiden and Levi waved them off from the table. Raiden felt like he was overflowing with love, for his friends who had traveled all this way to be with them, for the ones they would surprise back home, for his family who he hoped would be so happy for him. But most of all, for the man currently feeding him slivers of poke with chopsticks.

Despite there now being a free chair, Raiden stayed on Levi's lap, cradled to his chest. It was like he was a hundred feet high. "Thank you," he said again. He offered up a scrap of deep-fried malasadas to Levi's lips with his fingers. Levi took it, licking the sugar from Raiden's fingertips.

"For what?" he asked once he had chewed and swallowed.

Raiden kissed his neck. "For being you."

Levi tickled his side and grinned devilishly. "Even when I'm a Grumpy McGrumpypants?"

"*Especially* then," Raiden told him.

Without warning, Levi stood up, taking Raiden with him. Letting loose a squeak, Raiden hastily wrapped his long legs around Levi's waist and his arms around his neck, crushing the flowers on the lei.

"Just what do you think you're doing?" he asked with a laugh.

Levi kissed him possessively on the mouth. "I'm carrying you over the threshold, *husband.*"

Raiden shook his head. "Do you really think I want our first married fuck to be in a bed?" He tutted disapprovingly. "There's a perfectly good ocean behind us. And a private beach. I'm sure you can think of something a little more creative."

The warm night air stirred around them in the dark. Levi cradled the back of Raiden's head, his powerful body carrying him towards the waves. "Anything for you, my love," he said, wicked intent clear in his words.

"Anything," Raiden agreed.

———

To see the moment Levi and Raiden dive into temptation from Levi's point of view, sign up to my newsletter here: hjwelch.com/subscribe

The next book in the Homecoming Hearts series is Trent and Ashby's story, Steam. Turn the page to learn more…

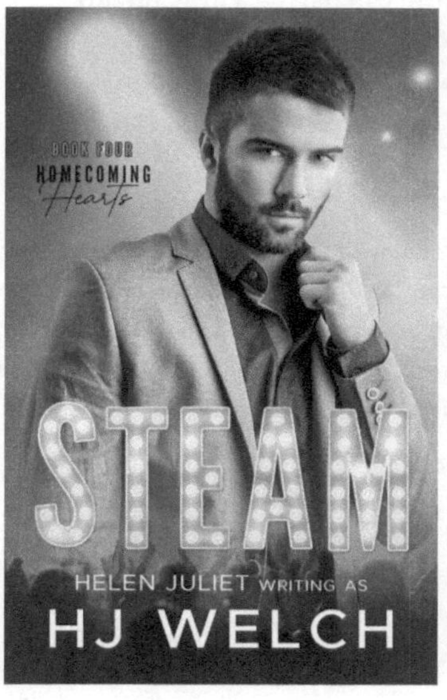

**Unlikely protector. Unwelcome crush. But is this true love as unstoppable as an avalanche?**

Bad boy Trent Charles is more famous for his outrageous behavior than he is for his acting these days. Long gone is his cute image from boy band Below Zero. After one scandal too many, his manager sends him home to the snowy ski slopes of Wyoming to get his life together. No parties, no fast cars, and certainly no women.

Ashby Wilcott is done with bad boys. His heart is broken from his last relationship disaster. A few weeks of peace and quiet in the mountains is just what he needs. He is absolutely not interested in moody Trent Charles, even if he is hot enough to melt snow with his rippling muscles and mysterious ways. Good thing Trent is straight.

But the two men can't seem to stay apart. Trent finds himself pretending to be Ashby's boyfriend, a lie that gets Ashby invited to a wedding as Trent's guest. Regardless of Trent's protests that he's not interested in the beautiful, feminine Ashby in that way, the chemistry between the two steams up. With only a few weeks together, what harm can having a little fun do?

As outside forces threaten to tear them apart, Trent realizes Ashby means more to him than just a fling. In fact, he'll do anything to protect him.

*Steam* is a high heat, low angst standalone MM romance. It's the fourth book in the **Homecoming Hearts** series, where these former pop stars swap the limelight for happy ever afters. This book features intimate snowboarding lessons, midnight skinny dipping, an adorable puppy, only one bed, a meddling reporter, and a guaranteed HEA with absolutely no cliffhanger.

Acknowledgments

There are so many people who I have to thank in helping me complete my first series in MM romance. Heck, my first ever book series! It's been a fair old journey and whether you've been here since the start or have only just discovered Below Zero and Homecoming Hearts, I couldn't have done this without you.

Thank you to the people who have been here all the way, behind the scenes, keeping me going and bringing these books to life with me: Ed Davies, Amelia Faulkner, Conrad Rivers, Meg Cooper, Cate Ashwood, Aria Tan, Tanja Ongkiehong, Leslie Copeland and LesCourt Author Services.

Thank you to my incredible husband, whose support I simply couldn't have done without. You believed in me when I didn't believe in myself and cheered on every milestone and accomplishment. Thank you for giving me my own happy ever after.

Thank you to my friends who make *me* feel like an international pop star!

Thank you to my fur babies for keeping Mummy company in her writing cave.

And finally, thank you to every single one of *you* who has enjoyed Blake, Joey, Raiden, Trent and Reyse's stories. Thank you for all the loving reviews, for the encouragement in our Facebook Group, <u>Helen's Jewels</u>, the emails you've sent saying how moved you were by a book, the excitement for each new release, everything. Without you this series wouldn't have come to life. You're the best and I have so much love for each and every one of you.

## PINE COVE BOX SET BY HJ WELCH

Welcome to Pine Cove, where true love lives happily ever after! **This 2000 page box set contains all six novels as well as all five companion short stories.**

———

### Safe Harbor

Robin Coal needs a fake boyfriend for his high school reunion. He asks his housemate: a gorgeous, totally straight ex-Marine. What could go wrong? There's only one bed, and Dair might not be so straight after all... When Robin's past threatens their future, only Dair can save him.

———

### *Sweet Spot*

It's Halloween and Robin has prepared a sexy little surprise for his boyfriend Dair when he gets home from work. Hold on to your horses, Marine!

### Troubled Waters

Bodyguard Scout Duffy doesn't know what's worse: the fact that his scorching one-night-stand, Emery Klein, is his bratty new client, or the fact that he doesn't even remember Scout. But Emery's life is in danger thanks to his out and proud charity work, and once he finally recognizes Scout, their chemistry in undeniable.

### Homeward Bound

Swift Coal just found out he's a father, and his daughter (and her cranky cat) are coming to stay. His best friend's younger brother, Micha Perkins, has nowhere to go and a wrongfully tattered reputation. He's relieved when Swift asks him to be a live-in babysitter. He just has to hide his lifelong crush. Easy, because Swift is straight—right?

### Bright Horizon

With sixteen years between them, baker Ben Turner and lawyer Elias Solomon have no idea their crush is mutual. But when Ben inherits his long-lost family's estate and becomes an overnight millionaire, Elias swears to protect the innocent younger man from the vultures circling him. To unravel the mystery of the inheritance, they must go to England to confront Ben's estranged relatives…and their feelings for each other.

### *Crossed Paths*

Raj Bhat is done living in the shadows. It's time for him to take charge of his own destiny and tell the man he's fallen for how he really feels.

————

### *Midnight Sky*

It's the night before New Year's Eve. Taylan Demir is all alone, and he's just lost his dog. Except when his handsome customer, Hudson Perkins, comes to his rescue, Taylan doesn't just get his dog back. He's suddenly got a hot date, and maybe someone to kiss when the clock strikes midnight.

————

### Memory Lane

Angel Shields saved Jay Coal's life in high school, and Jay has secretly loved his straight best friend ever since. Now Angel's back in town with amnesia after a suspicious work accident and it's Jay's turn to rescue him. He pretends to be Angel's fiancé to see him in the hospital, but with his scrambled-up memory, Angel's not sure it's fictional after all. He just knows he loves Jay more than ever.

————

### Thin Ice

Kamran's ex broke his heart, tricked him into aiding a bank robbery, and now he wants him to do one last job. There's only one way to say no: seek the protective custody of the biggest, grumpiest FBI agent ever, Lee Marshall. And pretend to be his boyfriend for a week-long family reunion in their giant mansion. Wait, what?

————

### *Calm Shores*

Gorgeous, sophisticated Dante walks into Oliver's bar and orders…a boyfriend?! Dante needs a man to keep his mother from setting him back up with his awful, cheating ex, and Oliver is up for the challenge.

————

***Fresh Snow***

Emery Klein is throwing the best Christmas party ever, but his fiancé, Scout Duffy, and all their friends have something more exciting in mind.

————

*Each Pine Cove book can be read as a stand alone and has its own happy ever after. But if you read the whole series, you'll see a lot of familiar faces!*

**Available as an ebook or audiobook.**

## PADDLE CREEK #1: HEAVEN SENT BY HJ WELCH

**Two rival jocks. One adorable nerd. A bet that changes everything.**

SETH

Being captain of the Paddle Creek Panthers is my life. I wouldn't care that my grades have slipped, except it could not only cost me my shot at the pros, but now the rich kid in town has wagered that if I don't graduate, I'll owe him *big* time. Can this gorgeous little freshman geek Gabe really save my degree and my reputation? All I know is that as soon as I laid eyes on him, I needed him. And I *don't* want to share.

MARTY

I've spent almost four years trying to get my captain Seth to notice me. He's hot as hell and knows how to boss a guy around, even one as big as me. To him, though, I'm just the team clown. But when he drags me into this graduation bet, it's no laughing matter. So why shouldn't this little cherub Gabe tutor me as well? In fact, I don't see why we can't share him in all *kinds* of ways. Seth is clearly a natural Daddy, Gabe thrives being doted on, and I'm happy to Daddy *and* be Daddied. Win-win, right?

GABE

Somehow, I've found myself standing up to the guy whose family pretty much owns Paddle Creek and put my neck on the line for two of the college's star players. Now we're spending every day together as I try and save their grades, and I don't know if I'm crazy but it's like they both *want* me. I've never had a boyfriend. I'm not even out to my overbearing parents. How could I choose between them…or do I actually have to when they *both* want to be my Daddies? After my life comes crashing down, it's their turn to come to my rescue. Maybe what me and these god-like men have isn't just a fling after all?

***Heaven Sent** is a steamy, standalone MMM romance. It's the first book in the **Paddle Creek College** series, where it's always the quiet ones who get up to the best kind of trouble. This book features a geek tutoring two hot jocks, two hot jocks tutoring a geek in a completely different way, a trash panda with a heart of gold, a human ice cream sundae, a revenge curse, and a guaranteed HEA with absolutely no cliffhanger.*

# *Also Available*

## PADDLE CREEK #2: YES, SIR BY HJ WELCH

**Two men. Two secrets. Can true love set them free?**

BENEDICT

Just one more year, then I can go back to my beloved Oxford University and leave this tiny town behind me. Teaching is my passion, but I have other desires that I know would get me fired if anyone found out. The only trouble is, my new TA is pushing all my buttons and I'm not sure he even realizes what calling me Sir does to me. That's nothing, however, compared to when he starts calling me Daddy.

JACKSON

Have I got hots for teacher? Oh, yes. Messing around is off the table, though, so in a way it's safe to flirt with him and see him lose that stiff upper lip. It's not like he'd be interested in me anyway if he ever discovered what I love wearing under my clothes. Tough guys like me shouldn't like satin and lace. They shouldn't want to feel pretty. But Sir makes me feel gorgeous, and I want to be *such* a good boy for him.

***Yes, Sir*** *is a steamy, standalone MM romance. It's the second book in the* **Paddle Creek College** *series, where it's always the quiet ones who get up to the best kind of trouble. This book features two people learning they don't have to be ashamed of who they are, a sassy brat who really wants to behave, a master in the bedroom who's a caring Daddy at heart, role playing so good it could win an Oscar, and a guaranteed HEA with absolutely no cliffhanger.*

## PADDLE CREEK #3: LITTLE PLEASURES BY HJ WELCH

**One jaded Daddy. One brand new boy. A fake relationship that becomes all too real.**

XANDER

It's bad enough I have to move back to Paddle Creek with my awful stepmom, but now my half-brother's best friend has decided he has to look after me—even pretending to be my new boyfriend for a family wedding to keep my stepmother off my back. What Ruben doesn't know is that I've been in love with him for as long as I can remember and spending so much time with him is torture. Until it isn't. I can't believe that he's interested in me and even wants to be my Daddy, unlocking something in me I never knew was there. But when my stepmom goes too far, can I rely on Ruben to be there for me seeing as no one else in my life ever has?

RUBEN

When my life-long best friend asks me to keep an eye on his half-brother, of course I agree. Except he's a young man now, not a kid, and he's tugging at every single one of my Daddy heartstrings. Xander has just moved back into town and between finishing his degree, part-time work, and hellish stepmother, he's stressing himself into knots. It's a long time since a boy interested me, but I just want to protect Xander from the whole world. No matter the cost.

*Little Pleasures is a steamy, standalone MM romance. It's the third book in the **Paddle Creek College** series, where it's always the quiet ones who get up to the best kind of trouble. This book features a Daddy introducing a boy to his inner little, the most loyal doggy best friend, a lot of dinosaurs, a heart-stopping rescue, and a guaranteed HEA with absolutely no cliffhanger. CW: Age play but no ABDL.*

Also Available

## PADDLE CREEK #4: FOUR PLAY BY HJ WELCH

**Three hungry wolves. One pretty little lamb. The hunt for love is on.**

HARPER

I'm here for a good time, not a long time. When a total cutie asks me if I'd be interested in him and his two Daddies chasing me down and having their way with me, it sounds fun. I'm only in this crappy town for the summer, after all. But what we share is *intense.* I signed on to get caught…not to catch feels. However, when I find myself being hunted for real, can I really expect my wolf pack to come to the rescue?

RICK

After my husband and I swapped military life for married life, we quickly met our sweet baby boy who we'll do anything for. When Brady says he's found a sassy little lamb for the three of us to stalk, I'm happy to indulge him. But this broken young man swiftly captures all of our hearts, even though he says he can walk away any time. There's a difference between walking and being taken, however. Now I have the scent of a fool who's about to discover what happens when he's stolen what's *mine*.

***Four Play*** *is a super steamy, standalone MMMM romance. It's the fourth book in the **Paddle Creek College** series, where it's always the quiet ones who get up to the best kind of trouble. This book features exhilarating primal play, one hell of a paint ball match, an underwater themed motel, so many smooches, an obsessive ex-boyfriend, and a guaranteed HEA with absolutely no cliffhanger.*

Also Available

## BEARS-4-U (MULTI-AUTHOR SHARED UNIVERSE): KEEP ME BY HJ WELCH

**Snowed in for a second chance at love...**

BECKETT

It's been over two years since I lost my darling husband, and my best friend is taking matters into her own hands. She's signed me up to a dating app for bears and those that love them, even encouraging me to attend a weekend mixer. I go to humor her, not expecting to rescue the most adorable boy...twice. But I'm not ready to open up my heart again, am I?

LAURIE

My last Daddy was bad news. It's taken a lot of courage for me to reach out on Bears-4-U and go to this mixer, only to find that the new Daddy I've been talking to is just as awful. That's when Beckett swoops into my life like a hero in a story book. I know he's not looking for love, but I want to mend his broken heart so badly. When a scary snowstorm blows in and strands us, I trust he'll keep me safe and warm. I want to be in his life, in his bed, in his heart…forever.

*Bears-4-U is a MM Daddy romance multi-author series, featuring a host of delicious Daddy pairings. The Bears-4-U dating app is all about putting Bears and Teddy Bears together for their honey-sweet HEAs. Psst, no real bears involved. Each book can be read as a standalone, but why not snuggle up with all the bears?*

*Also Available*

## DADDY'S FAIRY TALES BOX SET BY HELEN JULIET

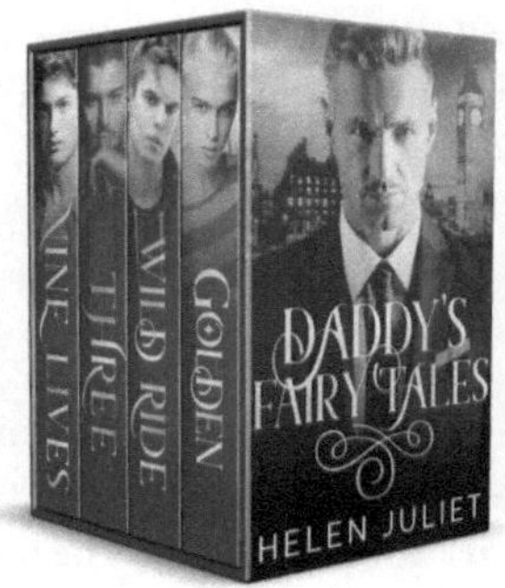

**Experience Goldilocks and the Three Bears, Little Red Riding Hood, The Three Little Pigs, and Puss in Boots as you've never seen them before in this box set of contemporary adaptations! Available together for the first time, each stand alone book features a caring Daddy finding his HEA with a loving boy (or boys!)**

---

### Golden

When Goldie's ex-boyfriend leaves him in serious debt with the adult entertainment company he works for, Goldie gets the chance to work off the money…in front of the camera. The idea excites him, but then his favourite throuple—Daddy, Papa, and Baby —*demand* he comes to play with them. No matter how scared he is, he can't miss this opportunity, not even when his past comes back to haunt him.

———

**Wild Ride**

When Red is chased into the woods, he seeks sanctuary at his estranged grandma's house. He doesn't expect to be rescued by his older brother's best friend, the man he was always madly in love with. Could Hunter be the Daddy of Red's wildest dreams? Especially when he unlocks a secret passion of Red's for beautiful lingerie. There's still a threat lurking in the woods, though, and Hunter realises he'll do anything to protect his beautiful boy.

———

**Three**

When three shy best friends sign up to a dating app to finally get some by the end of the year, they don't expect to all fall for the same gorgeous, slightly scary-looking Daddy. The only solution? Let him choose who he wants to bed. Except he doesn't. Daddy Wolf wants to spoil each little piggy, one after another. But when danger comes calling, will their love for each other be enough to save them all?
**Includes Halloween bonus scene!**

———

**Nine Lives**

When Charlie suddenly finds himself homeless and penniless, he decides to sell the only thing left he owns. Himself. For the very first time. Lucky for him he stumbles across Miller, the own of a London kink club, who saves him from those who would take advantage of him. As Miller discovers his inner Daddy, he also unlocks Charlie's kitten alter-ego. But with both their families meddling, will new love be enough to keep them together?

**Available as an ebook.**

# About the Author

HJ Welch is an author of contemporary MM romance series, including the international bestselling Pine Cove series. She lives just outside of London with her husband and two balls of fluff that occasionally pretend to be cats. She began writing at an early age, later honing her craft online in the world of fanfiction on sites like Wattpad. Fifteen years and over half a million words later, she sought out original MM novels to read. By the end of 2016 she had written her first book of her own, and in 2017 she achieved her lifelong dream of becoming a full-time author. When she's not writing she's usually dancing, singing, filming music videos, taking long walks, working on jigsaw puzzles, drinking prosecco, or talking about Eurovision.

She also writes contemporary British MM fairy tale adaptations as Helen Juliet.

———

You can contact Helen via the following:
Newsletter: https://www.subscribepage.com/helenjuliet
Website – www.hjwelch.com
Facebook Group – Helen's Jewels
Instagram – @helenjwrites
Twitter – @helenjwrites
Book Bub – @HJWelchAuthor
Facebook Page – @HJWelchAuthor

www.ingramcontent.com/pod-product-compliance
Lightning Source LLC
Chambersburg PA
CBHW061322190726

48288CB00002B/617